Susanne Wittpennig

Maya and Domenico: The story of an amazing friendship

www.fontis-verlag.com

To my sisters Aline and Julia

The author's website:

www.schreibegern.ch

Susanne Wittpennig

Maya and Domenico:

The story of an amazing friendship

fontis
BRUNNEN BASEL

Bibliografische Information der Deutschen Nationalbibliothek
Die Deutsche Nationalbibliothek verzeichnet diese Publikation in der Deutschen Nationalbibliografie; detaillierte bibliografische Daten sind im Internet über www.dnb.de abrufbar.

This book was first published in German under the title:
"Maya und Domenico:
Die krasse Geschichte einer ungewöhnlichen Freundschaft"
by Susanne Wittpennig

Translation into English by
Regina Kolb and Sara Saltalamacchia

Cover: spoon design, Olaf Johannson, Langgöns
Cover pictures: Andrei K, Jordi Vic Robles/Shutterstock.com
Backcover pictures: Zdenka Darula/Shutterstock.com
Typeset: Innoset AG, Justin Messmer, Basel
Print: East Print
Printed in Poland

ISBN 978-3-03848-045-7

Contents

1. Glad tidings

Honestly: until I turned fourteen, nothing much ever happened in my life. Nearly everything was just as it should be. I grew up well protected, was taught appropriate manners and wasn't very keen on school. That was *me* and I always dreamt that something would change. But I didn't quite know what.

And then, this story happened. All of a sudden, I was no longer invisible and I had to come face to face with life. This story now has a special place in my heart and, today, makes me laugh and cry at the same time.

When I tore Sunday's sheet with its red letters from my calendar, all that was waiting behind it was another boring Monday in black letters. There was no sign of the sensational news that would change my life on that particular Monday.

I dragged myself across the schoolyard in my worst mood. Those cheerfully singing birds had a nice life; they didn't know what tortures were waiting for anyone entering the school building. Neither did the sun, which was stretching its soft rays onto this slightly odd, old building with its green turrets. Many generations of students had walked through those gates and had survived school, I guess. That was a comforting thought – somehow.

The classes of secondary school had their classrooms

in the front wing of the building. Twelve classes spread over three floors. The cool hallways smelled of floor polish, chalk and dusty paper, and last year, in a misguided attempt to add a bit of colour, the doors to all classrooms had been painted bright orange.

I hurried over to the girls' toilets and stood in front of the mirror. Right above my head, there was a message written with pink lipstick in Delia's squiggly handwriting: "Kiss me!" And beneath it, a heart-shaped mark of a kiss. Mumbling in disgust, I got out a tissue and rubbed the tacky piece of art off. The face I was looking at in the mirror could only be described as average. I mean, I did have a few pretty attributes, like my big brown eyes, for example. They shone like polished chestnuts. And those cute freckles, dancing on my nose when I smiled. But that was about it. The rest of me was entirely plain and ordinary. My hair had the matt brown colour of tree bark and it was long and straight, no waves or anything that would have made it more interesting. I had tried to change it with Mum's hairspray once or twice, but it had always ended up hanging down in its usual dull way again, parted in the middle.

Delia and Isabelle did not look dull, at all, and they were much prettier than me. Delia's face was heart-shaped, just like her lips, and she had bright blue eyes with long lashes. Isabelle had a cute little nose and a bold, pointy chin that made her look very self-confident. There was nothing bold about my face, everything was flat and dull and round. I always wore my hair down so that it covered my ears, because Delia had once said that they looked like chimpanzee's ears. I would have liked to have had earrings, ever since primary school; really big cool silver earrings. But Dad would have none of that nonsense. He was absolutely against anything that would change the natural state of the body. Ears were not supposed to have holes. He probably thought that way because he was a doctor with his heart and soul.

I looked at my watch: it was half past seven. I pulled a long face, because it was high time I went into the chamber of torture.

Our classroom was on the top floor, room number 308, in the hall on the left, third door. I straightened my back and pulled my head up when I walked in. *Do not show your insecurity, Maya, act as though you were really confident. Yes, that is right – yep, nobody noticed you …*

I walked towards my desk in the back row and scanned the room with my eyes, looking for Delia Samantha. Yes, Samantha was really her middle name and she was incredibly proud of it. Her younger sister was called Linda Anastasia and she was in 6b. She was just as pretty as Delia, but the two sisters were never seen together.

Delia was standing at the open window with her two best friends Manuela and Isabelle, shaking her shiny blond hair. She was wearing a black top with glittery sequins. The top was cropped of course, so everyone could see her belly button piercing. And it was matched with low-cut jeans and a broad silver belt. All my tops were long enough to cover my bum; my dad would never have allowed me to wear clothes like Delia's. He always said that girls who dressed like that would end up as prostitutes. And Delia actually had had a lot of boyfriends, already. Boys never fancied me, and I didn't have a clue how to attract their attention. Who would want to even be friends with the outsider of 8a? I sat down at my desk, rested my head on my hands and waited for the bell to ring.

Danny and Ronnie had just finished their Godzilla drawing on the blackboard when the rusty bell rang and Evelyn, who had been standing at the door, shouted: "She's coming!"

Immediately, everyone ran back to their seats, Danny and Ronnie quickly wiped their stupid picture off the board and hurried back to their desks. Our form teacher was not someone to be trifled with. For some reason, Mrs Galiani had changed classes with Mr Lenz today. Just what I needed! In her classes, you had to be alert the whole time. Nothing escaped her keen eye.

She was fairly tall and looked sturdy; there was nothing much feminine about her. Her hair was cut short and she always wore jeans and trainers, even in the summer. She had a weathered face with a distinctive chin that gave her a hard, taunting look. There was a deep furrow between her eyebrows that became more pronounced depending on her state of alarm, and her sharp voice always got everyone's attention. But she was always very fair and we did learn a lot from her.

A short time after she'd said good morning and started the lesson, the door opened again. A small blond chubby boy slipped into the room. He kept his gaze on the ground and silently sat down at his desk. Mrs Galiani looked at him briefly but didn't say anything. She knew very well that Patrick was late every morning on purpose. This way he could avoid the others' bullying before the lessons began. So Mrs Galiani tolerated it.

With a sigh, I resigned myself to the fact that it was Monday again and was relieved that I didn't get picked.

In the short break before the next lesson, I wanted to write down the stack of homework Mrs Galiani had given us, but I didn't manage to. Delia staggered towards me in her heels and I could smell the cloud of her perfume coming closer.

"Aw, sweet little Maya! Make sure you don't forget anything! Wouldn't want to disappoint your daddy!"

"That is none of your business!" I mumbled awkwardly. Delia was not good at school, but of course that was not what counted. She was pretty enough to make up for it.

She sniggered and went back to her friends Isabelle and Manuela. They put their heads together and giggled and whispered and were watching every move I made with their heavily made-up eyes. I turned my gaze away and looked out of the window, trying to hide the tears that always flowed much too easily.

I only turned around again when the boys started to make their stupid comments. They moved closer to Patrick, like vultures circling their prey: the tall chunky Andrew and his two buddies Danny and Ronnie. Andrew was a six-foot-one hulk with size 10 feet, and he loved bullying weaker students.

I felt so sorry for Patrick. Not only was he small and chubby, but he had quite a bad stutter. Even though he was one year younger than everyone else, he was much more intelligent, because he loved reading. And he was unbeatable at maths. Which he had to pay for in PE classes; with his build he couldn't even do the easiest things.

"Right, fatty," Andrew started, "where is that maths homework then? Get it out! Where is it?"

"It's in m-m-my b-bag," Patrick whispered in agony.

"Oho!" Danny picked up Patrick's bag and poured the entire contents out on the floor.

"There it is!" He lifted a blue notebook with a carefully glued on picture of a Lufthansa airplane and threw it down onto the desk so violently that it flew right off it again. Patrick let it all happen without looking up.

"Hey, you fat pilot! The airplane's gonna crash under your weight!" scoffed Andrew, who was probably quite a lot heavier than Patrick himself. But he obviously didn't understand that with his pea of a brain.

I was boiling with rage, but I would never have had the courage to step in. Mrs Galiani had told Patrick very clearly that he would have to stand up for himself, that nobody else could do that for him. She had taken a lot of time to try and help him; she had sent him to self-help classes to strengthen his self-esteem. But Patrick didn't have a dad who could have shown him how to stand his ground as a man. He had died in a plane crash shortly after Patrick was born. And Patrick just wasn't a fighter, but the friendliest creature you could have imagined.

Finally, the bell put an end to his agony. Patrick sniffed and crept around the room to gather his things. I smiled at him discreetly but he didn't see me.

The next lessons were Maths and English, followed by the long break. I wandered sluggishly onto the schoolyard and sat down on the low wall next to the old lime tree, where I always sat the break out by myself. Nobody was by themselves except for me. Everyone else seemed to be part of a group of people they hung out with, laughed, talked and had fun. I had tried to talk to them many times – a while ago. I had tried to become part of those groups, but every time I got closer, there seemed to be an invisible wall building up, and I couldn't get through.

So I spent my time studying the small groups, and soon I knew exactly who was hanging out with whom.

There was only one girl who was by herself a lot as well: Janet Bonaventura. She was famous, because she always caused trouble and nobody dared get near her. But that seemed to suit her; she didn't seem to want anyone around her. The rumour was that she was the leader of a gang outside school, that she was a drug dealer and a burglar. Some even said that she was a witch. With her green cat's eyes she screened the schoolyard suspiciously and I knew that she was observing everything, just like me. Even though she had different reasons for it.

I would probably have remained "invisible" forever and I would at least have had my peace if the thing with the Bible hadn't happened one day. I thought that if I took the Bible to school with me, God would always be really close. It was a small book of the New Testament and it fitted perfectly into the pocket of my jacket. When I was wandering on the schoolyard by myself, I could slip my hand into my pocket and feel the soft leather cover. But one day, Andrew had nicked my jacket and thrown it right through the classroom. The Bible had fallen out and onto the floor for everyone to see.

And from that day on, I was the weirdo, the religious one who just didn't fit in anywhere. From that day on, I didn't dare take the Bible to school anymore, even though I never quite understood why other girls who wore lucky charms or believed in horoscopes weren't disrespected. Or Ronnie, who had a passion for aliens and was always talking about *"Star Wars"*. He kept thinking that he had seen UFOs in the sky. That was weird too, wasn't it?

At the end of the fifth lesson, Mrs Galiani surprised us with sensational news: "Tomorrow, a new student will join your class. He was at the Leonhardt School before and will repeat his eighth year with us."

Her words were drowned in a wave of hooting and the ringing of the bell.

"Hey girls, did you hear that? We're getting a new one!" Delia gushed, drumming her hands on the desk excitedly. "We could definitely do with a cute guy! Would make a change from those baby faces!"

Andrew looked at her angrily, and I really felt like grabbing her and pushing her cute little face right into the middle of the dates of the Second World War on the blackboard, so that she'd be covered in chalk. I truly hoped the new student would be ugly and that he'd have a ridiculous name like Ludger Edelkötter.

"What are you looking at, you little saint?" Delia, hands on hips, snapped right into my face. "The way you look, the new guy will probably start puking straight away when he sees you!"

"Ha, ha, ha! He's probably called Ludger Edelkötter!" I replied clumsily and even got muddled at the end of the sentence. Delia, Isabelle and Manuela looked at each other and then laughed out loud. "Did you hear that? Ludger Edelwhat ...!?"

"How cute!"

“Aw, poor little girl. Are you a bit jealous because you look so stupid that you’ll never get a guy?” Delia’s voice was full of mockery. Manuela and Isabelle were giggling, throwing their hair back arrogantly. And there it went, that tiny bit of courage I had built up and I hung my head, beaten. The three girls jeered triumphantly and staggered out of the room with swaying hips and their heads up high. I watched them sadly and angrily. Why did it always end like this?

2. The lantern in the forest

My home was only a fifteen minute walk from school in an exclusive area of the city. Our street was lined with beautiful magnolias; it was sunny and looked very peaceful. I was living in a big white house with a pretty well-kept garden. It was my mum's pride. My dad worked right next to the house in his own practice. It was well-known and booked out most of the time, so that Dad could barely take up new patients. Most people knew Doctor Fischer, because Dad had been on television and radio a few times. And a health guide had published an article by him. My mum had the theory that the other girls at school were jealous, because I was so privileged, but I didn't really believe that.

When I came home, Mum was usually making lunch. I generally got on really well with her, and she allowed a lot more than Dad. She kissed my cheek when I walked into the house and threw my jacket onto the clothes stand. "So, how was school, my big girl?"

"Rubbish!"

Mum was worried about me, because my class didn't respect me. Mrs Galiani had tried to send me to one of those self-help courses too, but I would have felt ridiculous. Self-help groups – they were for people with real problems, for complete losers. And I wasn't that bad, right?

We had talked about me changing classes once or twice, but Dad was worried that my education would suffer from that. A competent teacher like Mrs Galiani was not easy to be found, he said.

Dad arrived home shortly after me. When I heard his key unlock the door I raced to the clothes stand like lightening to hang up my jacket properly. To Dad, tidiness was a major issue and I couldn't stand his sermons. So I made sure he didn't have a reason to preach.

As he walked into the kitchen with a smile, he looked hungry. I think you could see that he was a doctor straight away even if you didn't know. His round metal-rimmed glasses and his full brown beard made him look like the typical good-natured, nice doctor.

"Hello, my girls! How are the two of you?"

"Fine. And you?" Mum and I replied at the same time.

"It was a busy morning and now I'm very tired. I'm lucky I could even get out to have lunch with you. Esther, could you maybe lend me a hand this afternoon?"

Mum worked part-time in Dad's practice; either in the morning or in the afternoon, depending on how much work he had. She was a doctor too; my parents had met and fallen in love at med school.

Five minutes later, we all sat at the table and said grace before we tugged into roast beef and mashed potatoes. Mum loved cooking and she was very good at it. She always made sure we had a varied diet.

I was relieved that Dad didn't ask anything about school today. To him, school was all that mattered. I knew his stories about his life as a student and his successful graduation by heart but he never grew tired of telling them again and again. His biggest wish was for me to follow in his footsteps and take over his practice one day. But I didn't know whether I even wanted to be a doctor.

We sat silent for a while, and I studied my parents' faces, wondering from which of them I had inherited my big nose. I probably had it from Dad, because Mum's nose was small. I was happy that my parents never argued when we were having lunch together, unlike other parents. Isabelle, for example, always told everyone with an annoyed expression how her parents were fighting all the time. Maybe that was why she was so aggressive. My parents hardly ever had an argument; sometimes I even wondered what they were talking about when I wasn't around. Mum was always much quieter when Dad was around.

All of a sudden, I remembered the big news: "We're getting a new student tomorrow!"

"Are you?" – "Mrs Galiani told us today." – "In the middle of the semester? That's a bit odd!" Dad didn't sound very happy about it.

"He used to go to another school and he's going to repeat eighth grade with us." I started thinking. Dad was right; it really was a bit odd. Usually, nobody changed classes in May.

"How chaotic these schools are nowadays! No wonder children don't learn properly anymore!" He was shaking his head.

After lunch, Mum got ready to work in the practice, which meant that I had to do the washing up. But at least, I could listen to the charts this afternoon at full blast, as I would be by myself.

After I had finished the dishes, I went up to my room and turned on my XBS Bass Boost stereo. My room was my castle, and it was furnished just as I liked it. It looked a bit like a sunny day in spring, with green and pink flower patterns on the wall and light, right silk curtains. It wasn't cool, but rather romantic. I liked flowers. And Mum's love of gardens might have rubbed off a bit: there were a lot of plants distributed everywhere in my room.

My desk stood right in front of the window. Dad didn't think that was a good idea, but I loved the view. To the right there was a shelf crammed with books, which I had read several times already. To the left, there was a slope in the roof, and in the niche underneath it, there was my bed. Right above the bed, there was another window through which I could see the sky.

I lay down on my bed and closed my eyes. My parents gave me almost everything I could wish for. Probably because I was their only child. There had been a really sad story in my family, but I could hardly remember any of it. I used to have a little brother, but he had died when he was only three months old. The only thing I remembered was my parents crying terribly. There was a picture, above the fireplace in the living room, showing little Michael sleeping peacefully in my mum's arms. Sometimes, I stood in front of the fireplace for a long time, looking at the picture, trying to imagine what my brother would have looked like now.

I preferred spending my evenings at my desk instead of downstairs with my parents in front of the television. They were happy with that because they thought that I was reading one of my books. But I wasn't. They didn't have a clue about what I was really doing.

In front of me, on the desk, laid an open notebook, baring all my secrets: my very own novel. Since I was eleven, I had been writing my own book, but I didn't tell anyone. The story was about a lantern in the forest that had magic powers. Through this lantern, the two children in my book, Jashnika and Michael, could enter a mysterious world, where they had to fight against evil forces to save that world and make the lantern shine brightly again. If my parents came into my room by surprise, I would quickly hide the book under my desk pad and act as though I was reading one of my school books.

It had already started getting dark outside and, like almost every evening, I was waiting for that one moment: the moment when the streetlamps were turned on. Because the lantern in my story had a special meaning.

Our street bordered on a park, a vast green area. Our

house was in the curve of the street on a slight hill. A bit further down, a narrow path led from the street through a small forest to an old mansion. The mansion was part of the park and had been made into a museum of local history. But the narrow path was private property, only the owners of the mansion and the employees of the museum were allowed to use it. To get to the mansion, everyone else had to make a detour via the public path, through the park, past the restaurant at the lake. The public path took about twenty minutes to walk, the private, direct path would only have taken five minutes.

It was not the mansion that was important to me, though, but the beautiful old lantern on the forecourt. I had to use the binoculars to see it better and I always got goose bumps when I saw that lonely light mysteriously shining through the trees.

In the night, I often had dreams I didn't want to wake up from again. I dreamt that I was riding through this green forest on the back of a white horse, surrounded by the light of the lantern in all its beautiful colours, like a shiny, wonderful rainbow. And when I reached my destination, the court with the lantern, I felt like I found the place where all my heart's desires, wishes and dreams came together. But this was usually the moment I woke up, disappointed that I hadn't managed to finish the dream. I had tried to tell my parents about it, but they didn't understand that kind of thing. So, I had started to write that novel.

I glanced at my watch. It was time! "I'm going to count to three." I murmured. "One, two, three!" Nothing happened. So I started again. "Okay, this time I'll count to ten."

I only got to seven. From one moment to the next, the park had been turned into a shimmering sea of lights in which my lantern was shining like an especially bright star in the night sky.

Dad hated the park. He preferred driving out to the countryside or to the mountains. A few years ago, we often used to go to the restaurant at the lake to have fish, but we had stopped doing that. Nowadays, some of the junkies from the other side of the park came wandering over as far as the restaurant once in a while, and ever since Dad had noticed used syringes in the grass, he didn't want to go there anymore. And he didn't allow me to go there anymore either. But Mum let me go every so often anyway. She reminded me every time, "Don't go any further than the lantern!" That was the limit.

Dad sometimes told us horrible stories about the other side of the park. All the crime that happened there and how neglected children were prowling around, stealing before they were old enough to go to school, even. He told us about men who would come home drunk, beating up their families. About poverty and drug misery. When I heard about that, I always went up to my room and thought about it. What would it be like to be a child who lives on the other side of the park?

Mum often told me that Dad struggled to come to terms with living in a city. He had grown up in a middle-class family in the country and he was quite traditional. But his desire to become a doctor had been so strong that he had been ready to give up that world that he loved so much. Maybe their way of thinking was also partly due to the fact that my parents were nearly fifty, already. They had had children quite late.

Dad generally struggled with modern things. With mobile phones, techno music and piercings. When I secretly bought a teen magazine half a year ago, his world caved in. I had forgotten to hide the magazine in the drawer of my desk, and Dad had discovered it on my bedside table. That had been one of the biggest arguments we had ever had, and I still blush thinking about it.

I wished my parents good night and went to bed, curling up underneath my duvet. And then I had to think about the new student again: it would definitely be an interesting change. I just hoped he was not going to be an idiot. Maybe it would help if I prayed. After all, I had once experienced a small miracle, which had made my faith stronger.

When I was about nine years old, my mum and I found an injured kitten on the street. The poor animal had been hit by a car and it had a horrible big wound. Blood was dripping onto the pavement. I will never forget that terrible sight. Mum and I had taken the kitten to the vet straight away. He shook his head sadly and told us that he wouldn't be able to do much anymore.

But I kept praying the whole day for God to perform a miracle and to heal the kitten. And really, three days later, the vet called us to say that the kitten was fine again and that they had found its owner. The vet himself admitted that it had been a minor miracle. I could not even start describing the joy I felt then.

I was thinking about that story too now, after I had finished praying. I prayed for a miracle that would change the situation in my class nearly every evening. But Mum said that these things didn't just happen over night.

I rolled over and pulled the duvet up to my nose. Soon, I was sleeping a deep, relaxing sleep, dreaming about the next day and the new student. In my dream, he came to school with a cat on his arms, his leg was bandaged and he had a very complicated name that didn't really exist and that I couldn't remember when I woke up the next morning.

3. Domenico

A friendly breeze filled the streets with life this morning as I walked to school a bit quicker than usually. I felt like I was going to burst with curiosity when I pushed the door to the building open. I ran up the last steps of the stairs and was nearly breathless when I arrived at the class room.

Everyone was gathered around Delia's desk, and they were unusually silent. The only voice to be heard was one I had never heard before; the hoarse voice of a boy that sounded cool and somehow really tough. Was he the new one?

"I swear, I'm gonna knock the stuffing out of your teachers! At my old swot shop, they all had to go to the nuthouse!"

I felt a shiver going from my head to my toes, leaving an electric feeling in my whole body. I stood behind Carol and Catherine and tried to catch a glimpse of the new boy. And what I saw instantly fascinated me.

Sitting casually on the desk was a freaky looking boy with ginger hair and a can of Red Bull in his hand. When I looked at him, he suddenly turned his face towards mine, and his expressive grey-blue eyes flashed at me. I wanted to say "hi," but then I realised that he hadn't actually noticed me. The way he was dressed was shocking and fascinating all at once: his washed out jeans and his black faded t-shirt were full of holes. To look dishevelled might have been trendy for boys at the moment, but that was a bit much. Nobody was wearing *that* torn-up clothes. Around his neck, he was wearing leather bands with a pointy, bent fang and a silver pendant that somehow looked like intertwining thorns.

I couldn't stop staring at him. I had never seen such a good-looking boy. I started studying every detail while I was listening to what he was telling Delia and the others.

"I heard your teacher's really uncool," he smiled dismissively. His eyes seemed to devour Delia. She moved closer and struck her well-rehearsed pose that worked with most boys. I grudgingly acknowledged that this new hope was lost already.

Andrew didn't seem to like the new boy either. He stood in front of him and looked down on him, snorting. "Hey, softhead, stop bragging about! I'm gonna bust your nose! I'm the boss at this school, everyone respects me!" he barked with his raucous voice.

"Do they?" the new one asked sneeringly, "I definitely don't."

I noticed that he had a slight accent. Where did he come from, anyway? And what was his name? I only knew one thing for sure: he was a complete idiot! Just what I needed!

"Oh, just shut up, you jerk!" Delia shouted. "You might be the strongest but Domenico is definitely the most handsome! And I think looks are more important."

Andrew grunted. His big fleshy nose and his closely-cropped hair didn't make him look like a Mister Universe candidate. But everyone feared him because of his strength and height.

Domenico! I had never heard that name before, but it sounded quite exotic and interesting. I was always collecting special names for my novel.

Domenico grinned and added coolly: "Keep it easy, Delia. At my old school, I was the strongest, too. That wimp ain't got no chance, relax!"

The girls were clapping their hands enthusiastically; everyone had always wanted to get their own back on him. Andrew snarled threateningly. There was definitely something dangerous brewing.

"Do you have a nickname?" Manuela asked. "Somethin' shorter than Domenico. That's so long!"

"You can call me Nico or Nick or Nicky."

He smiled at the girls seductively and I saw that he had a big gap between his front teeth, which made him look even bolder. His left front tooth was even chipped. He leaned over to Delia: "Tell me, sweets, how about I sit next to you?"

"Oh!" she breathed, flattered. But then, a disappointed look spread over her face. "Unfortunately, Manu's already sitting next to me."

"And where do I sit?"

They had a look around the room. My heart nearly stopped beating. I hadn't even thought about that.

There were only two free seats: next to me or next to Patrick. But Patrick sat in the front row, right in front of the teacher. And the way I judged Domenico, he wouldn't choose to sit where Mrs Galiani could see him best. So, he was probably going to choose the seat next to me. My stomach twisted into a knot.

"Pah, I'm afraid you're gonna have to choose between the fatty and the little saint," I heard Delia say. Domenico looked very disappointed.

"Bummer! And who's that supposed to be?"

The earth was trembling beneath my feet. That was definitely the most disgusting thing Delia could have done to me: ridiculing me in front of the new boy. I quickly hid my face. *Don't cry now, just don't!* Delia's eyes were looking for me and there was no point in hiding behind Catherine.

"There she is. Our little geeky saint!" She pointed her finger directly at me, and I could feel Domenico's eyes on me. These grey-blue, intense eyes that examined me thoroughly, shooting flashing arrows at me. I felt horribly clumsy and stupid and I wished the ground would open up and swallow me.

Was that an amused smile playing around his lips? I couldn't properly recognise it because the tears had won the battle again and they blurred my vision. I would so much have liked to give Delia a smart answer. I was not a saint little geek! I swallowed my tears and pressed my lips together.

He whistled through his teeth and leered. “Allora, where do you sit?”

“In the back, last row, at the window.” I tried to make my voice sound steady. He threw his paper bag, which he had brought some books in, onto my desk and strolled back past the other desks. I followed him grudgingly and sat down on my chair. Was God not listening? Domenico proved to be worse than my most horrible nightmare. And, of course, Delia had been lucky again!

“Guys, she’s coming! Watch out!” Isabelle shouted into the classroom. Immediately, everyone sat down at their desk. Delia smiled at Domenico expectantly and carefully draped her blonde mane on her shoulder. I sat there, head on my hands and sighed to myself. My eyes were still a bit wet. All hopes for Ludger Edelkötter had gone.

Mrs Galiani stepped into the room, followed by Patrick, who slipped behind his desk, as silent as a mouse. The class calmed down, and Mrs Galiani sternly looked around the room until her eyes reached Domenico.

“Welcome to 8a, Domenico! Have you handed in your documents to the headmaster?”

“Nah, the old fart overslept.”

The whole class started laughing, Delia the loudest.

“Be quiet, Delia!” Mrs Galiani ordered angrily. “Domenico di Loreno!” she pronounced his full name and made a note. At least his name was special, like in my dream last night. She looked at him attentively, she even seemed concerned. Nearly as though she knew something about him.

The first thing she made us do today was a writing exercise. I opened my notebook. I generally wasn't afraid of writing exercises. After I had written about four sentences, I peeked at Domenico. He sat there, holding his head, and scribbled something on the paper with a chewed pencil. Why didn't he use a proper pen?

I finished my sentence and started observing Domenico from the corner of my eye. First, I looked at his hair. Depending on the light, it seemed either light brown or ginger. Like a chameleon, I thought. It was falling into his face in cheeky, long strands, covering his grey-blue, almond-shaped eyes. His eyebrows, which were a bit darker than his hair, made a beautiful bow above his eyes. And, of course, he had a pointed, bold chin.

I noticed two other details: around his left wrist, he wore loads of leather bands, and he smelled of cigarette smoke.

Suddenly, he realised that I had been observing him and stopped writing. "What are you lookin' at?" he hissed. His voice was sharp and cold, and his eyes were piercing.

"I'm sorry!" I mumbled quickly, blushing. For the second time today, my eyes filled with tears. I missed the next sentence. And the one after that. Mrs Galiani's voice didn't reach me anymore. After a while, she stopped and came to stand next to Domenico. The furrow between her eyes became deeper when she picked up his notebook.

"Domenico ..." her voice sounded quite desperate. "Go up to the blackboard, please."

Domenico grinned at the teacher cheekily and remained on his chair.

"Now!"

"Alright, calma! Don't panic, lady!" He put some chewing gum in his mouth and walked to the front casually. The girls were following his moves with longing gazes. Mrs Galiani stayed next to his chair with her arms folded.

"Now, take a piece of chalk and write *February!*"

He rolled his eyes and scratched the chalk over the blackboard with a nasty squeak. His handwriting was not exactly pretty, but the word still clearly read "Febury".

"Retard!" Andrew grumbled.

Domenico grinned and flipped him the bird. The girls nearly couldn't suppress their giggling.

Mrs Galiani cleared her throat.

"Well, Domenico, it seems like you might need some extra tutoring in English."

Wham! That hit home! That would stop him trying to be funny. Mrs Galiani was really smart.

Domenico leaned against the blackboard and angrily looked at the teacher. "Whatever!" he said, without batting an eye-lid. Mrs Galiani walked towards him with vigorous steps and grabbed him at his shoulders.

"Let me tell you something, young man: don't try and play the rebel in my class. You are going to hand in that notebook at the end of the lesson and I will grade that exercise!"

Everyone, including me, was staring at Mrs Galiani in shock now. We all knew she was strict, but it had never been this bad before. The girls were looking at Domenico compassionately but he just shrugged his shoulders. I couldn't tell whether he really didn't mind that punishment. I took another look at his notebook. With all those spelling mistakes he would definitely get an insufficient grade. There was no doubt.

"I don't care about that stupid writing stuff!" Domenico commented after the second English lesson, when we girls had gathered around him in the schoolyard. I was incredibly curious about what would happen next. He was smoking a cigarette and studied every girl with his irresistible tooth-gap smile. Every girl, except for me, of course. Either he was quite a good actor or he really was not embarrassed at all.

"She's sharper than I thought, but I crack her. Gonna come up with summin' …"

"She really isn't easy to get to," Delia worried.

"I thought she went completely over the top!" Manuela commented.

But he waved dismissively. “Like I said: I don’t care!”

“If you manage to crack her, you’re going to get a medal!” declared Isabelle with her chin up, tying her dark brown, shiny hair up into a ponytail.

“You just wait and see. Got a lotta tricks up my sleeve!”

“We had some too. Don’t think you’re that clever!” Isabelle was not going to give up that easily, as usual.

“You just chicken out too easy, that’s all,” he said, “You’re too easy to scare.” He flicked his cigarette away, and it landed beside the bike shelter. The next one was immediately lit.

“Watch out Galiani doesn’t catch you,” Isabelle said, “smoking isn’t allowed on the grounds.”

“I don’t care,” he replied coolly and suddenly flinched when something in his pocket started beeping in a melody. He stuck the cigarette between his lips and fished out a smartphone.

“Wow! That’s awesome!” Delia admired it. “I’ve been nagging my parents for ages to get me one of those.”

He smiled at her smugly and checked the message on the display. His grin disappeared and his expression became hard and somehow worried.

“Gotta make a quick call. You gonna wait?” He moved away a few steps, just far enough for us not to hear his conversation.

I was boiling up inside. Delia had got her mobile out too and she was now pushing some keys with her fingers full of rings. I did not have my own mobile phone of course. Dad did not see the necessity of having one of those. After all, we had been living just fine without them before, too. At least I was allowed to borrow my mum's, and I could even take it to school. But it was just lying there in my bag. I didn't know anyone who would text me anyway.

When Domenico came back, Delia stretched like a purring cat. "Are you gonna give me your number?" she asked sweetly. I snorted a tiny bit too loudly and had to pretend I had a coughing fit.

"No," he said calmly and put his phone back into his pocket, "nobody gets my number."

I really enjoyed Delia's long face. "Man! What's that supposed to mean?!" she was sulking, but he wouldn't change his mind.

"What time is?" he asked. "I really gotta go."

We all looked pretty confused. We still had classes until lunch! But he was serious. He waved goodbye and just trod off, leaving the schoolyard as if it was a playground to which you only came if you felt like it.

"Man, this guy's got some nerve!" Isabelle muttered, saying out loud what everyone was thinking.

I touched my forehead and shook my head. What an idiot! It was all so frustrating and unfair! I really would have liked to cry out my anger, but I couldn't even cry anymore. I was standing in front of the biggest mystery of my life, and two hours later I was not even sure anymore whether it had all just been a dream or whether it was actually true.

I usually avoided talking about school at lunch with my parents but I just couldn't keep this morning's story to myself. "His name is Domenico di Loreno!" Despite all the worries, I let the letters of his name melt on my tongue.

I had never heard such a cool and resonant name before. What a shame that its owner was such a stupid poser.

"So, he is Italian?" Dad commented.

"I'm not sure. He has got reddish-light brown hair and Italians are usually dark-haired, aren't they?"

"Well, that probably means he comes from northern Italy."

"Anyway. He's a catastrophe for our class."

"What he did really sounds quite bad," Mum agreed after I had told them the whole story.

"It's horrific! An absolute disgrace!" Dad was railing. "Did his parents not teach that boy any manners?"

I shrugged: "I don't know."

"And you have to sit next to him?"

"Yes, unfortunately. All the other seats were taken."

"Did he leave you alone, at least?" Mum wanted to know.

"Oh well ..." I could not be bothered to tell them about the episode when he snapped at me at school. "Delia is just always lucky! Now there he is, her Mister

Universe with a big mouth that she can adore; just what she wished for. What a stupid idiot!"

"Now, now Maya!" Dad was telling me off. He did not like me speaking like that. "I'm sure one day he will have to deal with the consequences of his behaviour. I'm thinking about calling your teacher to have her move that boy next to someone else."

I wanted to reply but I could only gasp for breath. I had to think about this by myself in my room first and write the events of this morning down in my diary. Luckily, the art class of this afternoon had been cancelled, because Mrs Wilde was sick.

I took the notebook with my novel out and laid my head on my hands, thinking about the next lines I would write. Should I change the boy's name and call him Domenico instead of Michael? I probably should, not least because I had wanted him to have a special name from the start and just had not found one at the time. But I couldn't make up my mind. And anyway, I didn't even like that new boy. He was horrible. Arrogant, big-headed, stupid show-off, thinking he was Mister Universe.

4. Mister Universe

The first unbelievable surprise the next day was that Domenico did not show up at school. I couldn't believe his cheek! It did happen from time to time that somebody skipped a class or two. But like that!? The entire class was perplexed.

Mrs Galiani looked unusually serious when she asked where he was in the last lesson of the day. She shook her head silently and drew a big line into the register. She cleared her throat and looked at the class sternly.

"The spare keys disappeared from the teachers' room yesterday afternoon. I would like to ask you to keep your eyes open. I'm afraid someone might have misplaced them," she told us briefly and started the lesson without further ado.

I could not concentrate. The whole time I had to think about Domenico and stared at his empty seat. I couldn't have cared less about the lost keys. The teachers could worry about their stuff themselves.

I vaguely heard Mrs Galiani send Patrick home. His eyes had been glowing with fever all morning. Apparently, he had caught the flu and would be ill for the next few days. Oh no, not that as well! Even though we didn't speak to each other much, I missed Patrick when he was not around.

On Thursday morning, Domenico's seat remained

empty too, and I started wondering whether he would ever come back at all. But, in the afternoon, he showed up for the PE class; he acted as though nothing had happened. As it was warm and sunny, we went outside to the public sports field, close to the swimming pool.

Domenico was standing at the tube stop when I got off the bus. My heart beat fast as I walked past him and I said "hi" shyly. He looked down at me with a smug, cool expression, like James Dean, with a cigarette between his lips. Great! Now, I had made a complete loser of myself.

"Nico!" Delia, Isabelle and Manuela came around the corner and hurried towards him. I saw how he grinned at the girls and crossed the street to meet them. I left as quickly as I could. I was so angry with myself, I could have cried out loud.

I changed quickly and walked out onto the field. Some of our class were already sitting there, one of them was Domenico, who had not changed at all. He was still wearing the same clothes I had seen him in at the tube stop: his battered denim shorts and a black shirt with a silver tiger on it, snarling.

He had rolled up the sleeves over his shoulders and I could see his tattoo for the first time; an interlaced, probably Celtic pattern or something like that, which was drawn around his arm like a band. Coolly, he was smoking yet another cigarette and didn't seem to care about the surprised looks on the others' faces.

Mr Reuter, our PE teacher, sprinted over to us in his red and white tracksuit trousers. He was wearing the usual whistle around his neck. He probably even wore it in bed. He ticked our names off his list and then looked at Domenico from top to toe. “So, you are the new one, right? Smoking is not allowed here, by the way.”

Then he divided us into groups according to our heights. Delia and I were two of the tallest girls of our class and therefore we were in the same group. Luckily, Isabelle was even taller than us and so she was in the boys’ group. Domenico, however, was not very tall for his age. Smiling, he waited for Mr Reuter to make a decision and put him into our group. He was standing really close to me and I secretly tried to guess his height. I don’t know why, but somehow I would have minded if he had been smaller than me. But when we were standing next to the long jump bar, I could see that he was a few centimetres taller.

His turn was second to last. When he got into his starting position, I stepped aside so he had enough space and looked at him, curiously. He closed his eyes and concentrated like a real pro. Did he want to show off again or was he really good at this? I crossed my fingers nervously. And then he took off like a rocket. Exactly on the white line he jumped and flew through the air for what seemed like ages. Delia burst into a cheer and clapped her hands, thrilled. She ran over to him and measured the distance he had jumped. Her face was glowing with eagerness.

"Sixteen feet and ten inches!" she shouted happily. "Oh, Nico! That's incredible! That's crazy!"

It really was sensational. So far, Andrew had been the record holder of our school with sixteen feet and three inches. Domenico had just managed to beat him by an incredible seven inches!

He smiled at Delia, got up and cleaned the sand off his shoes. Delia grabbed his shoulders.

"Hey, where did you learn that? Are you in a club? Do you train a lot?"

He shook his head. "Not for long time. But I used to win lot of competitions."

Impressed, Delia looked at him admiringly and threw her arms around his neck. "Oh, Nico, you're so great! With you we're defo gonna win at the school competition! You gotta show that to Mr Reuter. Just wait, I'm gonna get him."

She ran off and came back with the teacher a second later. Domenico jumped again. Mr Reuter, who was usually hard to convince, was really impressed and scratched his beard ponderingly.

"You are astonishingly good. You should get advanced training."

Domenico looked at the teacher incredulously and seemed to forget about his arrogance, for the first time. Suddenly, he reminded me of a child who was happy about Christmas.

"I would like to see you in our booster club. After the

summer holidays, some kids are leaving and you could join. We will discuss that later," Mr Reuter suggested.

"Okay." Domenico was smiling and, in that moment, he even seemed to be a bit embarrassed.

Delia obviously had to spread the news immediately when we joined the rest of the class again. "Hey guys, did you hear that Domenico has set a new long jump record?"

"Wow, how cool!" the girls were impressed. Only I did not say anything. Now that bigmouth was the best at sports, too. Just what I needed.

Andrew's deep voice cut through the happy excitement: "Whatever! That's ridiculous! Big deal! I bet that skinny little jerk is not even half as strong as me!"

"Just shut up, you stupid poser!" Delia shouted. "You're just jealous, admit it!"

"Let me handle that, Delia," Domenico calmed her down. "I'm gonna beat the crap out of that wuss!"

He stood in front of Andrew with his arms akimbo.

"Hey, dumbo, I was the strongest in my old school, too. Wanna see who's gonna win?"

We were all terrified, staring at the two of them. He really wanted to compete against Andrew? Was he suicidal or something? That would definitely be the end of his career. Nobody ever won a fight against Andrew.

Andrew looked as though he had just won the lottery.

"Sure, you baby!" he jeered and looked at Domenico

as if he was a mouse in a trap. "And when do you wanna try it?"

"After school." Domenico's voice sounded very strong.

"Alright, loser! I'm gonna eat you up like antipasti!"

"We'll see."

"That's enough, now!" Mr Reuter interrupted the fight. "We are now going to play handball."

I moaned. I hated any type of ball game because I was too clumsy for them and the boys always threw the ball far too brutally.

Mr Reuter had the worst way of putting teams together: He designated three team bosses, and one of them was Delia. She got to start choosing her team members and obviously picked Domenico first. I was left standing there until the end, as usual, and finally got assigned to Nicole's team. It felt miserable, but there was one advantage to this: I was not in the same team as Delia, Domenico or Andrew.

Domenico was as good at handball as he was at long jump. Within a few minutes he had taken the lead in the game and he was moving so smoothly with the ball, the whole class was staring in amazement. He was not just talented, he was like a pro!

Andrew acted like a rabid dog and tried to push Domenico out of the field whenever he could. Mr Reuter was constantly blowing his whistle. The game ended in a very curious manner: Because Domenico had been throwing the ball so hard, it had deflated. All that remained was a floppy white piece of leather and we had to break up the game early. This was quite a blow for Mr Reuter.

"What a shame!" he was complaining. "If the keys had not disappeared, I could have brought a spare ball."

Secretly, I was thrilled, of course.

At four, when we went back to the locker rooms, Andrew growled: "We'll see whether you'll still find the retard so great once I've beaten him up!"

The other girls looked at each other uneasily. Andrew was dangerously charged and one thing was sure: This fight would be no fun. It was going to be dead serious.

"This is gonna be a tough one," Isabelle commented, "Andrew is a head taller than Nico!"

The others were nodding sceptically. I followed them to the locker rooms, lost in my thoughts. If Domenico was going to lose this fight, Mister Universe would belong to the past.

I did not go home but waited outside with the others for Andrew and Domenico to come out. When they finally arrived, the other boys were following them, shouting and cheering, getting the two of them fired up. We stepped aside to avoid getting pushed out of the way by them. The two adversaries threw their sports bags into a corner and stood in front of each other on the field, right outside the locker rooms. The girls were completely silent, but the boys were jeering. The difference between the two boys was really scary. Not only was Domenico considerably smaller than Andrew, he was also much skinnier. Andrew was quite sturdy and strong. I once heard that he even trained with weights.

Danny lifted his hands: "Are you ready?"

Both of them nodded grimly. I suddenly realised that I was trembling, because I was so apprehensive.

"Luke Skywalker versus Darth Vader!" Ronnie commented excitedly. "The rebel against the empire!"

"Stop your stupid space stories!" Delia shouted nervously.

"Alright guys!" Danny said. "On your marks, get set … GO!"

With a wild howl the two enemies lunged at each other. Andrew tried to grab Domenico straight away, but he missed. Domenico turned around like lightening and attacked Andrew from behind. With worried faces and clenched hands we watched the two of them wrestling, gasping, spitting, swearing and trying to knock each other down. My heart felt like it was going to burst.

"Nico! Nico!" Delia was screaming, and without even realising what I was doing I joined in with the cheers of the other girls. "Go on, Nico! Punch him! You have got to win! Wipe him out!" The boys stood opposite us and they were cheering for Andrew.

It was a really tough fight and it even hurt to watch. It looked as though neither of them was stronger than the other, despite their considerable physical differences. Domenico was extremely agile and he knew a lot of tricks. This was an absolute first: Someone who could take Andrew. So, full of hope, we cheered even louder than before.

"Nico! Nico! Nico!"

Andrew's expression was full of rage and hate – he brutally punched Domenico in the stomach. Domenico groaned and staggered backwards. We held our breath in horror. His face became completely pale and he breathed heavily.

But his counter attack came suddenly. Unpredictably. With all his might, he jumped at Andrew, grabbed his hands and pushed a foot into the back of his knees. Andrew could not keep his balance and fell on the floor.

"Yaaaaaay!" we screamed and jumped up and down happily. On the boys' side, there was complete silence. Domenico immediately sat down on Andrew and pinned his arms onto the ground. Andrew struggled and swore loudly but he did not manage to break free. Domenico had a grip on him. I was surprised how strong he was.

"Give up! You lost!" he triumphed.

Our cry of victory couldn't have been louder. One thing was sure: This fight would become a legend! The school had a new champion. Mister Universe was now definitely born.

Exhausted, Domenico got up and walked towards us

girls with a smile. There was blood on his face, he had a black eye and his hair was a complete mess. The girls ran to meet him and hugged him passionately; especially Delia, of course.

All of a sudden, my joy about Andrew having been beaten for once was gone. This would only give Domenico yet another reason to boast around. And it would make the atmosphere in our class even more violent. I was watching how Andrew pulled himself together, swearing, and how he joined the boys. They threw angry looks at Domenico. Andrew was red with rage and he would explode sooner or later. He would get his revenge one day.

While the other girls were celebrating Domenico, I grabbed my bag and left silently. How could I even have taken part in this! If only Andrew had won. Then everything would at least have stayed the same. Angrily, I was swinging my bag back and forth. It was high time I went home.

"Did this new boy ever come back to school in the end?" Dad served me a big spoonful of soup.

"Yes, this afternoon." I was definitely fed up with Domenico and really was not in the mood to talk about him. And still it just slipped out: "He and Andrew had quite a bad row!"

Dad was shocked. "My goodness! That new one has a really bad influence on your class. I am going to ask Mrs

Galiani to have you sit next to someone else. I do not like the thought of you having to share your desk with someone who behaves so badly."

This, however, alarmed me and I was suddenly interested in the subject again. "Oh no!" I burst out, "don't do that, Dad, please!"

Dad looked at me surprised. "Why not?"

"Because … because that would be really embarrassing for me. And … it's not necessary, I think. He … can do me no harm, really." I did not exactly know myself why I said this. Mum looked at me without saying anything. I blushed and turned my face away.

"But Mrs Galiani has to do something about this situation. Things cannot go on like this," Dad replied. "In any case, I want you to stay away from this boy, Maya."

Well, this was not going to be a problem. I kept silent and ate my soup, thinking. This afternoon, something had happened to me. Something I did not quite understand myself. I had been worried sick about Domenico during the whole fight. Even though I could not stand him.

In my head, I went through every single scene of this afternoon. He was really handsome, I had to admit that. And I really liked his smile when Mr Reuter praised him. But on the other hand he was just so full of himself that I didn't want to think about him anymore for the rest of the evening.

5. Strange incidents

On Friday morning, the way to the school gate was blocked by a police car that was parked in front of the building. Not completely awake yet, I squeezed my way through the small space between the car and the wall. Unfortunately, I managed to touch the side mirror with my bag and it was bent by a few degrees.

Oh no!, I thought and looked around nervously, before I finally realised that police cars do not usually belong on schoolyards. What on earth was going on?

I looked around. The schoolyard was nearly empty. I was incredibly late, though. Someone was moving behind the bike shelter, but I could not see who it was. I shrugged and turned towards the door reaching for the handle …

… but it was not there. The door was wide open, and a girl wearing lots of jewellery strutted past me. She looked a bit like Lara Croft with her thick black braid. Janet Bonaventura. Luckily, she had not noticed me. I followed her with my eyes and suddenly saw Domenico, next to the bike shelter. He was standing there in his cool James Dean pose, wearing his leather jacket and smoking a cigarette. He was looking down and his hair hid his face.

Janet walked straight towards him. I held my breath. I was extremely curious about what was going to happen now. Janet was only a few steps away from Domenico when he lifted his head and gave me a warning look.

Immediately I turned around, before his look could turn me into some wobbly mess. Better clear off now before I found out that Domenico was friends with this dubious girl. To be honest, I did not even want to know. It would have made me feel bad, somehow.

I arrived just in time. I stepped into the room at the same time as Mr Lenz. To welcome us, he distributed a sheet with boring exercises that included lots of highly complicated algebra formulas. Great! I would have been much more interested in the reason why a police car was standing in front of the school. Had the others seen it, too?

Domenico arrived a quarter of an hour later and sat down, as relaxed as always. I envied him for being able to act as though nothing bothered him.

We started calculating, but the numbers just did not seem to add up. I was no maths hero. Domenico was not even touching his sheet, instead he was busy with his smartphone.

His pack of cigarettes was lying openly on the desk and it nearly looked like they were on my side. I carefully pushed them over to his side and got a quick glance at his display. I read "TT2". Weird. Was that some secret language? The concentrated silence was suddenly interrupted by the beeping of a text message. Poor Mr Lenz winced and the piece of chalk he was writing with on the blackboard broke and fell to the floor.

As if that was not enough, someone knocked on the door loudly. Mr Lenz frowned angrily. There was nothing he hated more than being interrupted in his mathematical dreams. For us, however, it was a very welcome break.

"I am very sorry!" Mrs Galiani was not exactly the distraction we had hoped for. This smelled like serious trouble. Behind her we could see Mr Biedermann's red, sweaty face. Mr Biedermann was the janitor.

Domenico quickly hid his mobile phone and his cigarettes under the desk. Mrs Galiani's stern look seemed to impress him for once. There was a deep worry in her eyes, and the furrow on her forehead was exceptionally deep. She went over to Mr Lenz and talked to him with her voice lowered whilst Mr Biedermann looked at us threateningly. His black beady eyes wandered around, and he did not seem to know exactly what he was looking for. His nostrils quivered, and I would not have been surprised if smoke had started to come out of them. Like most students, I did not like him at all. You could smell his bad breath from miles away, and when you said hi to him he bared his unhealthy, rotten teeth at you.

Mrs Galiani finally turned to us and silently shook her head. It all looked like there was a catastrophe on its way.

"I am sorry that I have to interrupt your class, but I have something important to tell you. And that is ...," she looked at all the faces in the room as if she was searching for something she could not find. "Well, this morning someone broke into Mr Biedermann's empty flat and stole nearly two thousand euros. The police was here."

There was a gloomy silence, like at a funeral, only interrupted by Mr Biedermann's rhythmic panting. A few students were looking at the floor sheepishly as if it was their fault. I looked at Domenico; his eyes seemed frozen.

Mrs Galiani did not wait for a reaction and continued: "The set of keys that are missing also include the keys to the gym and the spare key to Mr Biedermann's flat. We therefore have to assume that the keys were stolen on purpose to break into the flat. I am currently informing all the classes. I am very sad to have to admit that there is an unscrupulous thief at our school."

"Sad? Ha! It's a colossal impertinence!" Mr Biedermann barked angrily and waved his arms as if he was swimming against the tide. "But I'm not surprised by this lot!" he said sarcastically, nodding at us with contempt.

Mr Galiani cleared her throat. "Mr Biedermann, please stick to the facts. We are going to try our best to find the culprit. So if any of you has any information or evidence, please do not hesitate to contact me. But, please do not spread any false rumours. That will be all for the moment."

A stunned silence fell on the whole class. With a brief nod, Mrs Galiani left to inform the rest of the school. Mr Biedermann threw another scornful look at us and followed her.

Mr Lenz could forget about the rest of his class now, and he wistfully looked at his carefully constructed algebra exercise. Obviously nobody was interested in any formula anymore. Until the bell rang, everyone was coming up with wild theories about the burglary. The wildest came from Andrew, Danny and Ronnie, whose imagination was limitless, thanks to all the mystery and science fiction they consumed.

"That's wicked, man! Finally something's happening in this lame dump! Even the cops came!" Danny was jeering and made the victory sign.

Great! These guys thought this kind of thing was funny. Delia, on the other hand, seemed to be straining her rather small amount of grey matter.

"This morning I saw this guy in front of the school. He looked suspicious. He had brown hair and was wearin' a tracksuit top!" Ronnie shouted so excitedly that he was spitting all over the place.

"Dimwit! Nearly everyone looks like that!" Andrew replied.

"I think that was a disguised purolitan!"

"Shut up!" Andrew barked and slapped Ronnie so

hard that he fell. “Stop droolin’ around, you creep! What’s that supposed to be, a purolitan?”

Well, everyone knew that Ronnie had a habit of inventing characters and names.

Even I could not concentrate on algebra, anymore. I was brooding over that burglary. Two thousand euros! That was an enormous amount! Who could have done such a thing?

Nobody from our class, that was for sure. Nobody, not even Delia, Isabelle or Andrew would have been so vile. A deed like that was beyond them. The burglar had to be completely rotten inside.

Almost automatically, my eyes turned towards Domenico. But I could not allow myself to even think that!

Janet Bonaventura, of course!, I suddenly realised. She had done things like that before. That she was still tolerated around here was probably thanks to her father’s influence. He was the highly respected head of a psychiatric clinic. Dad even knew him personally.

Domenico wrote another text. His lips were twisted into a smirk. What a jerk! He was definitely crazy.

In English class, Mrs Galiani returned Domenico his writing exercise, which she had graded as promised. I gave it a quick glance and saw that it was full of red marks.

With a grin, Domenico pulled the pages out of his notebook, screwed them up and threw them, all under Mrs Galianis eyes, into the bin. She shook her head. I could not believe it! Did he really not care at all that he might have to repeat the year? He was fooling around with his life, and one day he would definitely reach a dead end!

I moved my chair as far away from him as I could. How long would I have to bear sitting next to this jerk?

"It's up to you, Domenico." Mrs Galiani commented dryly. "If I were you, I would work really hard to straighten out that grade."

I was not the only one who thought Janet was suspicious. Andrew, Danny and Ronnie were so busy making plans on how they could set a trap for her that Andrew even seemed to forget his fury about Domenico's victory of the day before.

In the meantime, Domenico wandered over to the door where Delia was waiting for him, impatiently. Her very pink lips were pouting.

"Got any fags?" I heard her asking when Domenico had reached her. He nodded. I grabbed my jacket from my chair and carefully followed them. I hoped I was still invisible enough that they would not notice me.

They were holding hands as they wandered down the hallway. They looked pretty, I had to admit, even though I felt a sting in my heart. A dream couple.

Domenico let go of her hand and put his arm around her hips. His hand slowly found its way under her t-shirt.

I walked a few steps closer to hear their conversation.

"Scary, that burglary, huh?" Delia said.

"Nah, tough luck if that retard can't take care of his stuff!" Domenico replied. "I think that was a cool idea."

I was shaking with disgust. I could not believe it! His repulsiveness really topped it all!

"Janet Bonaventura does this kind of thing," Delia suggested. "D'you know her? This black haired Brazilian with green eyes."

"Yeah, I know her." Domenico did not seem interested. "Let's not talk about that anymore, babe."

They stopped in front of the toilets. Domenico pushed Delia into the corner next to the cleaning closet and started kissing her passionately. I felt sick. I stood at the wall next to the toilets and glanced around the corner. They could not see me here, as long as they did not turn around. But I had free vision. His hand slipped under her t-shirt and he fiddled around. Delia threw her head back and rubbed her hips on him. They might as well have taken all their clothes off right there, I thought. Jealously, I looked at Delia's nicely shaped curves, which were clearly visible under the thin fabric of her top. It was no surprise that boys like Domenico were into girls like Delia. And it was no surprise either that girls like me with hardly any bust did not stand a chance.

He kissed her neck and fished a necklace with a red love heart out of his coat pocket. Delia beamed and took it. He gave her a sign to turn around and put the necklace around her neck. Great! Why was that girl always so lucky? Even though she was so mean and stupid! I had really seen enough and left. I could not stand anymore of it. This was definitely the most annoying day I had had for ages.

With all these impressions in my head, I started my weekend by filling my diary. I did not tell my parents anything else about Domenico anymore. And I did not tell them about the burglary, either. That would only have upset Dad unnecessarily.

6. Andrew's revenge

On Monday morning, when I was on my way to the classroom, I walked past the teachers' room. At that moment, Mrs Galiani came out and asked me to come in. I was baffled. I had never before been summoned to speak to her. I never behaved badly. So what could be the reason?

Well, I would find out straight away. After Mrs Galiani had wished me a good morning in her usual dry manner and offered a seat, she asked something unbelievable.

"Would you like to swap seats with someone else, Maya?"

Speechless, I stared at my teacher. An uncomfortable thought began to dawn on me.

"Why?"

She cleared her throat. "Well, your father called me on Friday. He said that if Domenico was bothering you, I should make sure you could sit somewhere else."

My heart sank. "My dad really called you?"

She nodded. A big lump began to grow in my throat. Somehow, I had not thought that Dad would really do it. This was so embarrassing!

"Thank you ... it won't be necessary." I replied quickly, even though I did not know how I would bear sitting, even just one more day, next to Domenico. Mrs

Galiani did not say anything for a while; she seemed to be thinking about something.

"Okay," she nodded, "if you think that you are fine … But, if he is going to continue behaving so badly, I will make him sit in the front row, anyway. This way, I have better control over him."

"Why does he behave like this, actually?" I blurted out and immediately regretted it. I did not think I was allowed to ask any questions like this.

But Mrs Galiani did not seem to mind. "I cannot tell you that, I'm afraid. He behaved like that at his old school, too. It was also the reason why he was expelled. Nobody has managed to get to him, up to now."

The bell suddenly interrupted our conversation. I had to hurry to my classroom. Mrs Galiani let me go with one of her rare smiles and I sprinted off. I hoped the others would never know that my dad had called Mrs Galiani. In front of the classroom, I stopped to brush my hair out of my face.

What had Mrs Galiani said? Domenico had been expelled from his old school? Oh dear! That was something!

Just as I wanted to open the door, I heard shy steps and heavy breathing behind me. I turned around and saw Patrick. I was so happy to see him that I literally beamed at him. He smiled uncomfortably and rushed past me into the classroom, hoping, as usual, that nobody would notice him.

But they did, and I saw how Andrew and Danny were nudging each other and grinning at Patrick. I prayed that they would leave him alone and sat down next to Domenico, who was on time for once, but did not say hi or give any other sign that he had noticed I existed.

In the second break, Andrew jumped up from his seat and walked towards Patrick. "Hey guys, our little fatty's back!"

Danny and Ronnie followed him. Immediately, everyone was paying attention. Something interesting was going to happen! Delia and Domenico, who were sitting very closely to each other on the window sill, stopped talking. Domenico pulled his hand out from underneath Delia's t-shirt. I stayed on my seat and clenched my fist under the desk. Here we go again!

Andrew, Danny and Ronnie stood around Patrick, like three tall pillars. Patrick was whimpering desperately and begging for mercy.

"Oi, fatty!" Andrew taunted and planted a punch on his chin.

"P-p-please stop!" Patrick whined.

"Stop? But we only just started! If you beg very nicely, you might be lucky and we'll only chuck you in the skip outside." Andrew turned around to the rest of the class, waiting for applause. "What'cha think. That'd be very kind of us."

Some students were smiling sneakily. "I say lock him

in the toilets and steal his trousers." Isabelle suggested with a grin, shaking her shiny hair.

"And then, we'll throw the trousers out of the window!" Danny added.

"Great idea!" Andrew agreed with an ugly smirk. Delia detached herself from Domenico and approached curiously. Domenico stayed on the window sill, his legs pulled up, watching the whole scene with a frown. I got up and stared at him. His face twitched. He was probably just trying to understand what was going on.

"Yeah, that'll gonna be a cool show!" Danny jeered.

"Hey, why don't we pull down his trousers right here?" Andrew shouted excitedly. "We've only got five minutes left! Someone close the door, quick!"

"Are you crazy?" Manuela shouted, but the boys had already grabbed Patrick's hands and feet and Andrew tried to unbutton the poor boy's trousers. Patrick was crying and desperately begging for mercy, but everybody just laughed and looked at him indifferently. It was a horrible scene.

I thought I misheard when suddenly a loud, rough voice cut through the noise like a sharp blade: "Bastardi! You nasty bastards, you only got crap in your heads or what?"

Immediately the laughing stopped and everyone was looking around. I took a few steps away from my desk. Domenico had jumped off the window sill and was slowly approaching Andrew and the other boys, clenching his fists. Everything seemed to be happening in slow motion.

"You stupid losers. Leave him alone or I give you hell, ma veramente!"

"Get lost, you idiot!" Andrew hissed contemptuously and towered over him. "It's none of your business!"

"Yes, it is!" Domenico grabbed him. He was trembling with fury. "You imbeciles! If you do this again, I'm gonna take you apart so that nobody can put ya together again! Mi capìstevo?"

I shook my head, incredulously. Was this really happening? Domenico, the biggest jerk in history, had just stuck up for Patrick. That was the eighth wonder of the world! Andrew laughed evilly and tore on Domenico's t-shirt so forcefully that we could hear it getting ripped even further.

"You really think you got a chance against the ten of us, you mouthbreather?" he snapped at Domenico and pushed him so hard that he stumbled back and hit a desk. I shrieked and immediately felt like everyone was looking at me. Some girls held their hands in front of their mouths in horror. Domenico struggled back to his feet.

"Get ready!" he screamed in rage, "I'm gonna rip your heads off! Every one of you!"

"You must be suicidal!" Andrew mocked him. "After school you're gonna pay for this!"

After school! Everyone knew that Andrew always

meant his threats. The boys were nodding grimly and held up their fists to show that they were confident of victory. The bell rang. Andrew bent down to Patrick to pull him onto his feet, by his hair.

"Get up! This retard over there thinks we should leave you alone. You're lucky for today 'cause we're gonna make that ginger bastard bleed."

They let him go and returned to their seats noisily. Some girls were white as a sheet. I fell back on my chair numbly.

Domenico stood still in the middle of the room and stared at Patrick. His clothes were even more torn apart thanks to Andrew. Patrick nearly fell over his schoolbag. His lips were trembling and tears were streaming down his face. The two boys looked at each other. What was going on at that moment was hard to describe; it was like an invisible band that was tied between them.

But Delia interrupted them. She grabbed Domenico's arm, sulking. She looked disappointed, but also a bit insecure. "What's up with you, Nico?"

"They're such cowards!" he shouted.

I was so happy! I really felt like climbing on a table and jumping around like crazy. This was better than my wildest dreams!

"But it was only a bit of fun." Delia replied.

"Fun? Ma si scema? You're all nuts!"

He looked at his ripped t-shirt now and grimaced. And then he just pulled his arms in and turned the t-shirt around, so that the holes were now on the back. With a shy grin he left Delia standing there and slowly returned to his desk. Everyone in this room was observing him, attentively. Delia pouted and looked crestfallen. This was wonderful! She really deserved it. When Domenico was sitting next to me, I got all my courage together and bent over to him with my heart beating wildly, saying: "I think what you just did was great!"

He did not reply to that. But he looked at me with pensive interest in his grey-blue eyes. It felt a bit as if he was seeing me for the first time. And somehow that was true.

My cheeks blushed and became flaming hot. He smiled. It was a very special smile; one that was much profounder, very different to the smiles he usually reserved for girls. It made two cute dimples appear on his cheeks. But, since it was the first time he smiled when I was so close to him, it was also the first time I could see the unhealthy colour of his teeth. Was that because he smoked? It was the only thing on him that was not so handsome.

Mrs Lindner came into the room, but I really struggled to concentrate on physics.

During the ten o'clock break, I followed Domenico and Delia again and saw them making out at the school gate. I sighed with disappointment and anger. I felt somehow sad. The same sadness I felt when I woke up after dreams of the lantern in the park. But I would never forget what Domenico had done for Patrick, even if he decided to continue playing Mister Universe.

Nicky, I thought. Everyone called him Nico, because that sounded much cooler. Nicky, however, sounded nice. Was there anyone who called him that?

The last lesson of the day was history with Mrs Galiani. The class was so agitated that she had to extend the lesson by ten minutes in the end. And this time, it was not Domenico's fault but Andrew's and his stupid friends', who were acting silly like kindergarten kids.

When Mrs Galiani finally let us go, everyone ran out of the classroom. Except for me, because I had a question about the homework. Being the biggest nerd of the class, I did not dare handing in even one single piece of incomplete homework. Dad always had a close look at my homework.

When I came back to my desk, Domenico was the only one still there. He was looking for something in his plastic bag and, when I put my books into my school bag, he talked to me.

"Hey, can I ask you somethin'?"

Quite surprised, I stared at him and tried to grasp what was going on. He was talking to me! For the first time, he had said something to me!

We left the classroom together, and I pinched my arm to make sure that I was not dreaming. I felt dizzy.

"What did you think of this mornin'?" he asked, while

we were walking down the hall. "I mean, that they were so nasty to that guy …"

"That was so mean!" My voice sounded horribly throaty. "Patrick has been going through this for years!"

He did not reply anymore. Only when we arrived on the next floor, he mumbled: "Bastards! They ain't got no idea how that is!"

We were standing in front of the main exit. Something was wrong, it smelled of danger. Domenico hesitated a moment too, before he reached for the door handle. But then, he pulled it open quickly and we stepped outside.

Within seconds, we were surrounded by Andrew and his boys.

"No!" I screamed, terrified.

But before I could do anything, they had pushed me aside brutally and lunged at Domenico.

"There, you loudmouth, this will be the end of you!" Andrew bellowed. "Drag him to the fountain, guys! We're gonna beat the crap out of that dickhead and then drown him!"

"What, are you crazy? We can't do that!" Ronnie was worried. "They're gonna send us to prison for murder!"

"Idiot!" Andrew snarled, "we're not really gonna kill him. We're just gonna squeeze the air out of him, so he'll stop talking like he's the greatest."

"But he's gonna tell Mrs Galiani!" Ralph objected.

"No, he won't, if he wants to stay alive."

"Let me go, bastardi!" Domenico shouted, but they

had a tight grip on him. I watched in horror as they dragged him to the fountain. They pushed his head under the ice cold water again and again until his face turned blue and he was gasping for air. I could not believe how unfair this was! Ten against one! And they all seemed to be full of hatred. If nobody stopped them any time soon, they might hurt him seriously in their blind rage.

How lucky that they had completely forgotten about me in their eagerness to take revenge. Because, suddenly, I saw my chance to help him. There was just one way.

I turned around, pushed the heavy door to the school open and ran up the stairs, as quickly as I could, to the teachers' room. With my heart beating heavily, I knocked on the door, maybe just a bit too forcefully. I could hear someone getting up from the creaky sofa and slowly walking towards the door. It was yanked open and in front of me stood the janitor, glaring at me angrily. Apparently, I had disturbed his nap.

"I'm sorry ...," I stammered and felt very small. "In the schoolyard someone is being beaten up by ten students. Could you ... Could you maybe have a look?"

Mr Biedermann brought his round, shiny face down to mine a bit too closely, so that I could smell his fowl breath. Disgusted, I tried not to breathe. He grunted something incomprehensible and pushed me aside. Swearing all the way, he hurried down the stairs and out of the school building. I followed him. The screaming from the fountain was unmistakable.

"Bastards! Let me go!" I heard Domenico shout. Oh God, what were they doing to him?

And then, I saw what was going on: some boys were holding Domenico by his arms and legs and Andrew and Danny were kicking into his sides with their huge feet. It looked criminal! They were going to break all his ribs! His face was twisted in pain. I felt sick just looking at the scene. Mr Biedermann marched towards the boys and somehow he reminded me of a rolling pumpkin.

"Stop! Stop it immediately! What do you think you are doing?"

"Oh no! Biedermann!" Danny hissed. Immediately everyone stopped and stared at the janitor, scared.

"Have you all gone crazy? Ten against one! Do you want to kill him?"

"No! He only gets what he deserves!" Andrew dared to reply. What an idiot!

I was waiting at a safe distance and clenched my fists. I really hoped that the boys were going to be punished properly, for once.

"Really?" Mr Biedermann was steaming like an engine. "So, you don't think that ten against one is a bit unfair?"

Now it was silent. The boys looked at the ground sheepishly. But then Ronnie lifted his head and boldly said: "Yeah, but he beat Andrew up really badly, too!

We had to fight that injustice, 'cause I'm a Jedi, after all …"

"Shut up!" Andrew snarled and gave him a side blow.

The janitor was growling. "What class are you in?"

"8a," Ronnie replied meekly.

"And who's your form teacher?"

"Mrs Galiani," a few said simultaneously.

"Alright. I'm going to inform her about this incident. And now, off with you! And I won't have anything like this happen again!"

The boys picked up their school bags silently and left. Only Andrew turned around again and looked at Domenico with a gleeful smirk. What a creep! Luckily, nobody had noticed that Mr Biedermann had appeared because of me. I had been pretty worried about that, for a few seconds. Fortunately, these boys were definitely not the cleverest.

Now Mr Biedermann turned towards Domenico who was still lying on the floor, groaning. "What was going on here?" he barked.

"Those cowards!" Domenico managed to say." They're gonna pay for that!" He looked mangled. His lower lip was swollen and bleeding; from his temple to his ear I could see a long scrape. His hair was soaked and the water was mixing with the blood from the wound.

Slowly, I joined them. Mr Biedermann cleared his throat and looked at me.

"Well, if your friend here hadn't called me, they would probably have broken your ribs."

Domenico lifted his head carefully and looked at me. For one moment, the world seemed to stand still. I only saw his eyes, those grey-blue, glowing eyes that seemed to pierce me.

Mr Biedermann cleared his throat again, to remind us that he was still there.

"Uhm, can you go home? Or should we call an ambulance?"

"Nah, I'm gonna go home," Domenico said quickly.

"You can call your parents from the teachers' room if you don't have a mobile," Mr Biedermann added, to make sure he had done all he probably should.

"Nah, they're not there, anyway. I'm gonna be fine," Domenico assured him and tried to get up. But he immediately fell back onto the floor and held his right side, groaning.

Mr Biedermann scratched his bald head, indecisively.

"I'm fine, man!" Domenico managed to smile. "You go back to stuffin' yer face! Bye-bye! I'm okay."

I bit my lip. Domenico really stopped at nothing.

Mr Biedermann's face turned the colour of a tomato. "You're the new one in 8a, right?" he hissed.

"Yeah, I am. Why do you ask?"

"I've heard a lot about you. Nothing good. That's two hours' detention for you!"

He was done with Domenico and walked off with

quick steps to the school entrance and to the teachers' room, where he could finally get back to his lunch. Domenico seemed quite relieved that he was gone.

Now I was alone with him. He was still sitting on the floor, staring at me. My knees felt weak as I slowly walked closer, feverishly trying to think of what I should say to him.

"Can you get up?" Was it okay to offer help to a boy like Domenico, who thought he was Mister Universe, when he had trouble getting up?

But Domenico suddenly seemed to have forgotten who he thought he was, because he took the hand I was offering him and pulled himself up with my support. I was stunned. And then I had an idea, which I carefully pronounced: "Do you want to come to my place? Dad could have a look at you, he is a doctor."

Domenico looked at me as though I had just asked him to travel to Mars with me.

"To … to your place?"

"Yes."

"I can't. I … I mean it's not necessary, I'm fine."

"Are you sure? You look pretty bad …"

"Nah!" he managed a crooked smile again. "It's not that bad. I've been beaten up loads. There is nothin' undamaged on me, anymore. Listen, I gotta take care of somethin' important now. But anyway … thanks."

I had guessed that I would be pushing the boundary with my suggestion.

"Up to you. I just thought I'd offer …"

"That's nice of you." He gave me a regretful smile.

"Can I help you in any other way?"

"Nah … you already helped me get up; I'll be fine for the rest."

"Okay … I guess I should go home now, my parents will start to worry otherwise," I said and timidly lowered my eyes. Why could I not just stay cool?

"Okay, see you tomorrow. And thanks again!"

"You're welcome." Indecisively, I made a few steps towards the gate. My knees had turned into jelly by this point. And then, half way through the gate, I suddenly heard him call me again: "Hey, Maya, wait a sec!"

He knew my name! I could not believe it! I stopped and turned around. He hobbled towards me and laid his arm on my shoulder.

"Hey, Maya. I think … you're alright, you know."

A few seconds passed before I could reply. I would never have dared to dream of a boy like Domenico telling me something like that! It felt like Christmas, my birthday and Easter all at once.

I swallowed hard three times before I managed to say: "I think you are quite alright, too."

Like I suspected, my parents had already been worrying about me. "We nearly called your teacher," Mum said when she put down a plate of pasta in front of me. But I was on cloud number nine and I could not keep the exciting incidents of the morning to myself anymore.

The pasta remained untouched until it was cold and Mum had to heat it up in the microwave. The only part of the story I did not tell my parents was what Domenico had said to me at the end. His words still resounded like music in my ears. I wanted to keep them a secret.

"This boy seems to be more intelligent than we thought before," Mum said, but Dad did not agree at all.

"He rather sounds schizophrenic to me," he ranted.

"What does that mean, schizophrenic?" I did not always understand Dad's expressions.

"Schizophrenia. That is a split personality."

"No, he does not have a split personality!" I disagreed. Or did he? Mister Universe on the one hand and on the other hand … No, schizophrenia could not be the answer or the solution to the mystery.

"Oh, come on, Maya! He had a fight with ten boys! There is a fine line between mischief and madness. And you really went and helped him?"

"Yes … I wanted to return the favour. Because I thought that it was great how he stuck up for Patrick." Dad could not say anything against that now. After all, it had been my duty to get help from a teacher or someone else from the school.

I went up to my room, closed the door behind myself and jumped on my bed. I was filled with joy and I could have sung out loud. Domenico had stuck up for Patrick and he thought I was alright! This was better than anything that had ever happened to me before, and I could not wait to go to school the next day!

I got my novel out and opened it at the beginning. I would need a lot of correction fluid to change Michael for Domenico in the whole story.

7. The darkness in his eyes

We did not have to wait for Mrs Galiani's lecture, after the fight. Mr Biedermann had told her about it quicker than Andrew could count to three. And so she gave the boys a real what-for at the beginning of the first class and condemned them to two hours' detention.

But Domenico was not spared. He only arrived for the second class of the day. He looked very sleepy and dragged himself over to his seat with a can of Red Bull in his hand. I hoped that he would say something to me, but he did not even look at me. He rested his head on his arms and shut the world around him out.

"Good morning, Domenico!" Mrs Galiani said, warningly. "We generally start classes at seven thirty, in case this has slipped your attention. And now, sit up straight and wake up! Oh, and put that drink away. It would be much more sensible for you to go to bed earlier in the evening."

He grinned tiredly and stretched his arms. She told him that he would have to stay for the two hours' detention too, because of the incident of the previous day, plus another hour for skipping the first class of the day. He indifferently shrugged his shoulders; he did not even seem to listen properly.

"Now, let us talk about something more pleasant,"

Mrs Galiani changed the subject. "The school festival of next Thursday."

Every summer, the students who were graduating organised a big party. They arranged everything, and the younger students sometimes helped out. This year, they had looked for some voluntary helpers in our class, who would tend to the cake stand for a few hours. It was the opportunity for Delia, Manuela and Isabelle to be in the spotlight and flirt with the boys.

I stayed out of the whole thing. There was nobody with whom I could have gone to the party. But unfortunately, participation was obligatory.

"Woohoo, a real party!" Domenico grinned.

With another abrupt change of subject, Mrs Galiani shocked us all at the end of the class: "Next Tuesday we are going to have an exam on all the grammar we have discussed in the past six weeks. If you paid attention during that time, you should have no difficulties. Also, we will review some of the lessons in the next English classes, so that I can expect you to be on the top of your game next week and to achieve a high mark. The exam will include a dictation and two pages of exercises, which means you will get two grades. This is your chance to catch up!"

Everyone moaned. An exam, now?!

"Oh no!" complained Delia who was not the sharpest tool in the box, as everyone knew.

"A bit of discipline and pressure will do you wonders,

don't worry," Mrs Galiani retorted dryly. "And you have to take your exams at some point, so please pull yourselves together."

She turned to Domenico who had his head propped up on his hand and was lost in thoughts, fiddling with the volume on his smartphone lying next to him on the table.

"Domenico, put that thing away and concentrate on the lesson, please! I do know that you have not been with us for the past six weeks and therefore have not looked at the same subjects. I will make sure that I will not mark your exam as strictly as the others. Since you are repeating this year, however, you should be familiar with some of the subjects and you should be able to catch up on some of the lessons by next week."

Again, he just shrugged his shoulders as if he did not care in the slightest. Was I just imagining it, or did he seem gloomy? I wished I could think of something to say to him in the break. Immediately when the bell rang, I used the short moment before Delia came over.

"Does it still hurt after yesterday's fight?"

"I'm okay," he mumbled gruffly and proceeded to plug two small stereo speakers into his smartphone. We were all startled when a gravelly voice was suddenly screaming around in Italian. The girls squeaked in surprise and then started to giggle.

"Are you crazy, Nico?" Isabelle shouted.

"Hey, that's Vasco, man! You don't appreciate good music, guys." – "You're gonna get into trouble."

But Domenico just grinned and tiredly closed his eyes. I looked at him and tried to figure out what was going on inside him. He was probably still in pain from yesterday and just did not want to admit it. The boys had knocked him about pretty badly, after all.

Delia and Manuela started moving to the rhythm and sang along with their artificial sounding high pitched voices. It sounded so ridiculous that Andrew and Danny were snorting with laughter. The spectacle lasted until a raging teacher appeared in the door and summoned the culprit along with his smartphone to the headmaster.

"Uh-oh! He's definitely in for it," the girls worried. "Heehee! The moron's gonna get it in the neck. The headmaster's gonna give him a hiding!" the boys were jeering gleefully.

Ten minutes into the maths class, Domenico reappeared. He did not have his smartphone anymore. Poor Mr Lenz was visibly confused about the disturbance. He scratched his head, tousling his hair even more, and pushed his glasses, which were always slipping to the tip of his nose, back up. And then he went back to scratching over the blackboard with his piece of chalk, explaining an algebra exercise to us.

Domenico sat down slowly and stared straight into my eyes for half a second. I did not know what it was, but something in his glowing look hurt me terribly. It felt like it was cutting right through my heart. He flinched and nearly missed his chair. A dark shadow seemed to extinguish the sparkle in his eyes. Quickly, he turned his face away from me and began to leaf through his maths book, nervously. But I was very good at observing people closely without them noticing. And I observed his transformation; how he turned back into Mister Universe.

"Page 51!" I whispered shyly when I saw that he still had not found the right page.

After the ten o'clock break, when I came back to the classroom with my head full of the questions I kept asking myself over and over, Delia, Manuela and Isabelle were blocking my way. Their eyes were piercing me. I breathed in, stretched my back and walked past them, determined not to react to their teasing. But Delia pulled at my hair so fiercely and painfully that I spun around, shocked.

"Yuck, you should wash your wig from time to time, you nerd!" she scoffed.

"I … uhm … I …" I stumbled and fell against the door. Not again! Isabelle looked at me disgustedly and started pulling at my hair, too.

"Urgh, it makes your fingers all greasy!"

"I wash it all the time!" I shouted. My eyes filled with tears, I could not stop them any longer, even though I tried really hard.

"Oh God, she's already crying again!" Isabelle jeered.

Why could I not just look straight into their eyes and

laugh at their stupidity? Why could I never think of the right way to answer back? Through the mist of my tears their faces looked like grimaces. I was desperately searching for words to defend myself, but my head was completely empty.

“Hey, Nico!” Isabelle called Domenico, who was standing close to them. “Did you know that she always carries a Bible around with her?”

I saw him coming closer, and I could see the anger in his face. I became afraid. What would happen now? I wanted to run away but my legs felt like they were nailed to the ground.

“Stop it!” He grabbed Delia and Isabelle roughly by their arms and pushed them, along with Manuela, away with remarkable force. For a short moment, the three froze and looked at Domenico incomprehensively. It took me a moment to understand what an incredible thing was happening to me there. In my dizziness, I let Domenico carefully lead me into the classroom, and when I started to feel my legs again I ran to my seat to observe everything from a distance.

In the meantime, the three girls had apparently defrosted. Delia’s eyes were throwing out bitter sparks and she looked from me to Domenico and back. “You’re really strange, Nico,” she sulked and walked back to her seat, offended but with her head held high.

“So you’re protecting the nerd now!” Isabelle coolly commented and followed her friend. Manuela left, too.

"Women!" Domenico grunted and slammed the door closed – from outside. He did not reappear for the rest of the day.

On Wednesday during the last class of the day, Mrs Galiani brought us the exercises to prepare for next week's exam, as she had announced. We started working sluggishly. I had nearly no problems with the grammar exercises and advanced quite quickly. When I had finished the first page, I noticed that Domenico was still staring at an empty sheet. I got together all my courage and carefully tapped on his shoulder.

"Can I help you?"

For a moment, he looked at me sceptically. His right eye was hidden behind a strand of his hair. But then he seemed to relax a bit, he pulled the hair out of his face and handed me his exercise paper.

"I'm crap in English!" he mumbled. "But don't tell anyone!"

My heart was pounding like mad. "Of course not."

Whispering, I started to explain a few things to him, completely forgetting about Mrs Galiani's no-talking rule during classes. What was up with Domenico? He made mistakes like a seven-year-old! And he did not seem to find it funny anymore.

He seemed completely different, all of a sudden. Really serious. He was looking at his sheet, trying to understand it and he was nervously chewing on the end of his pen. Mister Universe had a problem.

Mrs Galiani scared me to death with her voice, right next to my ear: “Maya and Domenico, what are you talking about? I do not tolerate any talking in my classes. And you of all should know that, Maya.”

“But, I only explained a few things to Domenico.” I protested, surprising myself at how bold I was. I had never before dared to answer Mrs Galiani back. Only suicidal people did that, usually.

“Well, Domenico should come and ask me if he does not understand the exercise. I want you to concentrate on your own work, Maya.” She gave me a warning look and my hands and feet started to tingle. Obviously, ten pairs of girls’ eyes were on us, too.

“So, Domenico, what are you waiting for? Pick up your sheets and come up here.”

Domenico grimaced.

“Nah! Maya’s much better at explaining than you.”

Shocked and thrilled at the same time, I stared at him. The others were muttering, silently. Mrs Galiani’s lips became one thin line, and the furrow on her forehead deepened.

“Listen, Domenico,” she said coldly, “I am warning you for the last time: be careful! You should be aware, by now, that you will have to repeat the year again if your performance does not improve substantially. But it is up to you!”

She turned around and walked briskly back to her desk. Domenico pulled an ugly grimace and flipped the bird behind her back. Not even in her dreams would he ask for her help with the exercises. Instead, he started drawing a horrible caricature of our teacher on his sheet. I had to look twice before I realised that he was not just a very cheeky artist, but also a really talented one. The drawing looked so funny that I had to bite my lips to stop myself from laughing out loud. But secretly, I was actually worried about him. He really needed to work a lot if he wanted to pass the exams at the end of the year.

8. A triumph at dodge ball

The weather was amazing. The sun was shining in all its splendour, as if it had to win a competition. But that had not stopped Mr Reuter from making us play dodge ball. Why could we not go swimming in this incredible heat?

This time, Evelyn and Andrew got to pick the teams. Domenico grinned and showed the victory sign when Evelyn picked him straight away. I was grinding my teeth and nearly dislocated my jaw. Why did he have to act so arrogantly, again?!

While Patrick was put into Evelyn's team at the end, I had to join Andrew and Delia. Great! It seemed like I had the exclusive rights to bad luck, again.

I tried to be as invisible as possible, ran back and forth and acted as though I was eagerly participating in the game. But what happened was exactly what I had feared: I could really do what I wanted, I just was all thumbs. I overheard how Delia whispered in Isabelle's ear: "If we lose, it's gonna be that stupid cow's fault."

It hurt so much. I felt horrible. Domenico must think that I was a real loser. He was obviously fantastic, again! He hit the mark every time, caught every ball and never got hit himself. At the end, the only ones left in the field of our team were Delia, Andrew and I, whilst the other team still had six players in their field. I could not remember that I had ever managed to stay in the field that long. Usually, I was one of the first ones to get hit. But Domenico did not seem interested in aiming at me.

Andrew was furious because we were losing. Determined, he tried to put a halt to Domenico's success, but it was impossible. And when I managed to lose hold of the ball once again when I had the chance to shoot, he exploded.

"Pull yourself together! You suck!" he shouted so that his voice cracked, "can't you aim, you loser?!"

"Yes, I can!" I mumbled, pouted and swallowed the lump that had appeared in my throat. Now, I was completely embarrassed.

"Andrew, stay where you are!" Mr Reuter reprimanded him. "And you, Maya, make a bit of an effort, for once." In that moment, I wished I was far away.

All of a sudden, Domenico stood in front of Andrew and aimed at him with the ball. Andrew stood there, ready to jump, but Domenico hit his ankle with a merciless shot. Andrew howled angrily. Domenico celebrated his strike with a broad grin and flipped his adversary the bird. Somehow, this felt really good.

Now, I was alone in the field with Delia. The other team had the ball and they were aiming at her. She ran from one side of the field to the other, her face starting to glow red. The to and fro seemed to go on forever, especially since Domenico had forgotten how to aim properly, all of a sudden. I guessed that he missed on purpose, because Delia was his girlfriend. She screamed and swore and shouted over to me to catch the ball. But that white leather thing shot from one hand to the next like a flash, and I had trouble even following it with my eyes. When I finally gave up in confusion, Delia shouted: "God! How can you be so stupid!?"

I was so angry and desperate that I really felt like jumping at her and slapping her.

The ball had rolled over to Domenico. He picked it up and weighed it in his hands, looking at me. I could not have cared less, if he hit me now, the torture would at last be over.

He slowly lifted his arm and aimed at me. I did not bother trying to move out of the way. But then the ball slipped out of his hands, fell to the ground and rolled over to me. "Oh, no!" his team complained disappointedly. The ball lay at my feet now and I had to pick it up. The whole class was jeering and hooting. I looked around, hesitantly. What was I supposed to do with this stupid leather thing now?

"Give it to me, Maya!" Delia shouted. I wanted to throw it over to her when I suddenly saw how Domenico was subtly shaking his head and then nodded at me, expectantly. Did he want me to throw the ball?

I aimed. Delia screamed "No!" but it was too late. My shot was terrible, but the ball hit Domenico's foot! I could not believe it! Everyone was roaring, and Domenico left the field without batting an eye. Only now I realised something that made me forget to breathe for a second. It was so incredible that I did not pay attention to what was happening around me anymore.

He had done it on purpose! He let me hit him on purpose, I was sure about that. I was aglow with happiness and I had to pull myself together with all my might. I did not want the others to notice that I was nearly bursting.

The game was over at some point, but I did not even know who had won. And I did not care either. I was on cloud nine. Delia and Andrew did not say another word and furiously left the field.

Only in the locker room did Delia start to spew venom again.

"Stupid cow!" she hissed as she threw her sweaty t-shirt into her bag. "If she had made an effort I wouldn't have had to scream my head off!"

Isabelle came over to me, kicked me and slapped me with her t-shirt.

"Make an effort next time!" she kicked my shin again. I rubbed the spot where it hurt and hurried up, stuffing my clothes into my bag. Suddenly, Delia's pointy shoe flew in my direction.

I rushed to the exit, but suddenly I felt something hard hitting the back of my head. Delia had thrown her second shoe at me, too. For one moment, I thought I was going to pass out, the pain made tears come to my eyes.

I nearly ran into Domenico, who was hanging around

outside the locker rooms. Frightened, I stumbled back, but he looked worried when he saw my tears. He grabbed my shoulder.

"Hey, what's up with you? Why are you cryin'?"

I managed half a smile and wiped my hand over my wet face. "Uhm … because of the others."

He nodded understandingly. "Yeah, I know, they're really mean to you. Where are you goin' now?"

"To the bus stop."

"Alright, I'm goin' with you. It's on my way."

I nearly choked on my tears and smeared snot all over my face, because I was so nervous and because I did not have a tissue. It was so embarrassing!

"Sorry, I don't have a tissue." Domenico said, a bit helplessly. "Oh, but wait," he grinned and tore a piece off his t-shirt that was hanging down loosely. Before I could protest, he held the piece of fabric under my nose. "There you go. One hole more doesn't matter."

A bit overwhelmed, I mumbled a thank you and dug my nose into the piece of fabric. It smelled exciting. Just like Domenico.

He did not say a word about what had happened in the game. I tried to figure out whether I should mention it. What if I was completely wrong and if he had not done it on purpose, at all? That would be too embarrassing, so I decided to bring it up via a detour.

"You're really talented at sports," I said. "I bet it is your favourite subject at school."

"Yeah."

"Do you train a lot?"

He shrugged his shoulders. "Not for long time. We had competitions in the old swot-shop. And I was in the school team."

"Cool. Like here?"

He nodded. His eyes wandered off and he had this nice smile on his lips again. He seemed to be happier about Mr Reuter's offer than he wanted to admit. But now, I had to ask about the game, even though I was extremely nervous.

"I have never hit anyone before at dodge ball," I started. "I'm really bad at it …"

"No, you're not!"

"Why?"

"You hit me!"

"You didn't even move out of the way, though, right?"

He did not reply to that and I left it at that. It would probably remain a secret, even though in my heart I was sure that I knew the answer.

We had arrived at the crossroads now, where we had to separate. We were standing there hesitantly. I felt that Domenico was just as nervous as me. But I did not understand what it was about me that made him lose his cool.

"Uhm, can I …," he started but then he shook his head.

"Nah, forget it. I can't ask you that."

"Yes, sure you can! Go on!"

"It's that grammar exam … I don't think I can make it." His voice sounded hoarse. "I'm too bad."

"You mean, you need someone to help you?"

"Err … yeah, I guess …"

"No problem!" More exactly: there was nothing I'd rather do. I was incredibly happy.

"Whoa, that's great, Maya!" He lowered his gaze. "When would be a good time? Tomorrow after biology?"

I thought about it. Would Dad allow it?

"I think that should work," I replied without really knowing myself. "We could just stay in the classroom."

He looked up to the big clock next to the stadium. "Oh Maya, I gotta run! Gotta be downtown at half past four. Can't miss the next tube!"

"I would never take the tube by myself," I said, immediately regretting it! Did I really just tell him that? Surely, he was going to laugh at me, now. I was fourteen and I had never taken the tube by myself.

But he did not laugh. "That's probably best," he said with a serious tone. "Last week, I saw two guys beatin' the crap out of each other on the train." He looked straight at me again and fished a packet of cigarettes out of his pocket.

"Where do you live, actually?" he asked.

"On Magnolia Alley. Close to the park."

He whistled through his teeth in surprise. "Where all the fancy gardens are? Mizzica, that must be cool. Oh yeah, I forgot your dad's a famous doctor or somethin', right?"

"Yes ... but don't think I'm all stuck-up because of that," I defended myself.

"No worries, I won't," he said soothingly and took care not to blow the smoke into my direction.

"Is it true that you read the Bible?"

The question sounded honest and I could not see any sign of mockery in his eyes. Still, I was careful. I had been deceived many times when it came to that subject.

"Sometimes," I said shyly.

He smiled. "You believe in God?"

"Yes!"

"You sometimes take the Bible to school, righ'?"

"Not anymore. The others laughed about it."

"Senti, you really shouldn't listen to them! You know, if more people believed what's in the Bible, the world would be a better place ... somehow, maybe. I knew a few stories from the Bible too, you know. But it's a long time ago ..."

He waved his hand and turned around to leave. "Really gotta go now, my train's coming. See you on tomorrow. Ciao!" He grinned and waved good-bye.

"Bye!" I replied. "See you on tomorrow" he had said instead of "See you tomorrow". He made a lot of mistakes, even when he was speaking. I followed him with my eyes as he went across the street and snipped his cigarette away. That he – of all people – would encourage me to read the Bible more often was at least as strange as if Mrs Galiani had laughed at a mediocre joke.

That evening, Dad managed to spoil my mood entirely. Maybe the fact that he was a doctor with heart and soul made him treat me like one of his patients when I asked him, over dinner, whether he would allow me to study for the grammar exam with Domenico after school the next day. After dinner, he formally asked me to join him for a talk in the living room, where he pestered me with questions. Mum had joined us, silently.

"Why couldn't someone else help that boy with his studies? Did Mrs Galiani ask you to do it?"

"No, he asked me himself." I replied.

"Why you?"

"Well … just like that."

"But, he has to have a reason!"

"Oh, Martin!" Mum interrupted. "I think it would be very reasonable of Maya to help this boy at school. It would be good for him and for her."

"Reasonable?" Dad was not convinced. "So you think it would be reasonable for our daughter to spend time with that ill-bred boy? What if he infects her with his bad behaviour?"

"But you do not even know him, Martin."

"No, but what I have heard about him is enough."

"Oh, Dad," I shouted desperately, "there is nothing to it! I am just helping him." Now that things had finally started to change at school, it just could not stop because of his doubts. "And Domenico is really … really nice to me. And to Patrick too, by the way!"

"Hm. At least he wants to do something about his performance at school. That is at least something, I guess." Dad scratched his chin, in thoughts. The long silence that followed was nearly unbearable. What would I do if he did not allow it?

"You have to promise to be home tomorrow evening by seven o'clock sharp, Maya." He finally pronounced his well reflected decision. "I will be at a reunion, but your mother will be here waiting for you."

I sighed in relieved and flung my arms around his neck. Then I ran upstairs and happily danced around my room. I got my novel out, definitely determined to change the name Michael to Domenico.

Once I had finished, I took the Bible from my bedside table and put it back into the pocket of my jacket.

9. His secret

The whole next morning, I was hoping that Domenico would talk to me, but he did not. Had he forgotten what had happened between us the day before? I slid a piece of paper over to him on which I had written, "Tonight is fine!," and waited for his reply. But he did not react. Was the whole bubble going to burst again now?

In a sad mood, I made my way to the Zoo where we met with Mrs Schmiedle, our biology teacher, in the afternoon to study the life of sea lions. Mrs Schmiedle knew the friendly keeper personally and had asked him to give us a graphic description of those interesting animals.

They let us sit on the stand from where the public usually watched the show, and I hid in the last row, next to Patrick. Domenico sat right in front of us with the girls. I was still hoping that he would give me a sign, but nothing happened.

The presentation on the sea lions was great, and even though I was still sad, I admired the beautiful animals sliding elegantly and gracefully through the water.

At the end of the class, when I was gathering my things, I suddenly felt a piece of paper land on my lap. I looked up, but Domenico had already walked on with the girls and did not look at me. I unfolded the paper and read: B in scool @ 4 1/2

The water in the sea lions' pool was sparkling in a wonderful blue-green colour and drew mysterious patterns on the rock that was glowing in the sun. I hurried to catch the bus. Luckily, the school was only five stops away.

Domenico was sitting on the floor in front of the school entrance and just flicked a cigarette butt onto the bike shed when I arrived. He looked at me and showed me his nice smile again, so that my doubts shrunk immediately.

For the first time that day, I noticed how friendly and warm the sun was shining. The light was flooding the classroom. We took our schoolbooks out of our bags and spread them over two tables. We undecidedly looked at each other and did not manage to start a normal conversation, because all we could do was grin at each other shyly. I was incredibly nervous and I did not really know where to begin. We did not have a lot of time, either. I started by making a list of all the pages in the book that he absolutely had to read. Then, I tried to go through a few sentences from the exercises. But soon, I realised that I had to slow down; he seemed to have problems keeping up. He grinned at me contritely.

"I bet you think I'm really stupid!" he said silently. "Everyone thinks that I act like I'm dumb on purpose in the English classes but that ain't true. I really don't wanna repeat again! Man, I'm already two years too old for this class …"

"How old are you, actually?" I had wanted to ask that for so long.

"Fifteen. Gonna be sixteen in September."

So he was exactly one and a half year older than me, since my birthday was in March.

"I see. But why do you skip classes all the time if you do not want to repeat again?"

He shrugged his shoulders. He obviously could not really reply to that question. All of a sudden, I was worried he would think that I was a complete nerd, and I feverishly tried to find a way to convince him of the contrary.

"You know, I am not that bothered, either. It's not like I am interested in the stuff we have to learn all the time! But you still have to make an effort, you know. Skipping classes is not doing you any favours."

Oh no … What was I saying!? I sounded just like my dad! Must have been the genes. I was incredibly embarrassed, but Domenico did not seem to mind. I was surprised.

"You're so smart, Maya …" he said and it sounded honest and admiring. "Let's continue then, maybe I can do somethin' about my stupidness."

No, I did not think he was stupid at all. I could sense that he actually had to be quite intelligent, but that he had some kind of learning difficulty. We looked at a few questions from the exercises; I explained some complicated phrases to him and made him try a short writing exercise. The mistakes he made were terrible, and I did not really know what to do about it.

"You have to practice those texts from the book!" I said. "Mrs Galiani usually uses similar texts for the exams. I'm afraid that is all I can help you with."

"That's okay, Maya, thanks. You did really good."

I blushed. I had a look at the clock above the door.

"Oh no! I have to go. I promised my dad that I would be home at seven."

He looked at me intensely from head to toes, which made me feel dizzy.

"I can walk with you for some of the way if you want," he said, "cos I'm going in the same direction."

I started fidgeting awkwardly for excitement. My head turned hot, but I nodded.

We packed our things hurriedly. I made a neat pile (being orderly was in my genes, too) and put it in the shelf under the desk. He cleared the desk by stuffing the books and sheets under the desk in no particular order.

When I was about to leave the room, I saw the notice about the theft Mr Biedermann had pinned on the board.

"What do you think of that, by the way?" I asked him. I wanted to see whether he was really as hard-boiled as he always acted in front of Delia.

He shrugged his shoulders and stood behind me. "What I think of that? Don't concern me!"

"You do not think it is horrible?"

"Horrible?" He looked at me, questioningly. "You probably live in a really innocent world, huh? Hmhm…" he laughed dryly. "But then, this swot-shop's harmless compared with my old school."

"Maybe," I mumbled shyly. I was afraid I would ruin it all by saying something wrong. My stomach was aching; I was so worried when we walked out of the school building. The sun had disappeared behind a thick cloud, and I could feel a mild evening breeze.

"Man, I really need a fag!" Domenico sighed and searched his pockets.

"And I am hungry," I realised.

"Don't mention that!" he grinned and breathed in the smoke.

I decided to seize the opportunity. There was so much I wanted to know about him. I wanted to know everything.

"Domenico is an Italian name, right?"

"Yeah."

"Are you from Italy?"

"My Mum comes from Sicily."

"Hm, and your dad?"

"Don't have no dad." He smiled at me looking a bit sad, I thought.

"You don't have a father?" I could not even imagine that. "Is he … dead?"

"Dunno, don't even know him. He's German, I think, but I don't care, anyway." He kicked a stone against the wall and then another one. “I lived in Sicily, seven years.”

That sounded incredibly interesting and exciting. But somehow, I suddenly knew that I should not ask any more questions. I could clearly feel something in the air that made me stop.

“That’s why I’m so bad in English,” he said. And I finally understood. That explained a few things …

We did not say any more until we were nearly at my house. He stopped. “That’s where you live, righ’?”

I did not have a clue how he knew it that exactly. I had not realised it until then, but he had walked me all the way home. We saw Mum working in the garden. I glanced at Domenico’s torn jeans, the scars on his face and the cigarette between his fingers, and I secretly worried about Mum’s reaction.

Domenico slowed down and finally stood still. He peered at our house and our garden; he studied every line, every detail. I became more and more nervous. If at least he had got rid of his cigarette! But it was stuck between his lips and he seemed to have forgotten about it.

“Is that woman your mum?” he suddenly asked.

“Yes.”

And in that moment, Mum had discovered us and she was approaching with a smile. Her apron and her gloves showed signs of the work she had done. Our garden was known in the whole neighbourhood.

"Hi, you two." Mum was beaming, probably because I brought a friend from school for the first time.

"Hello … you must be the new boy in Maya's class? Dominic, I think, right?"

"Domenico." He finally remembered the cigarette between his lips and threw it away, embarrassed.

Smiling, Mum gave him her hand. "Welcome, Domenico! It's very nice of you to have walked Maya back!"

Nervously, I checked for the slightest sign in Mum's expression showing that she thought he was impossible, but I could not find anything. Relieved, I exhaled. Mum was always a lot more relaxed when Dad was not around.

"So, has Maya managed to help you, Domenico?"

"Yeah, I think so …"

"Would you like to join us for dinner?" Mum sometimes really surprised me. But I guessed that she would never have asked him if Dad had not happened to have this doctors' reunion tonight. I was completely overwhelmed by the idea. But Domenico seemed to be confused, for some reason.

"At yours? But … I can't!"

"Why not?"

"You wa-want me to have d-dinner with ya?" he stammered, as if it was the first invitation of his life.

"If your parents do not mind?" Mum was smiling. "You obviously have to ask them, first."

"They're not home."

"Oh, they aren't? When do they finish work then?"

"Uhm … late."

"Well then, why don't you stay here?" I begged and did not leave him a choice. Mum told us to go in and gathered her gardening stuff.

"Your mum's extremely okay!" Domenico commented and looked around impressed. He moved differently than usual, not as coolly as at school but much more attentively, carefully. As if he was worried about breaking something … I had never had anyone from school come to my place and I was already imagining how I would describe this historic moment in my diary.

We were standing in our huge, modern living room with the massive leather sofa, the broad coffee table and the soft, cream-coloured carpet. The glass cabinets were so clean that they were shining under the light of the little lamps inside them; Mum must have cleaned them right that afternoon. My parents had had the house redecorated two years ago and they had bought new furniture for all the rooms. I knew that we were well-off, but my parents had worked hard for it.

Domenico was completely gobsmacked and his eyes were wide open. He hesitantly walked around the living room and tried to digest the impression.

"Man, you must be minted!" he mumbled, unbelievingly. "Thi-this is as big as our entire flat!"

"Oh, I don't really care about all that," I blushed. I did not want him to feel uncomfortable. He did not say anything and kept staring. He discovered the pictures above the fireplace; I noticed that he was studying the photo of my little brother and then he looked at me. But he did not ask any questions. He did not seem to dare to, even though I would not have minded.

"Come on, I'll show you my room." I said and pulled on his t-shirt. With my heart beating loudly, I climbed up the stairs in front of him and nearly forgot to breathe. This was incredible! It was genius! Delia would have been green with envy if she had seen us, I thought triumphantly.

Silently, I opened the door to my room and walked over to the window straight away, to open the curtains that were protecting the room from the sun during the day. That made the room glow in a warm red light. Domenico stopped at the door and looked inside. In his eyes, I could see that he just did not know how to react to all this.

"Wow! It's all really tidy!"

"Hm … yeah. I don't like it messy, somehow."

"Really?" he sunk his head. He was still standing at the door, apparently afraid to come in.

I could feel that I had said something wrong and I could have bit my tongue. But it was too late.

"Come in!" I tried to encourage him.

And then I froze. Voices! I could hear voices coming from the living room! It was my dad! He had come home! But why? What about the reunion? My heart sunk. I could not believe it!

Domenico stopped and looked at me, intensely. He seemed to feel that something was wrong. “I dunno … maybe I better go home now.”

“No!” I replied decidedly and grabbed his arm. If he left now, this would be it. It would be over before it even started. But was it really a good idea for him to stay?

Dad. He would be shocked if he saw Domenico! I could hear Mum’s steps on the stairs. “Maya, your dad has come home! The reunion was postponed. We will eat in a minute, could you come down, please?”

I felt sick, I was so nervous and I had to hide it from Domenico, at all costs.

“Come on!” I said silently.

Dad was standing in the living room, waiting for us. He gave me a hug and then looked at Domenico. First at his face, with all the scars, and then at his long hair that fell over his right eye. Dad’s eyes wandered further down and he saw Domenico’s jeans.

He frowned sceptically and did not seem amused. I was feverishly trying to figure out how to save the situation.

“So you are this new boy!” Dad said in a very depreciative tone.

Domenico’s face turned hard from one second to the next. I quickly pushed him towards the kitchen and made him sit down.

“Come on, you can sit next to me!”

My parents sat down at the table, too. Dad folded his

hands and said grace. I was incredibly worried about how corny Domenico must have been thinking this was! But then, he suddenly said something unexpected: "We used to say grace too, before dinner."

Mum smiled at him and I completely forgot to say "Amen". I was so surprised by what Domenico had just said.

I could feel Dad's sceptical look; he was going to put him to the acid test. Domenico took his fork and picked at his salad as if he had never eaten with cutlery, before. I would not have cared, but Dad thought that table manners were indispensible. And Domenico clearly did not have any.

"Do you always hold the fork in your right hand?" he asked. I sighed with ostentation, but Dad ignored me.

Domenico flinched when he finally realised that Dad had been talking to him. He took the fork in his left hand, but somehow it slipped through his fingers and fell onto the plate, landing in the middle of the salad dressing. A few drops sprinkled on Dad's shirt sleeve. I looked at Dad, angrily.

When we got to the spaghetti, Dad started his interrogation.

"What do your parents do, Domenico?" Mum and I looked at each other and sighed. Dad just could not let go.

"Uhm ... well ... uhm." Domenico nearly choked on his spaghetti and was shaken by a coughing fit. "My mum ... she's ... she's a model."

Now, I nearly choked. “A model?” Wow, how cool! Or was he just inventing that?

“And your father?” Dad continued, determined.

“I don’t have one.”

Mum looked shocked.

“And where do you live?” Dad did not stop asking.

“Well, in the city ...”

“Where, exactly?”

“Does that matter?” Domenico mumbled embarrassed.

“Martin, would you stop now, please?” Mum said silently.

“Do you like going to school?” Dad completely ignored her.

“Yeah, I guess ...” Domenico looked at me coldly. Great! Thanks, Dad!

“What do you do in your spare time?”

“Uhm ... dunno ... different things.”

Dad’s eyes were burning through his.

“What, exactly?”

“Spend time with my brother.”

“And what do you do together?”

“Dad, stop it!” I desperately hissed. Mum put her napkin away and pleadingly looked at Dad: “Martin, please, stop asking all these questions!”

“Esther, I just want to know who our daughter spends time with!” Dad replied. How embarrassing! I rolled my eyes, ashamed, hoping that Domenico would understand the gesture. He was just sitting there, staring at the horribly, conservative looking picture of a fruit basket hanging on the wall, behind Dad's head.

After dinner, Dad wanted to sit in the living room with us. But Mum conjured him with looks to leave us alone and I pushed Domenico upstairs, before the catastrophe could be completed.

Domenico shook his head and turned away. "I think I better go home, Maya," he said silently.

"No, stay! Just for a little while!" I begged him. I had to make this up to him, otherwise all would be lost.

Domenico undecidedly followed me to my room. He still had this mysterious, dark look on his face which worried me a lot. I pushed the door behind us closed with my foot.

"I'm so sorry, Domenico," I sighed. "Dad can be horrible sometimes!"

"That's okay," he mumbled. He looked down at himself. "I really look a bit scruffy, huh?"

"No, that doesn't matter!" I hurried to say. I had tears in my eyes now, because I was so angry. Now, he definitely thought I was a loser.

Domenico stood behind me. "It's okay, Maya. Don't be sad. It's not your fault!"

Oh God! To spend time with Domenico really felt like a trip on a rollercoaster! It went from one high to the next low in no time. I turned around and tried to smile. "I am not like my dad, believe me!"

"I know that!" He smiled too now. I breathed deeply and tried to relax. I just did not want to make any mistakes.

"Now, tell me. You have got a brother, you said?"

"Yeah."

"How old is he?"

He could not stop himself from grinning. "Same age as me."

"What?" Sometimes I was really slow.

"We're twins."

"What? You never told me that!"

"You've never asked."

"Does he look exactly like you?"

"Mhm," he nodded, "he's even got the same tooth gap like me. But his hair's even more scrubby and he's got five piercings, there." He pointed to his left ear.

I really liked the thought that Domenico had a twin brother. I had always found twins fascinating; so many times I had wished that I had a twin sister myself.

"Oh wow! I would really like to see him!"

"I can bring a photo of him tomorrow. I've got one of us when we are seven."

"Don't you have any recent photos?"

He shook his head. I thought that was a bit curious. My parents had a thousand pictures of me at all ages and in all sorts of situations.

"What is his name?"

"Michele. But I always call him Mingo, cos his second name is Domingo. I've contracted that."

"Domingo? That sounds like Domenico!"

"It's the same name, in Spanish."

"But, I thought you were from Sicily?"

"Yeah, we are."

Strange, I thought. He still did not seem to want to talk about it properly. "Domenico is a very nice name," I said.

"You think? It's too long, though. Nobody can ever remember it. So, everyone calls me Nico or Nick."

"What about Nicky?"

"Yeah, sometimes." He blushed a little.

"Have you got a second name, too?"

"Manuel. Domenico Manuel."

"Cool. That sounds really nice. Do you get on well with your brother?"

He nodded but his eyes wandered off and he stared at the window next to my desk. "He's my best friend," he murmured. His lips were trembling strangely. He turned away and shook his head.

"What's up?" I asked. I just had to ask that.

He was playing with the leather bands that were tied around his left wrist and bit his lips.

"Nothin'. He … he's got some troubles, y'know."

"Oh …" I whispered, feeling sorry for him, but not really knowing what to say. Stop! I had to stop there. No more questions, otherwise I would risk hitting a raw nerve. I could not tell why, but I just knew that I had to respect this boundary. I would have loved to know everything about him, but he seemed to hate being asked all these questions.

"Well, I hope he is going to be fine." I ended up saying helplessly.

He nodded and pensively looked at me. I felt that everything inside me was trembling and I did not know where to turn my eyes or where to put my arms.

"I had a brother, too," I told him, to make him think of something else. "But I cannot remember him. He died when he was only three months old."

His eyes widened and he was looking at me even more intensely now. His gaze pierced through me again with this deep darkness, stirring up the same feelings in me as my dreams about the lantern.

"I'm sorry," he whispered.

"Don't worry. I really don't remember him."

"He's the baby on that photo, righ'? I thought, that wasn't you …"

How had he noticed that? Nobody who had not known about my brother had ever guessed that the child on the picture was not me. He had to have a really good eye for that.

"His name was Michael," I added.

"Michael … Michele!" he realised, fascinated, and looked at me attentively. "You know, I don't get why the others are so mean to you. You're really okay. You're

… you're the coolest girl I've ever met. I think … you're much more clever than Delia."

It was as if warm honey was running down inside me. A very old wound had started to heal. A wound caused by the constant doubts, doubts that something was wrong with me.

"You think?" I asked shyly. I would have to add a few pages to my diary, tonight! I had to write it all down in detail, even if that meant that I had to do it by the light of a torch, under my duvet.

"You are going out with Delia, aren't you?"

He shrugged his shoulders. "Pfff… I dunno. Sometimes she's really stupid. Really stupid!" He looked at me with clear eyes. "I know you think I'm into her. Cos I touched her and all. But that don't mean anything. She always wants to make out!"

"What?!" I blushed.

"Man, you know what I mean, righ'?" He smiled, embarrassed. I was offended.

"Of course I know what you mean! You don't have to … it's not my fault that my dad is so strict!"

"Hey, tranquilla! I ain't laughing at you! It's no problem, really!"

"Well, unfortunately I am not that cool."

"That's no problem. It's all just fake anyway. What do you think people are really like? But, you just gotta pretend if you wanna survive."

This was interesting. I would have to think about that

idea in detail later. Maybe this explained the whole Mister Universe mask.

"What do you think of our class, apart from that?"

"Hm, they're all babies." He waved his hand.

"And … what do you think about Mrs Galiani?"

"She's really clever." His look became tough again. "Much more clever than all the other teachers."

"I'm definitely scared of her," I admitted.

He gave me such a fierce look that, for a second, it felt like I lost my footing. Did he think I was a complete wuss now? I felt that we were already heading to the next low and I trembled inside. But he held his hand out as if to catch me and grabbed my arm gently. I was staggered. Did my feelings show that clearly on my face, or could he see right into my heart?

"What do you think of … Andrew?" I quickly changed the subject.

"He's an idiot!" He let go of my arm and looked out of the window. It seemed as though he was staring at one specific spot. I stood next to him and tried to see what he was focussing on. His eyes looked straight at the mansion where my favourite lantern stood. It was a shame that the sky was still bright and that the lantern was not on yet, otherwise I might have told Domenico that …

"You can see it from here, righ'?" he mumbled silently.

"What do you mean?" I asked, stunned. What was he talking about …

"That lantern up there!" All of a sudden, his voice sounded as though it came from a different world and his thoughts seemed to wander off to a place far away. A place, where most people never went. Only those who were a bit strange (something I was very familiar with) … What on earth did that mean? Was I dreaming or was I awake? I stared at him as if thunder had struck me.

"W-what are you saying?"

"Sorry, Maya, you'll probably think I'm crazy," he said a bit embarrassed.

"No! No! Not at all! Please tell me what you mean! What lantern?"

"That old lantern, next to the mansion. It's … It's … I dunno how to tell you. This might sound crazy, but I have these super freaky dreams sometimes …"

"I … I …" I swallowed excitedly. Should I tell him about my freaky dreams, too? About my book? I was definitely crazier than he was!

"I … I have weird dreams sometimes too, Nicky. Wonderful dreams, actually. In which I am riding on a white horse through this beautiful forest to the lantern. And every time I get there, I wake up …"

My face was glowing hot and I could feel his eyes staring right into me. He was probably thinking that I had completely lost my mind now. He shook his head as if I had just told him I really was an enchanted fairy.

"You don't even know what you just said, Maya."

"What do you mean?"

"Nothin'." He stared past me at the window sill. "I always thought I was the only one with such crazy ideas."

"I always thought that, too!"

"You know what? We've got a lot in common."

"Hmm." Up to now, I had been convinced of the opposite, rather. But thinking about it, he was completely right. I felt more and more like I could tell him everything. Even the weirdest things, that other people would only laugh about.

"I even write a novel about this lantern. But my parents don't know that."

"A novel? You mean a story?"

"Yes. A whole book. And … and the main character is called Domenico." Maybe I had taken it a bit too far now.

"Really?" he was completely baffled. His cheeks blushed. "After … after me?"

"Uhm… I just really like your name! It … it is so special."

He was grinning broadly. He did not manage to hide his delight behind his cool mask. But suddenly, he became strangely quiet again and he stared into the blue. His face was so tense that it twitched from time to time. His phone went off with a loud beep and brought him back to reality. He took it out of his pocket.

"Yeah?"

And then he continued in Italian. He lowered his

voice, but I still listened. I was fascinated, even if I did not understand a word. The conversation was brief. His eyes looked really dark now, and he seemed nervous when he put the phone back in his pocket.

"Is everything okay?" I asked.

"Yeah. But I gotta go now."

I nodded sadly. "That's a shame. Was it your brother?"

"Mhm." He did not look at me and turned towards the door. I walked him out to the gate, once he had said goodbye to my parents. The temperature was still nice and mild, outside. The church bell rang: it was quarter to nine. Domenico stopped and looked over to the park. We could see the lantern from where we stood.

"I'm there almost every night," he suddenly said. But then he was quiet again and looked scared, as if he had already said too much. But I had good ears.

"Out there, by the lantern?" I could not believe it. Was he allowed to do that?

"And what do you mean, nearly every night?"

He grinned embarrassed. "Not important. I'm a bit strange sometimes."

Indeed! I thought. In the forest, at night? Every normal teenager was in bed at night. But, maybe he was just making things up.

"My parents would never allow me to go to the forest by myself in the middle of the night. That must be quite dangerous, I think."

He waved dismissively. “Nah, whatever. I do what I want anyway.” His voice sounded tough.

He was probably just bragging about now. I knew that some parents were a bit weird, but that would definitely be too extreme.

“I have never gone out there at night. I would really like to see the lantern up close when it is on. But then, my parents would have to come with me and I would be too embarrassed to ask them …”

“Yeah, I get that …” He looked to the floor. “I mean … if you want, we can go there together sometime,” he shyly suggested.

My heart was beating fast. “I would love that! But … my dad would never allow it.”

“Are your parents always at home?”

“Most of the time, yes. They never leave me alone in the evening.”

“Really?” This seemed to be a strange thing to him. “They never go out or somethin’?”

“Yes, sometimes they do. But then, my aunt comes around,” I replied contritely. He had to think I was a baby, because there was always someone looking after me. Dad was too worried to leave me alone in our big house at night. There had been two or three burglaries in our neighbourhood.

Domenico did not know how to reply, and I could feel that he was astonished. I was pretty sure by now that his parents were neglecting him quite a bit. Or rather his mum was. Maybe that was the reason why he did so many crazy things.

"How long will it take you to get home?" I asked.

"Depends on which way I go ..."

He smiled and held out his hand. "Gotta go now, Maya. Take care! And thanks for all. See you on Monday at school."

I took his hand, which felt rough and warm. I would have liked to hold it forever.

I lingered outside the gate for a little while and watched him walk away. Before he turned around the corner, he stopped to light a cigarette. He really smoked a lot. Was he not worried about his health?

None of us had mentioned it. But it was absolutely clear now. No doubt about it. I knew it, and I knew that he knew it: we were friends!

But there was something else.

"Domenico ..." I murmured silently, while I was walking back to the house. "You thought you could hide it from me, but I know: you have a secret!"

This gave me loads of thoughts to fill my diary with over the weekend, and I felt light with joy. I was happy about the incredible fact that Domenico seemed to like me, that he had come to my place, that he knew the lantern in the forest. I was happy that we had so much in common and that I felt like he understood me. But at the same time, the secret that I sensed around him and that I could not wait to explore made me shudder.

Dad did not say anything the whole weekend, and Mum was more nervous than usual. She had probably somehow managed to keep Dad from telling me off about Domenico. I hid in my room, busy, using up a whole bottle of white-out to exchange all the Michaels in my book for Domenicos.

10. The forbidden spire

On my way to school, I was humming "Morning has broken," picking leaves from the hedges. After thinking about it thoroughly over the weekend, I had decided that it was impossible that Domenico would ever fall in love with me. But we were friends, and even that was better than anything I had ever dreamed of. I had not expected, though, that he would be waiting for me in the schoolyard. So I was very surprised when he suddenly stepped out from behind the bike shelter and walked towards me.

"Hey, Maya!"

"Hi, Nicky!" It had just slipped out of my mouth. He smiled, a bit embarrassed. I let the leaves that I had collected on my way fall to his feet. He grinned and tried to catch them.

"So, you plucked all the trees for me, huh?"

"Not exactly. My hands are not that big …" I said and looked at my fingers.

"Mine aren't either. Let's see!" He splayed out his fingers and held his hand carefully against mine. And he was right: his hand was not much bigger than mine, but it was tanned and covered in scratches. His fingers were yellow from the nicotine. Suddenly, he pulled his hand back again, almost as if he was a little ashamed. But I was not sure.

"Hey, Maya, I wanna show you somethin' wicked! Come on!"

"But, the bell is going to ring in five minutes!"

"That's enough time! I've got a secret hiding place, come on!"

He ran off in front of me and pointed to the roof of the gym: "It's up there!"

"Where?" I looked up at the old building in disbelief, the angled roof and the small spire sitting on the top, making it all look like a fairy-tale castle. When I realised what Domenico was up to, I stared at him in shock.

"You mean the spire? But that's forbidden!"

He just grinned. "What's *not* forbidden around here?"

I hesitated. "Domenico … I … I would rather not go up there! What if we get caught …"

"We won't. Nobody can see us. Come on!"

I gave in and followed him. He really had nerves of steel! But we did manage to enter into the building unnoticed and climbed up the stairs to the attic. In front of the low brittle wooden door we stopped. It smelled like the inside of an old boat.

"I'm sure it's locked!" I protested.

"No, it ain't."

"Nicky, we could get into really bad trouble for this. Let's go back. Please! I don't want to go up there! And we are going to be late for first period!"

"Hey, don't worry. I'm telling you, it's completely safe."

He seemed to be determined and was not going to stop now. He opened the door and pulled me along with him. The wooden stairs creaked loudly. The attic was full of junk, mainly indefinable old gym equipment and deflated balls. Creepy spider webs were covering every corner, like in a haunted castle. Right at the back, there was a half-broken ladder leading up to the window in the roof. Great!

"You go first. I'm gonna catch you if you fall," Domenico said when I was hesitating, again. I really did not want to go up there. Anything but that!

"Go on. It's amazing, I swear!"

Holding my breath, I climbed up the steps. The window was open and sunlight was shining onto my face. I took a last step and I had made it. Domenico was right behind me.

I stood up and carefully leant against the balustrade. I was speechless. The view was fantastic! I could see the entire schoolyard, the roofs of the city all the way up to the park. Seen from the ground, the spire had always looked so unimpressive. I imagined what it would feel like to be a bird, to spread my wings and fly away to … Where would I fly to? I did not want to be anywhere else. And I did not have to fly anywhere; I could just stay here and do somersaults high up in the air. But obviously only if were able to fly. And sometimes I was, but only at night in my dreams.

Domenico stepped next to me. “Beautiful, righ’? You miss too much if you never break any rules.”

“Wow …” I sighed. I closed my eyes and felt the soft wind in my face. What was so bad about this? If nobody caught us …

But I could not fool myself. I did not manage to ignore my conscience, even with the great view. It was high time we went back, anyway. The bell would ring in just one minute!

“Let’s go back now, Nicky! I do not want to be late.”

“Pah, no maths! Let’s stay up here. It’s awesome.”

“Yes, it is really nice, but we can’t just skip the class! Are you crazy?”

“Why not? What’s gonna happen, anyway?”

I shook my head uncomprehendingly. He was just so different from me.

“But if my parents find out about this …”

“They won’t.”

“But what if somebody calls at home and asks where I am?”

“Nobody’s gonna do that. Even you can oversleep one day. It’s really easy! And Mr Lenz is harmless, anyway. He’s never gonna call no one.”

I leant against the balustrade and looked down on the schoolyard that was still full of students. Skip the class. Now that was one thing I really could not do. If Dad found out about it, he would be livid. But what if nobody was ever going to know? I started to go through all the possibilities.

"Mrs Galiani could notice something!"

"No, she won't. We're gonna be there for the next class, before she's even there and she will never find out."

"But, Mr Lenz has to write down in the register that we were not in his class." This was definitely a good argument.

Domenico only shrugged his shoulders. "And even if he does …"

Why did he not take this seriously? Now I heard the angry sound of the school bell. Everything inside me was screaming and shouting. I could feel Domenico's insecure look on me.

"That's really important to you, the whole entry in the register stuff, huh?" he said, and it made me realise that he too had to make an effort to understand my point of view.

"Well, we would have to hand in an excuse signed by our parents. And you know my dad now …"

"Alright, alright," he replied and scratched a line into the withered wood. His thoughts definitely started to drift off and if I did not say anything now he would not move for another half hour. The school yard started to empty.

"Doesn't your mum mind at all that you skip classes all the time?" He did not answer that; he just continued scratching. Irritated, I looked down through the open windows of the classrooms and saw the students arrive. Soon the teachers would appear. If I left now, I could still pretend that I was just a little bit late.

"I'll forge the signature, if you want," Domenico finally suggested. "I'm good at that!"

Oh yes, I could imagine that! Suddenly, I understood how important it was for him that I stayed up there with him. But, I just did not have the nerve to do it. Apart from the fact that I read teen magazines without my parents' knowledge and that I had cheated on my homework once or twice, I did not have much on my record.

"No, Nicky, I don't want to lie. I am going down, now. We have still got time." I turned around but my legs would not move. The old Maya that I was so familiar with, wanted to run off and make it in time. But a different, new Maya protested inside me, and this Maya wanted to stay up there on the roof with Domenico, to stare into the vast blue sky and dream. I was nearly a bit relieved when I saw that in some of the rooms, the classes had started and that it was too late now, anyway. Time had made the decision for me.

Domenico was looking at me, confused. "What are you up to, now?"

"I'm staying here." What was so bad about skipping one single class in seven years? I thought. Everyone did that at least once.

"You don't have to if you don't want to, Maya," he said, still insecure. "I'm not gonna be mad at you. You're just a bit different in these things …"

"I know."

"I can make the note in the record disappear for you," he suggested, "I just put white-out on it. Galiani will think that Lenz has made a mistake."

I did not really believe in that plan, but it did sound better than forging my parents' signature. I nodded while I had a glance at the window of our classroom, where I saw Mr Lenz slowly walking towards the blackboard. Fingers crossed that this would go well!

The clicking sound of Domenico's lighter woke me from my thoughts and I looked at him.

"You smoke quite a lot."

"Yeah, so?" he snapped.

"Why do you do that?" I only realised now that this was exactly the kind of interrogation Dad always put me through and I hated so much.

"Dunno. Cos I need it?"

"But it's really unhealthy." Another one.

"I know that myself. Everything I do is unhealthy! I couldn't care less." His voice sounded incredibly bitter and cold. He sat down on the floor and leant against the balustrade.

I did the same and sadly stared into the blue summer sky. Now I had definitely spoilt it all, how stupid! But then, he suddenly dug a photo out of his pocket and handed it to me.

"Look, that's Mingo and me."

I took it and looked at it interestedly.

There were two pretty little boys, about seven years old, who looked like two peas in a pod. I held the photo next to Domenico who was sitting by my side looking at me attentively. The red shine in his hair seemed to have faded a bit. I tried to find a clue to show me which of the two in the photo was Domenico, but try as I might, I couldn't make it out. I shook my head in awe. I still could not believe it, even though I held the proof of it in my hands.

"It's amazing! Who is who?"

"You gotta guess!"

"I am trying but I can't find a difference!"

"Alright, I'm the one on the right, with the stupid grin."

I looked at the photo again. I could have done that for hours. The other boy, Mingo, looked very sceptical.

"Will you introduce me to Mingo?"

"We'll see." The reply came very hesitantly. There it was again, the boundary. The boundary that said: up to here and no further. He tried to hide it, but I could feel it very clearly. As clearly as the wind that was blowing around our faces. He got up, put his cigarette out on the balustrade and flicked the butt down onto the school-yard.

Carefully, I changed the subject by asking about the English exercises.

"Have you read all the texts?"

"Oh, man! Don't mention that again! Mingo said I was crazy to study that stuff. I'm too stupid to get it, anyway. And I only get a headache from studying."

If I was skipping a class, I might as well make something useful of it, the sensible, good-mannered Maya thought, and so I suggested: "Why don't we use the time we have to look at that again?"

He yawned and stretched his arms. "If we have to."

We had to, I insisted. After all, his future was at stake. And while he was studying, I tried to sort out my thoughts. I was breaking out of my usual boundaries, and somehow it did not feel right. How would everyone else at school react to all this?

The ringing of the bell brought me back to reality. I had to stop turning the thoughts in my head around and around. Domenico picked up exactly what I had been worrying about: "I bet there's gonna be chaos when the others find out about us!"

"Aren't you afraid of them?" I asked.

"Nah, you can't be. If they notice that you chicken out, they're gonna bully you even more."

He was right. But how could I overcome my fears and get rid of them? They were just there, and I could not stop them from creeping up inside me, once they were awakened. They sometimes just took over.

When we climbed down the ladder, she was there again, the old, worried Maya: "Nicky … you know, I really like it up there, but I do not want to go up from now on anymore. I'm sure we would get into trouble otherwise."

He wrinkled his nose scornfully. "Trouble? Do you think I'm gonna take any crap from them?"

"That is not the point! I just … You know, my dad can be really difficult. And then it gets really uncomfortable at home."

We were back in the dusty attic with all the gym equipment. It was dark, but I could still see a twitch in Domenico's eyes and how he turned his face away from me.

"Man! I sure don't want that!" he mumbled.

"You mean about my dad? Don't worry! Now, let's go downstairs, or we will miss the next class too."

Sometimes things turned out differently than you would have expected, but our confrontation with Delia was not one of those exceptions. She immediately saw us when we came into the classroom. She jumped up from her chair and gasped, as if she had an asthma fit.

"Where were you, Nico? And what are you doing with that stupid cow?" she screamed, her voice nearly cracking. I anxiously tried to avoid her cat-like eyes, but Domenico was not impressed. He even stepped in front of me, as if he was trying to protect me.

"Take the stupid cow back, Delia!" he commanded loudly.

The entire class was staring at us, and for the first time ever since I knew her, Delia turned into a sobbing mess in front of my eyes. Her tears left a black mascara mark on her cheek. "You … you're a mean bastard! You said you loved me! You even wanted to sleep with me!" Her eyes lit up angrily and full of hate she pointed at me with her manicured finger: "I know what happened! You have fallen in love with her! I know it! Just admit it! You have! Haven't you?"

My heart stopped beating for a couple of seconds. What was she saying?

"That ain't none of your business!" Domenico hissed.

"Coward!" Isabelle snorted.

"Stupid bastard!" Delia screamed with such a shrill voice that some of the boys started to grin. "I hate you! You and your stupid little slut!" She yanked on the necklace with the red heart-shaped pendant and threw it on the floor in front of Domenico. "There! You can have that back, too!"

Seething with rage she stamped back to her seat while Andrew, Danny and Ronnie were screaming with laughter.

"Haha, our great superhero and the holy little cow! What a dream team!" Andrew shouted and rolled around the floor, pretending it was that funny. "What a joke!"

Isabelle built herself up in front of Domenico and stared at him, her cold eyes looking even more menacing with the black eye-shadow she was always wearing.

"Really, Nico, you must be mad, hanging out with that ugly witch!"

"Just leave us alone!" Domenico pushed the tall girl – yes, she was actually taller than him – roughly out of the way and led me to the teacher's desk. I knew what he was planning to do: We had to delete the entry next to my name before Mrs Galiani saw it. She remembered every absence. The register and the writing material were in the drawer. In everyone's plain view, Domenico got them out and painted a white line over my name.

"Nicky! You are crazy!" I whispered anxiously, because everyone could see what he was doing.

"So, you've made her skip a class?" Isabelle jeered meanly. "How interesting!"

I was sure that she would tell Mrs Galiani. She knew exactly what we were doing. But I had underestimated Domenico's willpower. He stood in front of the class and looked at everyone menacingly. I did not know how he did it; he did not even have to say anything. He could silence them all with just one look; even I felt huge respect for him in that moment. There was something about him that was hard to describe.

Only Isabelle kept looking at him angrily, even though she did not say anything anymore. Domenico took my hand and walked back to our desk with me.

And really: the first thing Mrs Galiani did when she came in was check the register. I was terrified. She picked it up and when she looked up her eyes aimed at Domenico.

"Missed the first class again, have you? Do you never look at the timetable, Domenico? What am I supposed to do with you? Do I really have to keep you here again, this afternoon?"

He rolled his eyes annoyed but did not reply.

"We will discuss this later," Mrs Galiani concluded and closed the book, without wondering about the mysterious white stain. I breathed a sigh of relieve. Delia and Isabelle, however, gave me evil looks.

What did Delia say? That Domenico had fallen in love with me? I nearly exploded just thinking about it. But I pulled myself back down to earth. It was just impossible.

In the break, Isabelle started attacking us again. "You're making such a fool of yourself with that wall-flower!" she spat out when she stood up from her desk. "Everyone's gonna make fun of you."

"I don't care! Laugh how much as you want!" Domenico replied annoyed.

"*How* much as you want? It's *as* much as you want! You can't even talk properly!" she scoffed and then turned to the others with a grin: "Did you know that he doesn't know how to spell *dead?* He spells it without an e! Like d-a-d!"

"Teehee!" Andrew was sneering. "Wonder what his daddy thinks about that! Bet he's not gonna be very happy with his sonny boy."

"No, I think his dad must be dead proud of him!" Ronnie joined in happily. "He's probably just as brain-dead!"

Suddenly, everyone had fallen silent. They seemed to sense that Andrew and Ronnie had brought up a dangerous subject. I felt a freeze creeping up my neck and I let go of Domenico's hand. His face had become rigid and ice-cold, he looked really scary. A few seconds passed and then, something happened inside me that I would never have thought possible: I turned around and furiously looked at Andrew: "Just shut up, you big bragger! In geography, you didn't even know that Madrid is the capital of Spain!"

Dead silence. Andrew stared at me. Domenico stared at me. The entire class stared at me. Frightened, I turned my face away. What had I just done? This would probably have really bad consequences for me …!

"Interesting …" Isabelle murmured, "She fights back!"

Domenico looked at me surprised, as if I had achieved a miracle. He bent down, picked up Delia's necklace that had still been lying on the floor, and put it in my hand. "I give this to you. Do you wanna go out with me, Maya?" he hoarsely asked.

My "yes" was nearly inaudible. My heart was beating

like crazy. I took the necklace and looked at the red heart. Hadn't he bought that necklace for Delia? And now I should have it? He put it around my neck and fastened the clasp. I felt thousands of butterflies in my stomach when his fingers touched my skin. And then I straightened my back. It was high time I got over my fears.

I did not say much during lunch and I was glad that Dad did not want to talk about Domenico again. I was very busy hiding the necklace, as well as the new Maya that had skipped a class for the first time in her life this morning. I avoided looking my parents in the eyes, focussing on the rice on my plate instead.

When I helped Mum wash the dishes after the meal, the necklace slipped out from under my t-shirt and Mum immediately noticed it. I blushed. Mum bent down and curiously touched the red heart-shaped pendant.

"Where did you get that necklace, Maya?"

"Domenico gave it to me. It used to belong to Delia but she did not want it anymore ..."

"Really? It looks very pretty!"

Mum smiled her smile that made me go crazy. Why did mothers always have to make that face when they found out that their daughters had a boyfriend for the first time?

"Are you always together now, at school?"

"Uhm, yes …" I snarled. "He is the only one, at school, who likes me."

"Are you sure?" Mum looked over her shoulder, but Dad was in the bathroom.

"I thought he was very nice," she said. "But he is a bit shy, isn't he?"

Domenico? Shy?! I thought laughing to myself. But I guess in a way Mum was actually right.

11. Three friends

On Tuesday morning, I woke up with a huge lump in my stomach and immediately knew why. The English exam! If Domenico failed, he would get into really big trouble. I sat down at the table in a bad mood, forced myself to eat some cornflakes and hoped that Mrs Galiani would be off sick today.

But Mrs Galiani was in rude health and her tongue was especially sharp when she distributed the exam papers. "I hope you are well prepared. If you fail this exam, you will struggle to catch up." Her eyes stopped for a moment on Domenico, and she gave him a stern look, as if she wanted to warn him in particular. He tried to stay as cool as possible, but he did not really manage. To be honest, I do not think I had ever seen him this nervous before.

"Nicky, you are going to make this!" I whispered to him. He did not seem to hear me; he was just clutching his pen so tightly that his knuckles became all white.

And then Mrs Galiani gave the starting signal. For forty-five minutes, we worked our tails off, struggling, agonising and sweating our way through the first part of the exam. There was complete silence, except for the scratching sound of our pens on the paper, the rustling of turning pages and a weary sigh from time to time. I was glad to see that three of the questions were based on the subjects I had studied with Domenico. I glanced over to him quickly when Mrs Galiani was busy with Andrew and Ronnie. He was writing very slowly and his face was so close to the paper that his hair nearly touched it. He was the last one to hand his copy in, and I was surprised to see that he had not skipped any of the questions.

After a break of five minutes, Mrs Galiani continued with the dictation part of the exam. And again, luck was on our side, since the text she was dictating was exactly the one Domenico and I had revised.

When the bell announced the ten o'clock break, Domenico just sat there staring into the air until I carefully nudged him.

"Hey, Nicky! How did it go?"

He turned his face towards me.

"Dunno. Not bad, I think. Let's go downstairs, Maya, I'm knackered. I need a fag!"

And I needed something to eat. So I picked up my purse, and we left the classroom.

In our hurry, we completely ignored Patrick, who was standing next to the toilets, and Domenico, probably still dizzy after the exam, ran right into him. The two boys stumbled and held on to each other, but they could not keep their balance and fell to the floor.

"Oh man! I'm sorry!" Domenico stammered. "Are you hurt?"

Patrick's eyes widened, when he realised who had

walked into him. He looked at me and then back to Domenico, as if he was watching a match of tennis. The craziest boy of the class was friends with the wallflower! He probably struggled digesting this information.

"I should really watch out where I'm going!" Domenico said, shaking his head, and stood up.

"Tha-that's okay!" Patrick mumbled, but he was so perplexed that he did not manage to get up. Domenico gave him his hand and helped him, which confused Patrick even more. The two boys looked at each other, not saying anything, and again there was this invisible bond that was being tied between them.

"Hey, how about you … you could come downstairs with us, if you want," Domenico suggested. He was breathing heavily, as if his heart was beating too fast. "I'm gonna make sure those idiots leave you alone."

Patrick's eyes widened again, and his cheeks were flaming red with excitement. He swallowed hard several times, but he wasn't able to say anything. Domenico, who had managed to compose himself again, smiled at him and gave him a pat on the back.

"Y-yes, I-I would like that!" Patrick stammered, and there was a glow in his eyes. "B-but I don't wa-want to bother you."

"You don't bother us," I replied, "not at all!" I had always liked Patrick, and I was really happy that Domenico had made this connection.

When we heard Andrew's booming voice approaching, Domenico quickly pulled us with him. "Come on, guys!"

In the schoolyard, Patrick and I bought a sandwich at the stand and we went to sit behind the big lime tree that shielded us a bit from the view of the others. This way, Domenico could smoke his cigarette without being caught. The weather was cloudy and dull and it looked as though it would soon be pouring with rain.

Domenico looked at Patrick with curiosity. "You've got all those planes on your schoolbooks. You wanna be a pilot?" he asked.

Patrick blushed again.

"Oh, yes! Tha-that's my b-biggest dream! I-I collect everything about p-planes. I have got m-many b-books and posters."

"Really? That's cool! I'd really like to go on a plane one day, too!"

"You mean you have never been on a plane, before? Do you never go on a holiday or anything?" I flew on holidays once a year with my parents. To France, to Spain or to the Canary Islands.

Domenico smiled a bit sadly. "Nah, we've never done that."

"I-I am going to take you with me, w-when I'm a p-pilot!" Patrick tried to comfort him quickly. "Y-you know, m-my dad was a Lufthansa p-pilot. B-but he died in a plane crash."

Domenico took a long drag on his cigarette and

looked at Patrick earnestly. His eyes seemed to absorb him. And Patrick was equally fascinated by Domenico. There were some drops of sweat along his hairline.

"Man, I'm really sorry," Domenico said silently. "I ain't got no dad, either. You know what … I got a poster of a plane at home, too. You can have it, if you want."

This seemed to be nearly too much for Patrick to handle. If Domenico had not been a superhero to Patrick before, he had definitely turned into one right now.

"W-what do you want to be w-when you are grown up?" I could see that Patrick was nearly bursting with curiosity and the sheer amount of questions he wanted to ask.

"When I'm grown up?" Domenico was slightly amused by Patrick's question. "I guess that's gonna be quite soon … I'm a couple of years older than you, Patrick. What I wanna be? Don't know, really …"

"I want to become a doctor!" I declared. I had never thought about becoming anything else. But I had not always been as good at school as I was now. The first four years at primary school and at the beginning of secondary school, I thought that only the other kids were clever enough to understand everything we learnt, even though Dad had helped me with my homework all the time. I was shy and inconspicuous from head to toe, and I had come to terms with my situation. But one day when they handed out our school reports against all odds I found myself at the top of our class. After secondary school, I would go on to do my A-levels and then I would be able to go to university, where I would study medicine. And I never argued with my dad when he decided that one day I would take over his practice, even though I did have a different dream for my future.

"A doctor?" Domenico asked, "Like your dad?"

I nodded.

"I thought you're gonna be an author … write books and stuff!" He was very serious. I gasped. What was he saying? His comment aimed right at my heart. I had never dared to think seriously about this dream.

"Yes, I guess that would be my dream," I admitted. But how would I do that on top my job? If I was a doctor I would be really busy.

"I don't even need to dream about anything like that … I'm not so clever as you guys." Domenico sadly shrugged his shoulders and lit the next cigarette. "I can't even write without mistakes. How do you spell dead, actually? With an e?"

"Yes."

"Aw, man!" He looked at his feet, ashamed. "Guess, I'm pretty stupid."

"No, you're not!" Patrick and I protested at the same time.

"I don't think intelligence has got anything to do with that," I added. "You are just not used to studying. And on top of that, your mother tongue is Italian."

"When I was younger, I wanted to become a famous athlete." He grinned as if he was laughing at his own idea, but the melancholy in his voice was clearly audible.

"And why don't you work on that? You are really talented!" I encouraged him.

He gave me a piercing look and then shook his head in resignation "It's not possible anymore, Maya."

I did not get it. "Of course it is! Mr Reuter even wants to put you on the school team!"

"I could only start in the new semester when some of the team have left," he explained. "And if I've gotta repeat the semester again ..."

"Nicky, don't say that!" I replied shocked.

He shrugged his shoulders and turned around, when we suddenly heard a too familiar jeering coming closer.

Andrew, Danny and Ronnie were approaching the lime tree and we made sure we were gone, before they got there.

Domenico extinguished his cigarette under his foot and we walked back to the school building. Domenico in the middle, with his arms on Patrick's and my shoulder.

The art class in the afternoon showed me another of Domenico's incredible talents. Since he had skipped last week's class, this was his first. Mrs Wilde put us in teams of two and got big white sheets of paper out of the cupboard. I had always been looking forward to having so much space to draw on, and I was impatient to find out what would be our assignment today. I really liked drawing and painting, even if I was not the most talented. I was definitely better at writing. Mrs Wilde briefly explained what she wanted us to do: we should draw a portrait of our partner with carbon pencils.

I had not discussed with Domenico who would be the model this time, he just decided without asking me. He arranged a chair for me and carefully clipped a sheet of paper to the easel. I sat down and waited for him to get ready.

There was a mysterious smile on his face, when he picked up the carbon pencil.

"Move a bit to the right, Maya! Turn your head to the side … only a little bit … Yeah, like that! And let your hair fall over your left shoulder. Ecco, così …!"

I smiled at him and obeyed, curious what he was going to do. From the corner of my eye, I glanced at the others. They looked like they were part of a cartoon rather than an art class: Andrew was sitting on his chair like a sack of potatoes, making an ugly grimace. Danny, his partner, was laughing out loud, but Mrs Wilde told them off.

And then it was quiet, and I felt like Domenico and I were alone in the room. For a long time, he only looked at me before he started. His focussed grey-blue eyes studied every line on my face. He smiled again and began to draw. I had never had this much time to look at him, before: his face, handsome and rough at the same time, the tenderness and the dedication he invested in what he was doing, and his hands, which were completely covered in carbon by the end. I would have loved to touch them.

The first period was over in no time, and when I got up to have a look at the portrait, he quickly hid it from me. "Not before I've finished!" he commanded with a sneaky smile. During the second period, Mrs Wilde came to stand behind Domenico several times and interestedly studied his work. She also went to see what the others were doing, but she definitely came to us most often. When he had finished, she picked up his drawing and contemplated it for a while. I fidgeted on my chair impatiently. I was nearly bursting with curiosity! Mrs Wilde collected all the sheets and spread them over the tables.

I was the first one who walked over to have a look and I saw many mediocre, clumsily drawn pictures, unrecognizable grimaces with big noses, goggle eyes or small beads. And there, in the middle of all those strange masks, was *my* face: drawn with fine, delicate, perfect lines, just the right shading, like a black and white reflection of me in the mirror. I swallowed hard and carefully picked it up without even noticing that Mrs Wilde was standing next to me.

"Great work!" she praised in a friendly tone. I was startled and put the picture back on the table. I looked for Domenico. He was standing next to the easel and was writing something with the carbon pencil on a brown piece of paper. I went over to him.

"It is incredibly ... beautiful! How did you do that?" He smiled absentmindedly and drew an indefinable shape on the brown paper. Even that looked great, somehow! And then he just shrugged his shoulders.

"You are a genius, did you know that?"

"Rubbish!" he replied, blushing.

"Yes, you are! You ... you could draw pictures for my book one day!" I suggested hoarsely and he looked at me, his face glowing with excitement.

"Are you serious? You ... you mean ...?" But that idea seemed to make both of us far too nervous.

"Urgh!" Isabelle said when she held up Domenico's drawing. "Just thinks he's the greatest at everything!"

Mrs Wilde walked over and carefully took the picture out of her hands, putting it back on the table. I went over again and looked at it. I saw that it was more than just talent. He had put everything he had in this drawing: his feelings, his hopes, his friendship. He had literally submerged himself in this picture when he was creating it. And I felt as though he had looked right into my soul while he was drawing. For the light in my eyes in that picture expressed exactly what I was feeling inside.

12. Janet's vicious rumour

The next exciting event was not far away: the school party. With my head full of so many other things, I had nearly forgotten about it. But now, the evening was almost there, and for the first time, I was actually looking forward to it. I could not guess then, however, that I would find out a lot about Domenico and that some of my questions would be answered.

We had agreed to meet outside my house at seven; exactly the time my parents would sit down to have dinner. I was sure that Dad only let me go because the party was organised by the school.

The clouds had moved aside and let the evening sun shine through. Domenico was just crossing the street when I stepped through our garden door. His slightly ginger hair looked great in the small ray of sunlight that was falling right onto his face. My stomach was full of butterflies when I saw him. He stopped in front of me and admiringly looked at me from head to toe. I was wearing my new red dress, and I had put one of Mum's flowers in my hair. But I found myself still miles away from beautiful.

"Wow, y-you look amazing, Maya!" he stuttered and touched the flower in my hair very carefully, as if it was made of glass. Nobody, apart from my parents, had ever said anything like that to me! I would have loved to be able to turn back time to hear his words again, but I guessed I could hardly ask him to repeat what he had just said.

"Guess I look pretty scruffy again, huh?" Embarrassed, he looked down at himself. He was wearing his oldest pair of jeans and the t-shirt with the snarling tiger on it. Why did he turn up in his worst outfit at the school party? Did he not have anything reasonable to wear? I decided not to worry about it. Sometimes life was just so much easier when you stopped trying to find a reason for everything.

The schoolyard was brilliantly decorated. The rows of different stands made it look like a fun fair. The stands were linked with chains of fairy lights and colourful garlands. The entrance of the gym was covered in posters advertising the disco. There were a lot of people already there when we arrived. We wandered past the different stands and looked at what the older students had come up with. There were proper shooting galleries, charity stands and raffles, and some students were even performing a little play. And, of course, there was tons of food.

Domenico took my hand and pulled me over to a stand where they sold sweet waffles, but I rather wanted something savoury. When we had made up our minds, we went over to the old lime tree to tuck in: Domenico had chosen a chocolate waffle, the sauce of which was dripping onto his shoes, and I ate a hot dog. We laughed about his chocolate mess and I felt light and happy, as if someone had lighted fireworks inside me.

The cake stand was right next to the gym entrance. Mrs Galiani was there together with Delia, Manuela and Isabelle, whose turn it was to take care of the stand. They were all dressed up, and Delia was wearing really nice drop-shaped silver earrings that perfectly matched her baby blue dress.

Sadly, I touched my “naked” ears. But then, I reminded myself that I was at the party with the best-looking boy, not Delia, and I felt great again. I could feel the jealous looks of the girls, they were stinging my neck like needles, and I looked at Domenico. He smiled at me proudly. I was not a nobody in the schoolyard anymore!

I noticed that Mrs Galiani was observing us. Her eyes wandered back and forth between me and Domenico. There was a slight smile on her lips. Whenever my eyes crossed Mrs Galiani’s that evening, she gave me a knowing look.

Patrick arrived a bit later. We suddenly discovered him next to the gym, hiding behind a group of teachers. He beamed at us happily when he saw us too. The three of us wandered around on the schoolyard for a while, bought some more snacks (Domenico wanted another sweet waffle) and admired the other stands.

Finally, we walked towards the gym to have a look at the disco. Excited, I imagined what it would feel like to dance with Domenico, held closely in his arms … but I was suddenly interrupted in my dreams: In front the door, I bumped into Janet Bonaventura. Not again! Her green, cat-like eyes burned me down to a small lump of ashes. Her nose stud was sparkling like an ice-cold diamond. On her upper arm, I could see her impressive tattoo of a winding snake.

"Hey, Nick, got something to settle with you!" Janet grabbed Domenico's arm.

"Leave me alone, Janet!" Domenico replied and shook her hand off.

She pointed at me suspiciously. "Got a new girlfriend, again? Still changin' them like your underwear, huh?"

"Piss off!" he hissed. I could physically feel the cold that emanated from this girl and how it went under my skin. Patrick looked at me insecurely, his lips quivering.

"We still got a score to settle, Nick. Don't forget about that!" she smiled evilly.

"Yeah, but not now!" he replied angrily.

Janet was looking at Patrick and me again. "And you, babies!" She spat in front of our feet. "Need some nappies?"

"Hey, you're not gonna do that again!" Domenico clenched his fists and was trembling with fury.

With a grin, Janet put one of her black varnished fingernails under my chin and looked at me as if I was a cow on the cattle market. "Oh sugar, you've got no idea who you got involved with! Who do you think broke into Biedermann's flat, huh?"

"You're lying!" Domenico snarled hoarsely. "Don't believe a word she's saying, Maya!"

But Janet kept staring at me, as if she was trying to hypnotise me.

"It's not his fault he's crazy, the poor thing nearly suffocated when he was a baby," she continued meanly.

What was she saying? I had no idea what she was referring to. But Domenico did. His eyes became ice-cold.

"You mean slut!" he shouted, and then he swirled around and ran into the building. Patrick and I looked at each other horrified. What had just happened with Domenico? I wanted to run after him straight away, but Janet roughly grabbed my arm. Her lips were twisted into a disgusting smile.

"You two really don't seem to know him at all. Otherwise you'd never be friends with him!" She came even closer to me. "You'll see, he's gonna leave you for another bird, in no time. Mark my words. And shall I tell you something?"

My whole body was trembling and I was not able to reply. I did not want to hear it! I just wanted this horrible girl to leave us alone, but Janet held my arm to tightly that I could feel my fingertips become numb. "I know everything about him. My dad's got all the records on his mum! You know why Nick's so crazy? Cos his mum wanted to kill him and his brother after they were born! Strangled them. Like this."

She put her hands on my throat, but before she could squeeze them together I jumped back. No, no, no! I could not believe this!

"You are completely crazy!" I screamed. "You're a liar!" Furiously, I pushed her away and ran into the gym. I did not even realise that I had just insulted the most dangerous girl of the school and that I was probably in for some ugly act of revenge. But, what she told me was so incredibly horrible and mean that I had completely forgotten all my fears.

I could only concentrate on one thought, and that was to find Domenico. Where had he gone? I even forgot to make sure that Patrick had managed to follow me. There was a huge mess in my head. I remembered things that had happened; they all merged into one picture. The dark circles around his eyes, the fact that he always avoided speaking about his family, his mum neglecting him, his dad who he was not in touch with, dead without an e, his anger, his brother's mysterious problems … there was so much.

But what Janet had just told me – no, it just could not be true! She just wanted to get her own back on him. And still, he had seemed strangely powerless against her, even though he could have taken on everyone at this school.

Following my instincts, I had gone through the door leading to the attic without even thinking about the rules. Right behind me, I could hear Patrick breathe heavily; he obviously had no idea where I was leading him.

We crossed the dusty room, climbed up the wonky ladder and through the window in the roof. And there he was: Domenico was standing at the balustrade. I exchanged a look with Patrick and slowly approached Domenico.

"Nicky!" I whispered. He turned around to face me. His grey-blue eyes looked cold and they were staring right through me. Or inside me, it was hard to tell. He held a cigarette in his right hand. He always smoked when he was nervous or sad. I did not know what to say. I put my hand on his shoulder.

"What did Janet tell you?," he asked harshly.

"N-nothing in particular!" I stammered and looked at Patrick, imploringly. He had just joined us.

Domenico grabbed my arm. "She's a dirty liar! Don't listen to her!"

"Don't worry, Nicky. But … I can feel that something is bothering you. Why don't you talk to us?"

"I'm fine!"

"I don't believe you." I would not give up easily this time.

"W-we want to help you, Nicky." Patrick assured him. "W-we are friends, now."

Domenico lowered his eyes and took a deep drag of his cigarette. Then he shook his head gloomily.

"Just leave me alone, please," he said bitterly. "I don't

wanna talk about it!" He flicked his cigarette away over the balustrade and immediately lit a new one. We sat down on the floor and helplessly looked at each other.

"Man, I'm okay, really! Don't worry about me. I just don't want ... you know ... you to be afraid of me or somethin'!" His voice was quivering and he turned his head away.

"We are not afraid of you!" I objected.

"I dunno," he mumbled silently. I just did not know what to say. I could not think clearly at the moment.

"Please don't believe what Janet was saying about the burglary at Biedermann's," he suddenly said. "She was lying."

"Is it possible that she did it herself?" I asked.

He looked at me again. "She does stuff like that, yeah."

"Why does she hate you so much?"

He looked down at his feet and blinked as if the sun was blinding him even though it was nearly dark.

"Alright, she's my ex-girlfriend. But I split up with her, and she never got over it." With a dismissive wave of his hand he showed that this was all he was going to say about the subject.

Janet was Domenico's ex-girlfriend? Oh dear! That was something I would have to chew on! This criminal, violent girl, nobody dared to get close to? It cost me a huge effort to reign in all my questions, and I felt it was only possible at all if we got out of here double-quick. I got up.

“Come on, let’s go downstairs. Otherwise we could get into even more trouble,” I urged them. There was a storm in my stomach. Patrick held me back for a second and whispered: “I-I need to ask y-you something, Maya. C-could we meet at the toilets in a minute?”

We returned to the stairs unseen. Luckily, nobody had come up here. They were all downstairs at the disco; we could hear the muffled music in the hall.

“I-I need to go to the toilet.” Patrick said and looked at me expectantly.

I nodded. “Me too.”

“Should I come with you?” Domenico asked.

“No. But you could wait for us at the fountain,” I quickly replied. Obviously, Patrick wanted to ask me something he didn’t want Domenico to hear. He nodded and got out another cigarette. We hurried off, but in front of the toilets we stopped.

“I-I don’t really need the toilet,” Patrick said, “I-I just wanted to ask you something.”

“Yes, I got that,” I laughed. “What is it?”

“D-do you think J-Janet was lying?”

“I don’t know. It would be horrible if it was true. I cannot imagine that parents could ever be so cruel!”

“M-me neither.” He frowned. “B-but he always looks so sad, d-don’t you think?”

So Patrick had noticed it, too. It was not just me who had made it all up. Sometimes I was afraid I over-analysed things because of my curiosity.

"I get sad a lot too, b-because I do not have a dad," Patrick continued, "but that's d-different somehow. 'Cause I have g-got my m-mum. B-but with Domenico … I think he m-might not have a-anyone! I-I have b-been watching him si-since he joined our class."

"Yes, I thought the same," I agreed. "His mum does not seem to take care of him properly. No wonder he is so … so crazy sometimes!"

Patrick nodded sadly. "W-we should g-go back now, Maya. Otherwise, he will notice that we were talking about him!"

It was nice to be able to talk about these things with Patrick. We went over to the fountain. Janet was standing next to Domenico and was whispering into his ear. Oh no! Why could she not leave him alone?

Janet gave me a contemptuous look. "Your babies are coming back, Nick! Tell your ugly little girlfriend that she better be careful about what she's saying in the future." She wanted to give Domenico a playful, but somehow still serious, punch but he fended it off quickly. He lifted his hands in resignation and came over to us.

Ugly? This horrible word left a burning mark on my heart. I bravely swallowed down the lump I had in my throat. It was not the time to think about that now.

"What's up?" I asked.

"Nothing. It's alright. Come on, let's leave. I don't wanna stay here." He put his arms around me and

Patrick and pulled us away with him. In front of the school gate we stopped.

Even though I had tried to be brave, a few tears were pushing their way through my lashes now. I was very tired all of a sudden. I tried to wipe the tears off before Domenico noticed, but it was too late.

“Hey, sweetie, don’t cry!” he carefully put his arm around me. “Don’t worry. I’m gonna look after you. Janet won’t hurt you.” He held me even closer.

“W-What are we going to do now?” Patrick asked.

“Let’s leave! Or do you wanna stay?”

Neither Patrick nor I wanted to. Somehow the atmosphere was ruined. The church bells were ringing half past nine. Since we all agreed that we wanted to go home, we said goodnight to Patrick who lived in the opposite direction.

Domenico and I stood there for a moment, looking at each other. “Hey, Maya, do you wanna go to the lantern with me? It ain’t very late, yet. And I walk you home afterwards. But only if you want ...”

Immediately, I had a warm feeling in my stomach. But at the same time I was shivering. It was a very strange, wonderful sensation! We would not get another chance like this. And Dad would never find out about it.

He looked at me and his eyes were glowing. Could Delia have been right, after all? My heart was beating excitedly.

“I would love to!” I replied.

13. First love

We took the path that led through my street. Luckily there was a soft wind that cooled my glowing cheeks. I looked at Domenico from the side when we were standing in front of the gate to the park.

"You must live close to the park too, if you go to the lantern so often."

"Yeah," was his only reply.

"Where exactly do you live?"

"I explain it to you another time."

I looked at the path we were going to take. If I closed my eyes and thought about it, I could probably have imagined it. But Domenico pulled me with him so that I had to keep my eyes open to see where I was walking. He seemed to guess what I had been thinking about. But he could not stop me now.

"Can I come to your place one day? I would really like to meet Mingo."

Now he had to say something, either yes or no. I would not settle for a maybe this time.

"Come on, we need to turn right here," he said, ignoring my question.

I knew that myself of course; after all, this was not the first time I walked up to the lantern. He had actually found a fourth possibility to react by not saying anything, neither yes, nor no, not even maybe. I felt I should not insist if I did not want to spoil the evening. Those were the unwritten rules of the game. His rules, which he had never spelled out, but which were very clearly set between us.

In the dark, the park was somehow scary and mysterious at the same time. Only when we arrived at the brightly lit restaurant at the lake there was pulsating life again. The lights were reflected in the water and it was shining like liquid gold. It nearly looked like a fairytale castle.

We took the dark side path which led us through the botanic garden and over a small wooden bridge. This was the only way to get to the mansion.

We climbed up the path in the light of the lamps. It was all quiet, like a small world apart, where the only noise was the chirring of the crickets. Walking next to Domenico, my hand grazed his lightly and I secretly hoped that he would take my hand.

"I really like to be here," he suddenly interrupted the silence. "But the nicest part is yet to come!"

When we arrived at the small square, I had to pause for a few seconds. The lantern was even brighter and more beautiful – much more beautiful! – than I had imagined. The light seemed to have a soft pink tint, but maybe I was just imagining that. I slowly walked closer and touched the lamp post in awe. Domenico stood quietly next to me.

"I would never have thought it would be so beautiful," I said. He carefully put his arm around my shoulder. I did not dare to move, afraid I would wake up from this wonderful dream. For the first time, I did not feel like a child anymore or like a teenager, but like a young woman. It was amazing. For a long time, we just stood there, in the light of the lantern, not saying anything, only communicating in our thoughts.

You still keep your door locked in front of me. But I can feel that there is something dark waiting inside. Something dangerous. Something I am not familiar with. What kind of world is it you are living in? A world I do not know, I cannot imagine?

And his thoughts replied: *Maybe you would understand if I explained it to you; yes, maybe you would, because you are something special. But the risk of losing you is too big. This is why I do everything I can to keep my door locked.*

And I replied: *But I will find the keys, even if I'm the first person in your life who is going to do it. I am going to find them and then I am going to open your door. I will see and understand.*

And once again he replied: *You will see, Maya. You will see very soon, because I won't be able to hide it all forever. But will you really understand? I doubt it ...*

We looked at each other. His eyes had a nearly golden glow in the light of the lantern.

"Nicky ... I have to ask you something!"

"What is it?"

"Were you showing off when you said that about the lantern? You know … that you are here every night?"

"No," he said briefly. "I like that lantern, that's all."

I did not believe that that was all. The light of the lantern suddenly seemed to flare a bit. Something was wrong. In my head, everything started to turn all of a sudden, and I felt tears on my face. Somehow, a whole world crumbled down inside me.

"Hey, sweetie …" his fingertips carefully stroked my cheek. "Are you crying because of what Janet said? Please don't believe her! You're not ugly, at all! You are amazing! The most beautiful girl in our class! And you've got gorgeous eyes."

What was he saying there? I could not believe what I heard.

"Are you serious?"

"Course I am! You think I lie to you?" He looked at me so intensely that I had to close my eyes, trembling.

"If I'm saying it, you gotta believe me," he continued, "you're much cuter than Delia!"

"What?" I opened my eyes wide again.

"She wears too much make-up. You should see her without all that stuff. I bet she's really pale without it. I know what makeup can hide."

"But you were really into her, when you first arrived."

"She's a floosy, a loose girl. That gets boring very quickly."

He carefully put his hands on my shoulders and looked at me pensively.

"You know what would look really cool on you?"

"No."

"A ponytail and big loops in your ears. I know it, cos I know your face really well! After all, I've drawn it. Sometimes, you gotta do things like that. Not cos of the others, but for yourself."

His words went straight to my heart and woke this strong desire again. But it would remain an unrealisable wish. Dad would never allow it. He would not even let me wear t-shirts that might show a bit of my stomach. Not even in the hottest summer. And there was another reason too.

"I … I don't know. I don't think the ponytail is such a good idea. Everyone could see my ears and Delia said I have monkey ears."

"That's a fat lie!" he carefully pushed back my hair. "You've got normal ears, absolutely, just like everyone else. She's only saying that to tease you. Don't listen to her. She's not happy herself, you know. You really don't need to be afraid of her. There is another girl in our class who's much more dangerous than her!"

I knew that he was talking about Isabelle. He squinted his eyes as if he was trying to see something more clearly.

"Why don't you wear earrings, actually?"

I made a suffering face and looked at my feet. Domenico had found my sensitive spot.

"Dad just does not want me to," I explained. "He would not want me to poke holes through my ears."

"Really, your old man's so strict?"

"He means well, you know. But somehow he is very fond of the past century, where everything was still as it should be, according to him."

"Do you wanna have earrings?" He smiled at me encouragingly.

"Oh, I would love to, but …"

"I'm gonna buy you a pair. We're gonna go to the city together and then you can have your ears pierced."

Oh dear! As if it was that easy!

"But I'm not allowed to …"

"You could just tell them *afterwards!*" He was grinning broadly. "You can't let them decide everything!"

I breathed in deeply and nearly forgot to breathe out again. Domenico was not afraid of anything. The thought of going to the city with him and to have one of my greatest wishes fulfilled was very tempting, and it was hard to resist. In my heart, I had actually already made a decision, but my head was still hesitating anxiously.

"You are completely crazy! I could never accept that! You don't have the money for that!"

"Course I do! I've got as much dough as I want!" He sounded a bit offended and looked disappointed because I was about to reject his offer. I pondered the possible consequences. What was the worst that could happen? Well, Dad would definitely be furious, disappointed, he would tell me off. He could ban me from seeing Domenico. But then he did not need to know that it had been Domenico's idea …

"Wouldn't I need my parents' consent? I mean, they are probably going to ask about it in the shop."

"Nah, I know someone who's really good. And he ain't gonna ask no stupid questions. Honestly! You don't have to be afraid."

"Okay, then." I finally said. "When do you want to do it?"

"Next week?"

I nodded and he looked at me happily. I held my breath, trying to stay in this wonderful moment for another second or two.

"I know how it feels when people laugh at you," he said. "They always laughed at us because of our hair. Cos we had red hair when we were kids. Guess you saw it on the picture. But the red's nearly gone now, luckily …"

"Why luckily? I really like red hair. I wish mine was red!"

"No, you shouldn't. They always called us devil's sons. That really hurt. But I guess you know the feeling. And then, one day we just beat 'em all up. All of them!"

I was surprised at the bitter expression on his face when he said all those words. What was up with him? I tried to find a better direction for our conversation.

"I would never have thought that anyone could ever laugh at you. You look really good!"

"Me? You think?" He was embarrassed now. "I don't think so. I look scruffy."

"You are nuts! You're the coolest boy in the entire school!"

"Yeah, right!" His smile looked a bit sad. "I used to look lot better. Alright, Andrew still looks more stupid than me! He's got a face like a football: all you wanna do is kick it!"

We both laughed. With his chunky face, Andrew was really not the most handsome boy.

"Have you really had as many girlfriends as Janet pretended?" This was another question that had bugged me for a while.

"Yeah, that's true," he replied a bit embarrassed again. "You probably think that I'm gonna break up with you soon, righ'? But I won't. You … you're different."

I was glad that it was dark so that he could not see how I blushed. His hand was trembling when he carefully touched my hair. I could feel my heartbeat in my throat. And then, he kissed me. He leant forward until his lips touched mine. Gently and softly. It was a fantastic feeling. He closed his eyes and kissed my cheek, my forehead, the tip of my nose. I was shivering from head to toe. I had always hoped that my first kiss would be a special experience, but I had not thought that reality would be so much better than my imagination. Domenico opened his eyes again and smiled at me. But suddenly his expression changed and a dark shadow seemed to cover his eyes.

"I shouldn't do this. Cos of your dad."

"What about my dad?"

"He don't like me."

"So what? My dad does not have a reason not to like you."

"Yeah, he does." He squinted. Suddenly, he seemed to be miles away and I helplessly tried to reach him. Now, the light of the lantern seemed blinding.

"You're a year and a half younger than me, Maya. I'm somehow responsible for you, I guess. I can't treat you like Delia or the other girls. You're different … innocent somehow. I really like you. Mi piaci davvero."

I was overwhelmed and I did not manage an answer. It was hard to believe that we had only been friends for a few days. He was closer to me than any other person I had ever known. Except for my parents, of course.

He took my hand, and we interlaced our fingers. "I'm never gonna break up with you!" he promised. "And I'm gonna make sure that the others don't bully you anymore. Even if it means that I have to beat 'em all up."

"No, Nicky, I do not want you to beat anyone up for me. But it is sweet of you to say that. And I will always be on your side. No matter what. And you should always remember that when you are here at the lantern. It's going to be the symbol of our friendship. Okay?"

Could I have guessed then that my words would be put to the test very soon? I could feel it somehow, but I did not want to think about it then.

To seal our promise, we held up our interlaced hands in front of the light of the lantern. When we loosened our fingers and separated our hands again, the church bell was ringing half past ten. I had to go home! "Domenico, I have to go now!"

"Yeah," he said, "I'm gonna walk you back."

We did not talk much anymore on our way back. I could not have said a lot anyway with the turmoil of conflicting thoughts in my head. Domenico – Dad – the conflict – the mystery – our profound friendship – and my first kiss! I tried not to think about the problems that were lying ahead of us and tried to focus on the new, strong bond we had discovered that night.

Domenico stopped in front of our door. I saw that the light was still on in the kitchen. I knew that Mum was up, waiting for me to come home.

"Your mum worries about you lots, huh?" Domenico said. "Man, you dunno how lucky you are, Maya!" he kicked a small stone with his foot and swore silently.

"Oh, Nicky …" What should I reply to that? I could so clearly hear the longing in his voice and the look in his eyes pierced my heart. I would never forget this.

"Remember my promise," I said before I rang the door and had to leave him behind in the darkness. But I could not get him out of my head.

Domenico, you have managed to do something that nobody has done before: You have helped me to leave behind what had been blocking, even crushing me. For the first time in my life I do not feel ugly anymore. I am never going to forget what you have done for me!

Mum opened the door and put her hand on my shoulder. I turned around to look at Domenico again. He had stopped at the garden gate and was waving goodnight hesitantly. With all my willpower, I tried to chase away the thought of Janet's story about Domenico's mum. It was just too horrible to be true.

Upstairs in my room I opened the window to let some fresh air in. Happily, I looked up to the park and at our lantern. And then I discovered a shadow at the garden gate, a shadow that was not usually there. Something was moving and I saw the glow of a cigarette. I stood at the window for another fifteen minutes, but the shadow remained where it was.

Finally, I lost the fight against my tiredness. When I sunk onto my bed, I felt that I had come very, very close to my dreams about the lantern tonight. I touched my throat and found the necklace with the heart on it, pressing it against my skin.

14. A crazy dare

The next morning, I found four cigarette buds in front of our garden gate. A very unusual sight on our usually immaculate street. While I swept them onto the lawn with my foot so Dad wouldn't notice them, I tried to calculate the time it had taken Domenico to smoke four cigarettes. I felt like something between a wandering zombie who had not had enough sleep and an over-excited butterfly. In my head, I was still somewhere out there in the forest next to the lantern, rather than on my way to a normal school day.

Domenico was waiting for me in the schoolyard again. I immediately sensed that something was wrong. He had dark circles around his eyes and his smile seemed somehow contorted and lost. My spirits sank straight away. What had happened? Was something between us not okay anymore?

"What's wrong, Nicky?"

"What should be wrong?"

I took his hand. "You look gloomy."

"Man, just leave me alone. I'm tired, that's all. And I've got a headache." He turned around and disappeared through the door. I did not understand anything anymore! What had I done wrong?

On top of it all, Mrs Galiani seemed particularly grumpy today. Why did these things just always coincide?

"I have started to correct last week's exams, and it is not looking great, ladies and gentlemen. I expected more from you!" she said in the English class.

She made a little pause so that her words could sink in fully. I was not worried about myself, because I had quite a good feeling about my exam. But what about Domenico? If he had not managed to get a satisfying grade at least, it looked pretty bad for him.

"Up to now, only two of you have obtained a good grade. Six were inadequate. I really do not know what I should do with you." Her voice had become even more serious. She paused again. Domenico was as pale as a ghost. Mrs Galiani gave him a piercing look. I took his hand under the desk; it felt really hot.

"Over the weekend, I will correct the rest of the copies and I will hand them back to you on Tuesday. We will see how we will continue then."

We were finally saved by the school bell, and the tension in the class loosened a bit. Only Domenico did not manage to move.

"Man, did you see how she stared at me? I bet I screwed it up. Ah, what the heck! Doesn't matter, anyway," he added bitterly.

"Don't give up just yet. You could still catch up in the other subjects!" I pulled him up from his chair.

"I'm too stupid anyway!" He gave a dismissive wave and searched for his cigarettes.

Carefully, I took the packet out of his hand. "Please

don't. You really should not smoke that much! It won't fix anything. And you are not stupid. You are very intelligent! I know you can make it! Remember the promise we made to each other yesterday."

Patrick was waiting for us at the door. "M-Mrs Galiani w-was quite t-tough this morning, right?" he said and looked at Domenico compassionately. "I r-really hope that you w-will pass, Nicky!"

"I don't think so," he mumbled coolly. "I'm off for an hour. Gonna be back for PE, in the afternoon." There had been a few changes to the timetable due to the school party and so we had PE instead of Biology in the afternoon.

"No, don't skip any classes again!" I sighed.

He smiled at me tiredly and pinched my cheek. "Don't worry, sweets, I'm just gonna get myself in a better mood!"

"It's up to you," I murmured in resignation. "But don't forget your swimming things, we are going to the pool in PE."

In the afternoon, the temperature rose to 32 degrees Celsius; the perfect weather to go swimming. We met Mrs Galiani at the pool. She usually taught PE in some other classes and replaced Mr Reuter today, because he was teaching the 8b on Friday afternoon. Patrick was extremely happy about that, because she allowed him to just sit on the wall and watch the rest of the class. With Mr Reuter, who was obsessed with sports, this would have been impossible. But Mrs Galiani made an exception, because she knew that Patrick was bullied even more during swimming classes.

Domenico lay down next to Patrick as if it was natural and stared up into the blue sky.

"Hey, Nicky, what's up? Are you not swimming?" I asked, disappointedly.

"Nah, not today. Don't understand why we gotta go into the cold water. It's much better out here in the sun, anyway. Come here, sweets!" He smiled at me with his eyes half closed and reached out for me, as if he had completely forgotten about his bad mood this morning and as if nothing in the world could trouble him. I could not keep up with his mood swings.

"Stop that! I do not like it when you act like a jerk. Plus, you are going to get a sunstroke if you stay there in the blazing sun!"

Mrs Galiani came over and sternly looked at Domenico. "What are you doing? You cannot just do whatever you feel like, Domenico," she said coolly. "Go and get changed."

"Nah, I forgot my swim stuff."

Surprisingly, Mrs Galiani did not say anything to that anymore. She suddenly looked as though she had solved a tricky mathematical problem. She first looked at me and then at Domenico again and said: "Okay, then. Go join the others in the pool, Maya, we will start in a minute."

But then, Andrew turned up. He had immediately sensed Domenico's weakness and now built up in front of him.

"Heehee, you chicken! You can't swim, admit it!"

I rolled my eyes. Not again!

Domenico stood up and fixed Andrew with his look. "I'm gonna jump off the ten metre board and do a back flip if you need proof," he said calmly.

"Nicky!" I shouted, irritated.

"Yeah, right!" Andrew sneered. "You're wetting your pants, cos you would drown!"

I was looking for Mrs Galiani to get help, and, luckily, she was just in time to stop Andrew: "Stop fooling around, now. Get in the water, Andrew. And you, Domenico, stay with Patrick. I don't want to hear another word!"

For the next few minutes, I could not concentrate on anything other than the ice-cold water of the shower and then of the pool. I really had to clench my teeth. Usually, the water was heated, but today of all days the heater was turned off because of some repair work. I waved to Domenico and Patrick when I stepped carefully into the pool. It was a shame that they were not joining us! It would have been so much fun! Slowly, I got used to the temperature and plunged into the refreshing, prickling flood. Mrs Galiani was standing at the edge of the pool counting the laps we swam.

It was only after about the eighth lap that I realised that Domenico was not sitting next to Patrick anymore.

"Hey, Patrick, where did Domenico go?" I asked him, shouting from the pool. Patrick looked around. He did not know.

"I-I don't know. He just left. I thought th-that he m-might need the toilet."

I shrugged my shoulders and wanted to continue swimming my laps, when I suddenly heard Isabelle screaming. She was screeching so loudly that her voice nearly cracked. "Oh, my God! What is he doing up there?! He's completely lost it!"

I turned around and looked at the ten metre tower. And then I saw the reason for Isabelle's hysteria. I was so shocked that I nearly forgot to swim. Domenico was standing on the board – in his normal clothes – with his arms spread to both sides. He looked like a motionless statue. Was he completely mad now? Did he really want to jump down there to impress Andrew? Also, the tower was out of use today! So he must even have climbed over the barrier! Why did he always do these things?

"Nicky, please, don't be stupid!" I shouted but my voice was not as loud as Isabelle's and Andrew's. He did not even hear me. It was too late.

Everyone held their breath when Domenico jumped off, head first, his arms spread, doing two perfect back flips. I nearly choked on some water when I saw it. But the splash that followed when he hit the water surface hurt my ears. The echo could be heard in the entire swim park. Or was I just imagining that? He had gone completely off the rails! Muffled by the water in my ears, I could hear some of the others cheering and applauding. Swimming over to him as quickly as I could, I did not know whether I should laugh or cry.

Mrs Galiani had been even quicker than me. Her face looked as though she had just seen a very creepy ghost. "Domenico!" she shouted breathlessly, even though he had still not swum back to the surface and could not hear her. Why was he still down there? I bet he did it on purpose to scare everyone. I started to become really mad at him.

I only understood that he was not fooling around, when Mrs Galiani jumped into the water and dived down to the ground. The whole class gathered at the edge of the pool, together with other onlookers. "Oh, my God!" Delia screamed and fell down on her knees. "Please, don't let him be dead! Please!"

I got water in my nose and my ears. Everything was turning in my head. Coughing and spitting, I tried to get the water out of my lungs. I just about managed to swim to the edge of the pool, holding on to it desperately. Everything seemed so surreal, as if there was a thick fog hanging over everything. Domenico … no, this could not be true! What kind of a nightmare was this? Why on earth did he always have to do these crazy things?

Mrs Galiani reappeared at the surface. She was holding Domenico in her arm. He did not move and gave no sign of life! Some of our classmates were crying in shock. Even Andrew looked sorry. A young pool attendant came running over breathlessly and helped Mrs Galiani pull Domenico out of the water. His face was dead pale. It was nearly transparent with a blue tint. His clothes were sticking to him like a second skin and I saw how skinny he really was. Oh, Domenico …

In my desperation, I began to cry and I felt so weak that I did not manage to get out of the water anymore. Only vaguely I realised how a pair of hands grabbed me carefully and helped pulling me out of the water. I staggered into Patrick's arms and watched how Mrs Galiani tried to feel Domenico's heartbeat.

The crowd around them became bigger from minute to minute. Mrs Galiani seemed as calm and concentrated as ever, but I could see that her face had become entirely pale too.

"Stupid dares!" she was mumbling very silently, but I had good ears. Finally she announced, to my greatest relief, that she could feel his heartbeat. But then, she added: "But he is not breathing!"

"We have to take off his wet clothes! Otherwise he is going to catch a cold," the pool attendant warned and started to pull off his t-shirt.

"No!" Mrs Galiani replied quickly and vigorously pushed his hands away. "Please, go and get the paramedics!"

There was a heavy silence in the crowd when Mrs Galiani started the reanimation measures. She put his head back by lifting his chin and holding down his forehead. Then she began to breathe air into his nose in regular intervals. Again and again. I thought about calling Dad when suddenly Domenico opened his eyes and turned to the side, groaning. He chocked and coughed and spat out a lot of water. His eyes were flickering.

"I feel sick!" he groaned.

The pool attendant came back with two paramedics and a stretcher.

"Take the boy straight to the first aid room!" Mrs Galiani commanded briefly. The pool attendant nodded and the paramedics lifted Domenico onto the stretcher. I could not stop myself from squeezing in between the two men to touch Domenico's pale face. "Nicky? Nicky, can you hear me?" But he did not reply. His eyes were closed again and I could see thin, red veins, shining through his skin. I felt panic creeping up inside me again.

"Everyone back to the locker rooms and get changed. This class is over!" Mrs Galiani's voice was quieter and softer than usual, and the exhaustion had made a few more wrinkles appear on her face. I nervously tugged at her swimsuit.

"Please ...!"

She turned around to face me. "I'll be right with you, Maya!"

"Can Patrick and I go to the first aid room, too?"

"Yes, okay." She gave me one of her rare smiles.

Luckily, the room was not very far away. We followed the paramedics and the pool attendant to a dimmed room where they lay down Domenico in the recovery position.

"He is going to be fine!" Mrs Galiani promised. "He had a shock, because he was very hot and had jumped into the cold water too quickly. It was very unlucky that the heater was turned off today of all days."

"Why on earth did this boy do such a stupid thing?" the pool attendant snarled. Again, he started pulling on Domenico's t-shirt. Mrs Galiani tried to stop him, but it was too late. We saw Domenico's naked torso.

"Oh no!" I gasped in shock.

He was covered in scars. Long, red, horrible scars starting on his stomach and going up to his chest. They looked like deep knife wounds. Terrified, I held my breath and did not know what to think. Slowly I sank down on my knees. Patrick swallowed hard.

"Let me do this, please!" Mrs Galiani ordered strictly and covered his body with the t-shirt again.

"Where do those scars come from?" I whispered.

Mrs Galiani looked at me and shook her head, looking very severe. It hit me like lightening. She knew it. She knew exactly what was going on with Domenico, but she did not seem to want to talk about it. My head felt like it was going to burst while I was trying to put together all the pieces but did not manage to create a logical picture.

Mrs Galiani bent over and carefully patted his head. She did not look like the disciplined, strong teacher right then.

"Domenico, wake up!" she said with a worried tone in her soft voice and it worked. He opened his eyes and blinked. Mrs Galiani shook him a bit and finally his eyes began to clear.

"Whassup?" he asked weakly. "Whatcha shakin' me about for?"

"You were trying to be a hero and fainted after you jumped off the ten metre tower," Mrs Galiani said dryly.

"Man, I'm dizzy!" he groaned and carefully sat up.

"No wonder! Your back flips were quite impressive. But I really do not understand why you keep risking your life to impress others!"

He was still looking around him in confusion, and his eyes finally stopped on us. He suddenly started shivering and his teeth chattered.

"My clothes are wet!"

"Well, yes! This happens when you jump in the water without taking them off first." Mrs Galiani was smiling grimly, and Domenico grinned back weakly.

"I did that?"

Patrick and I nodded vehemently. “We are all glad that you are still alive. This could have turned out really badly!”

“Now, we need to get rid of your wet clothes and dry you, otherwise you are going to catch a cold.” Mrs Galiani decided. And looking at Patrick and me she added: “You can wait for him outside, if you want.”

“Shall I call an ambulance?” the pool attendant asked.

But Mrs Galiani shook her head. “No, I think we will be fine. This boy is a survivor.”

“We could walk him home,” I suggested. And suddenly, Domenico was wide awake again.

“No!” he said and jumped onto his feet. “I’m fine. I’m gonna go home now and put some dry clothes on.”

“This is out of the question, Domenico! You are going to catch pneumonia!” Mrs Galiani objected.

“No way! It’s hot outside!”

He held on to his t-shirt as if making sure that nobody could take it off him.

“This story is not quite over yet,” the pool attendant interrupted. “It is strictly forbidden to climb over the fence. This is going to cost your parents a fine!”

“Let me handle that,” Mrs Galiani said.

Suddenly, there was a shy “hello” coming from the door behind us. I could not believe my eyes when I saw Manuela and Delia at the entrance, carrying Domenico’s trainers and mobile. Delia stayed in the background, while Manuela explained their appearance: "He left that next to the tower."

Mrs Galiani thanked them, took the things off them and handed them to their owner. Delia avoided looking at me as they quickly made their excuses and disappeared again.

Domenico hurried up to put his shoes on.

We could see that he was freezing in his wet clothes, but he did not come to his senses. Mrs Galiani grabbed him by his shoulders.

"Listen, Domenico, I cannot make you do anything and I know that there is no point trying to persuade you. But you should really take care of your health!"

She gave Patrick and me an encouraging look as if she wanted to ask us to keep an eye on him.

We left the first aid room together and, once we were outside at the pool, all the feelings I had kept back burst out: "Seriously, Nicky, why are you doing these stupid things?" I ranted. "You could have died!"

He shrugged his shoulders. "Wouldn't have mattered, anyway." He laughed bitterly, getting his soaked packet of cigarettes out of his pocket. I stared at him, not knowing what to say anymore. His lips were trembling and they were entirely blue.

"Sometimes you are just so weird, Nicky," I finally sighed. Patrick nodded.

"What I was wondering though: where did you learn to do back flips like that?"

Unfortunately, the tube arrived right in that moment. I this part of the city, it ran above the ground. Domenico smiled tiredly and ran across the street, just about missing a car driving past fast.

Patrick and I exchanged a look.

"Now, he is definitely crazy!" I commented. "He has been acting like a complete mentalist, all day! This morning he was really depressed and in the afternoon, suddenly, sky-high! What on earth is up with him?"

"D-do you think that he m-maybe ..." but Patrick did not finish his sentence. He shook his head and looked at his feet. "No, t-that's not possible."

I did not understand what Patrick tried to say.

Worried, I looked after the tube that had started its way towards the city with a monotonous clicking on the rails, taking Nicky into a world I was not even allowed to set foot in. The weekend ahead was going to be a long one, long and tedious.

15. What is going on with him?

Domenico's leap into the cold water triggered a whole chain of reactions which I was not even really aware of to start with. He became ill gradually, and he tried to fight it with all his strength. On Monday, I noticed straight away that he was unusually pale. He was coughing quietly during classes, trying to stay unnoticed, and in the ten o'clock break he walked off to the toilets without saying anything. Patrick and I followed him and listened at the door. Inside, we heard how Domenico coughed heavily. It sounded painful.

I closed my eyes and tried to think of something I could do. When he came out, he joined us hesitantly and looked at us pleadingly. But I did not really understand how I should interpret his expression. At the moment, I did not even know anymore what I should feel for him. It was as though I could see through the fabric of his t-shirt and looked right at the horrible scars on his chest. Whatever fate they stood for, I knew that the explanation lay beyond the boundaries he had set for us.

His legendary back flips from the ten metre tower had quickly become the topic of the day and earned him incredulous, but also respectful looks. Somebody even came running to him with a copy of the local newspaper which had published an article on his crazy dare. He just grinned knowingly and took another drag at his cigarette. For the first time, I did not feel comfortable around him. Andrew went nearly crazy with envy and was lurking around us the whole time.

At the end of the last period, Mrs Galiani asked Domenico to go to the teachers' room with her. She had probably noticed that he looked like a zombie. I could not go home without knowing what she had told him. So I waited for Domenico in front of the teachers' room.

Twenty minutes later, he came out with a dark look in his eyes and slammed the door closed behind him so violently that it felt like the whole hallway was shaking. Mrs Galiani must have been really hard on him. I felt a wave of fear washing over me as I sensed once more how threatening his anger could be. He did not even notice that I had been waiting for him and stormed past me towards the exit.

"Nicky, wait!" Worriedly, I ran after him.

"Leave me alone!" he snapped, but he stopped and turned to face me.

"Nicky, I'm really worried about you. Something is going on with you. You are ill!"

"I'm not ill." He took out his last cigarette, crumpled up the package and angrily fired it to the ground.

"Yes, you are! You are coughing like crazy! You really should not smoke! You are practically chain smoking!"

I should not have said that. His eyes became even colder.

"That's still up to me, innit?"

In the ten o'clock break he had smoked four cigarettes in a row, and my clothes were impregnated with the horrible smell. I was exhausted from all the recent turbulences.

"You could at least have a break from smoking until your cough is gone," I gave in tiredly.

"Just stop nagging about that, okay?" He squinted as he always did when he tried to hide what was going on inside him. "I don't care! A sermon from you is the last thing I need now! And I gotta go, anyway. See you tomorrow!" He just left me standing there slamming the school door closed behind him.

I stayed there, stunned, when suddenly desperation hit me with incredible force. What on earth was going on with him? Ever since Friday, he had been unbearably moody, even though the night before we had been walking on clouds, in the park under the lantern.

I had tried to force my way through his boundaries again. This was never going to work. I knew that much now. It was like an extremely difficult operation, where you had to work step by step, very carefully.

Where did he go now? What did he do in his spare time? Did he have a lot of friends? What did he do in the city? So many questions I did not have an answer to and that I was apparently not allowed to ask, either.

On top of this definitely totally messed-up day, Dad had decided that we were going to have the long feared discussion that evening. I had arrived home twenty minutes late, my clothes smelled of smoke and my parents were at the edge of a nervous breakdown.

"We nearly called the school," Mum complained, while she heated up some of the dinner for me in the microwave. "What were you doing for so long?"

"It is all that boy's fault!" Dad started. "Enough is enough! I have not said anything for a whole week, just because you, Esther, thought we should not interfere. But I am not going to watch this any longer!"

"Martin, I do not think ..."

"No! I am fed up!" Dad bent over to look me straight in the eyes. "I did not like the boy you brought home a few days ago, Maya. He looks like a criminal from the streets. And I would not be surprised if he was taking drugs. I would not be surprised at all!"

"How can you say something like that?" I burst out so violently that I accidently pushed over the plate with my dinner. The chicken stew spread on Mum's lovely flowery table cloth.

"Maya! What is going on with you?" my parents asked, shocked. Dad's eyes looked sad behind his glasses and I could not hold back the tears any longer.

"Oh, Maya, honey," Dad whispered. "I do not recognise you like this. What has this boy done to you? What has he done?"

"Martin ..."

I felt the desperation grab hold of me and I let my head and my arms hang down tiredly. I knew too well what Dad meant and my guilty conscience was torturing me in the depths of my heart.

"Nothing. Nothing at all. He did not do anything to me," I mumbled and felt like I was running around in a maze of dead ends.

"Well, you know, Maya, your dad is right," Mum continued. "Maybe this boy needs help."

But Dad shook his head with determination. "This is not our job, Esther. I do not want Maya to spend time with such a ... such a tramp!" He wrinkled his nose. "You have been smelling of cigarettes for days, Maya!"

"I don't smoke!" I shouted.

"But this boy smokes, doesn't he?"

"A lot of people at school do."

"Martin, do you want our daughter to close her eyes to reality?"

"Esther, I want our daughter to grow up decently. And I want her to pass her A-levels, so that she can take over my practice, one day," Dad replied with an imploring tone in his voice.

This was too much for me to take. My nerves were already strained and I could not bear hearing this. Should I not have the right to decide over my life myself? Before I realised what I was doing, I had jumped up and stormed out of the kitchen. When I heard my parents call my name, I was already lying on my bed in my room, weeping in desperation. What on earth was I supposed to do?

I was staring into the sky outside, feeling completely miserable, and not even the beautiful weather helped in the slightest to improve my state. I had managed to alienate everyone. Dad, Domenico … and even Mum had not called me anymore this afternoon. I felt horrible, and I had resigned myself to the fact that I would have to hide in my room until the end of my life, when suddenly Mum knocked on the door.

Even though my "come in!" must have sounded anything but friendly, there was a hint of a smile on her face when she handed me a smudged envelope.

"I found this in the letterbox," she said mysteriously and left me alone again. I looked at the envelope. There was nothing on it except my name, written wonkily with a black pen. I tore it open excitedly and unfolded the letter.

Deer Maya,
I'm sorry that I was mad at you. Pleas don't be sad. Becos I like you lot. Can you come out at the half past ate tonite? I will wait 4 you outside your hous. Your frend. Domenico

I let the letter fall onto my bed. They were simple words in his clumsy handwriting, but they still cast a ray of light into my misery. Half past eight. That was in twenty minutes. But there was a huge obstacle to overcome: Dad. He would never let me go out. With the letter in my hand, I hurried to Mum, who was in the kitchen.

"Dad is busy in his study, and I guess he is going to stay in there for another while," she said. "He is reviewing his medical reports so that he can take the weekend off. But …," she added silently and with a strict tone in her voice, "the two of us are going to talk about this later, Maya!"

At half past eight exactly, I sneaked out of the house, mobile phone in my pocket. I saw Domenico stand behind a magnolia in the golden light of the sunset. A dark, lonely shape that looked strangely lost. In the few seconds it took me to walk over to him, I tried, once more, to imagine what his life outside school must look like: his mum, his brother, his house … But they all remained shapeless, blurred silhouettes, and for a moment, I wondered whether they even existed at all.

"Hi, Nicky!" I said and watched the lost shape come to life. He lifted his head and smiled at me. It was a nice smile, even a bit shy; not a Mr Universe smile. He gave me a rose that had nearly wilted.

"Hi, Maya. This is for you."

He could not have made a better choice. Carefully, I

took the rose and happily touched it with my fingertips. "It is beautiful. Thank you."

"I guess I was a real idiot," he said sheepishly. "I didn't wanna hurt you."

"It's okay." I could not stay mad at him for one second. "Things like that happen. You just had a bad day."

"More than that! And you're right, somehow," he replied, "I screw things up, all the time."

"Oh, Nicky, I just worry about you, about your health. And I do not want you to get expelled again."

His eyes became very small. "How do you know that I was expelled before?" he asked suspiciously. I was startled. Was that a secret? Was I not supposed to know that? But Mrs Galiani had told me herself, when she asked whether I wanted to sit somewhere else. I explained it to him.

He did not say anything anymore and was about take out a cigarette, but he stopped and put the packet back into his pocket.

"I decided I don't wanna smoke anymore, when I'm with you ..."

"But this is not about me. It's about you and your cough. You caught a cold on Friday after all, and if you continue smoking so much, it is never going to get any better!"

He bit his lip and played with the leather bands around his left wrist. Before his eyes showed me what he was thinking, he squinted.

"I can't just stop," he admitted.

"How long have you been smoking for?" I asked very, very carefully.

"Much too long!" he laughed bitterly, and I did not ask anymore. This definitely was a delicate subject.

He let his arm sink and touched the garden gate, looking at Mum's yellow roses. Suddenly he gave a little smile.

"Hey, Maya, you wanna go to the city tomorrow to get your ears pierced?" he asked and finally looked me in the eyes again. "I promised that I buy you some earrings, remember?"

"If I manage to persuade my parents, I would love to," I sighed. "We had a really bad argument today."

He opened his mouth in surprise, but this time he was the one who did not dare asking any questions.

"Just let me know tomorrow," he said silently and kissed me goodbye on my forehead. "I gotta go. See you in school, tomorrow."

"Wait!"

He stopped and looked at me questioningly.

"Could you give me your mobile number?"

I knew that this was a lot to ask and that I was pushing the boundaries pretty far. He hesitated and his face twitched nervously but then he took out his mobile phone from his pocket.

"Gimme your number," he just said.

I gave it to him. Within a second he had typed

something into his phone and I received a text. Then he waved goodbye and left quickly.

Mrs Galiani was standing in front of the class with the important exam papers in her hands, and her sharp tongue was hitting us like whip lashes. I was dying with anxiety, and Domenico looked pretty nervous too sitting next to me.

"Three of you have managed to make less than seven mistakes. Only three! And half of you have an inadequate grade." She shook her head disapprovingly.

There was complete silence when she started to hand out the sheets. Nobody dared to move. You could hear nothing but a groan here and there from those who were struck especially hard by fate. Delia seemed to be one of the unlucky ones again. And then Mrs Galiani approached our table. I felt like I was glued to my chair, partly due to the damp heat in the room, but also due to my anxiety.

"Well done, Maya!" Mrs Galiani praised and gave me my sheet. There were two big As on there. Of course I was happy about them, but I would have put up with Ds if it had meant that Domenico would have gotten the two As.

"Nerd!" Delia hissed contemptuously. "Bet daddy's gonna be real happy!"

Patrick was one of the lucky ones too. And finally, Mrs Galiani only had one copy left in her hands: Domenico's.

She was standing there and looked at him. He completely forgot to be cool and nervously grabbed my hand.

Mrs Galiani slowly came closer and put the sheets on our table without saying a word. He nearly squashed my fingers. A second later, Domenico was so surprised that he nearly forgot to breathe.

There was a huge B on one side of the copy. I could see that he had not known all the right answers but Mrs Galiani had been indulgent. He turned the copy around quickly to see the writing test. There were loads of red marks and some of his mistakes were unbelievable, but Mrs Galiani had still given him a sufficient grade. Counted together that was a C! Satisfactory! I thought that was great of her.

"Wow!" Domenico was really excited.

Patrick turned around to us, beaming.

"There you go," Mrs Galiani said dryly. "You can do it if you put your head to it, Domenico. Calm down now, though. We are going to continue the class."

Domenico just smiled and tore a page out of his exercise book. He drew a big, beautiful heart on it and, in the middle, he wrote MAYA. I looked at him, completely over the moon. Unfortunately, Mrs Galiani took the sheet away from him.

"Now," she said coldly, "friendship is a great thing, but English classes are not for writing love letters, Domenico."

The class grumbled and sent some withering looks our way.

Getting the permission from Mum was easier than I thought. She did not find anything wrong with going to the city for an ice cream after school with Domenico and Patrick.

"But watch out on the tube!" she smiled. "You are fourteen and not a little child, anymore. I am happy that Patrick will be there, too. But promise me that you will be home before Dad gets back, okay?"

"Of course," I mumbled and lowered my head guiltily. Mum did not deserve that I lied to her. What was going on with me? And I tried to ban the thought of my dad from my mind altogether.

The weather was playing along perfectly. The sky was as blue as it could get when we left school after the art class.

Obviously Domenico had been looking forward enormously to our trip. He was in a great mood and pulled on my ear playfully when we were sitting on the tube.

"My sweet girl's gonna get some hot earrings today!"

"Heehee!" I squeaked, "that tickles!" I was not feeling as happy about all this as I sounded.

One stop before the train station we got off and started walking towards the high street, where I usually went shopping with Mum. Domenico had put his arm around me, and I enjoyed the envious looks of some girls who walked past us. Domenico was the best looking boy in this street by far. Patrick was beaming, walking circles around us excitedly. I guessed that he had never gone out with friends before.

"Does it hurt to get pierced?" I asked Domenico.

He shrugged his shoulders. "Mingo even pierced his ear himself with a needle."

"Where is that shop we are going to?"

"You see in a sec."

We turned into a narrow side lane and suddenly stood in front of a small, almost entirely hidden piercing studio.

"Here!?" I hesitated and sceptically peered into this strange room with the red lighting, a waft of frankincense hitting my nose.

"Oh, Nicky … can't we go somewhere else?"

"Why?" He looked at me, honestly surprised. "What's wrong with this shop?"

"You know … I thought we would go to a … to a normal jewellery shop or something!"

He lowered his eyes. "Nah, I think they'd kick me out straight away," he murmured, looking at his scruffy clothes.

"Listen … you don't want anyone asking for a signature from your parents or anything, righ'? Cos then, you can forget about the earrings. And I know the guy who works here, he's really good! I got the tattoo on my arm here, too. He's okay, definitely. Trust me!"

I was still hesitating when I suddenly heard Domenico's voice quite close to my ear.

Trust me, sweets! It's all gonna be fine!

I closed my eyes, took a deep breath and let him pull me into the dodgy shop. Patrick followed us like a silent shadow, but I could feel exactly what he thought about the whole thing.

The man who came out from behind a red curtain fit perfectly into the oriental interior of the shop. He was a real Hippie with a mysterious look in his eyes, long hair and colourful clothes. He was probably pierced from head to toe. I did not dare looking up and wondered how I would turn this man into a nice jewellery shop assistant when I explained all this to my parents that evening.

"Hi Nick. Long time no see," said the pierced hippie monster.

Domenico switched to cool again immediately. "Hi Robbie! Can you pierce my girlfriend's ears?"

"If you pay straight away this time, yeah," was Robbie's not exactly encouraging answer, and my eagerness to get earrings faded more and more.

"Course! I saved some dough, man," Domenico explained.

"Yeah and I'm gonna marry my gran," Robbie laughed and waved me over. "Well then, let's see." He told me to sit down on a small spinning chair. "Let's get this done. It's gonna be quick and it won't hurt."

At that moment, I would have loved to turn back time to the evening in the park, to tell Domenico that I did not want to have earrings. I sat down on the chair stiffly as a poker and quickly chose a pair of silver hearts when Robbie showed me a range of different studs.

Domenico and Patrick were standing on either side of me while Robbie marked the right spots on my earlobes with a pen. I felt like I would rather be dead right then. Or in a tiny little coma at least. Just until it was over.

"I feel sick," I mumbled.

"Shall I hold your hand?" Domenico asked and held his hand out. I grabbed it and closed my eyes. In the middle of my dark thoughts I felt how warm and soft and strong his hand was.

It really was over quickly. Two deep breaths, and that was it. Robbie grinned at me happily with his pierced face. "There you go. Did it hurt?"

"It only stung a little bit," I admitted, infinitely relieved that it was over. My ears burned quite a bit. Now I could not make it undone anymore and Dad would have to get used to it. Robbie gave me a few tips about care and disinfection.

"It looks amazing," Domenico and Patrick agreed with each other. Domenico carefully put my hair behind my ears and looked at me with satisfaction, as if he had accomplished an important mission.

"You want anything else, Maya? A hair band, maybe? Or a necklace? I'm gonna buy you whatever you want! The other girls are never gonna laugh at you anymore." He looked around in the shop and pulled me over to a box of Indian hair bands.

He wanted to be nice, I could feel that, and I was really touched. But he was going completely crazy again! He could not just spend all his pocket money on me!

"No, listen. I could never accept that! It's far too expensive! Have you really got that much money?"

"Yeah, I told you," he sounded offended, "I've been saving it, even if no one believes it. I just want you to remember me forever." Something in his words made me shiver but I tried to ignore it.

"I would remember you without any of this!" *But I hope that you will never become just a memory!*

I let him pay for the earrings, but I could not accept anything else from him. My conscience would not have let me. He insisted, however, on inviting us to an ice cream and we could not say no to that. Patrick, who had been really quiet up to now, became very lively at the thought of ice cream. We found the next ice cream van and a minute later wandered down to the river with big cones in our hands. Domenico held his ice cream as though it was made of china and ate it slowly and with devotion. "I could live on sweets," he declared. His face was hidden under a baseball cap, which he had said he wore to protect his face from the sun. But I did not really believe that. Maybe he thought I had not noticed it, but I had seen him peeking around worriedly.

The sun was glittering on the surface of the water. A small flock of ducks swam to the river bank. We found a hidden spot under the trees where we sat down. Domenico pulled his cap even further down on his face.

"Is the sun blinding you?" I asked.

"No. I ..."

"What is it?" I hated my own stubbornness but I just could not stop myself from asking.

"Just a few people 'round here I don't wanna see."

He ate up the last bit of his ice cream and took out his cigarettes. "Can I smoke? Do you mind?"

"No," Patrick and I said at the same time and looked at each other meaningfully. But then I blew my top after all. I did not want to be annoying; I wanted to leave him alone and to stop asking all these questions. But I had put up with his secretiveness for so long now that I felt I was going to choke.

"Nicky, why can't you start talking to us about what is bothering you? I can't stand this any longer! You always make a big secret out of your life. But why? Don't you trust us at all? We are your friends!"

His mouth started to quiver. He clenched his fists and his whole body was trembling all of a sudden, as if he was going to burst. I had not expected this reaction.

"You don't understand that," he gnarled. "You

couldn't understand. But anyway. I tell you now! My brother's doing really crappy. That's the reason I always skip classes, man!"

Now, I had to be careful what I would say next. I was not allowed to make any mistakes. Carefully, I put my arm around him.

"Is he … ill?" I tried.

"No … or maybe he is … somehow he is, yeah." Suddenly, I saw a tear rolling down his cheek. He nervously wiped it off and bit his lip so hard that it started to bleed. He threw his half smoked cigarette into the river and sniffed. "You can't imagine how stupid all of this is!"

He drew a deep breath. His body was shaken with a coughing fit. He pressed his hand against his chest and gasped, struggling to breathe. It looked horrible.

"Nicky, this does not sound good!" I warned him worriedly. "You probably have pneumonia. I will ask Dad to have a look at you."

"No! I'm fine. It's gonna pass." He ground his teeth and held his breath. His face was red, and he was sweating. What should I do? How could you help someone if you did not even know his problems? And if you were not even supposed to know what you did know about him?

In that moment we were interrupted by a sharp voice.

"Hey, Nico, we were looking for ya! You gotta come and pick up your nutty twin brother."

We looked up immediately.

Behind us were two guys, a bit older than Domenico, with black, studded leather jackets and beer bottles in their hands. One of them had a tattoo on his neck, and his head was shaven. Behind them, there was a third person, moving like a cat. I was shocked to recognise Janet Bonaventura. The sight of this scary girl made Domenico turn into a nervous wreck within seconds.

"Nick, if you don't go pick up that rat right now, I'm gonna tell your little babies here about your criminal activities at night," she said tauntingly and gave Patrick and me a triumphant look. I gasped.

"You dirty lying bitch!" Domenico hissed.

"Shut up, Janet!" one of the tattooed guys warned her and stepped over to Domenico. "Hey, man, everything alright with you? Come on, we really need you!" He looked at Patrick and me. "Sorry, guys! Didn't mean to interrupt your little session, here. It's an emergency, I swear!"

"You go, Mike, I'll be there in a minute," Domenico said while he got up and turned his face towards us with a cold expression. "I gotta go. Mingo's in trouble. Are you mad at me?"

"No," Patrick and I said nearly at the same time again. I stood up, too, and put my hands on his shoulders. "It's okay, Nicky, we understand. And we will not ask any more questions. But please think of what I promised you!"

“Okay,” he mumbled and followed the others who had already disappeared in the hedges. I sank back to the ground, feeling angry and desperate.

“I’m starting to get fed up,” I said and yanked a leaf off a plant that was tickling my neck. “What on earth is going on with him? And now Janet claims that he is a criminal! I don’t know what to think about all this anymore …”

“J-Janet is just a l-liar,” Patrick tried to reassure me. “D-don’t listen to her.”

I was glad that Patrick was here with me. But the guys Domenico was hanging out with were scary. And I did not like the fact that Janet was his ex-girlfriend.

“Mingo is his t-twin brother, right?” Patrick asked.

“Yes. You did not know that? I would really like to know what is going on with him. Can you imagine what it is?”

“N-no. First I-I thought that it was a b-bad illness, but j-just now it sounded rather a-as though …”

“… he had mental issues?” I asked silently. Patrick nodded hesitantly. I stared onto the river. The flock of ducks waddled out from behind the bushes, but I did not even notice how cute they were. I was thinking about Mingo, who I had never met, trying to imagine what he was like. But I couldn’t. He was like a phantom, which I began to be afraid of.

On our way home, I was torn between my worries about Dad and Domenico. My burning earlobes reminded me of the discussions I would have to endure soon. What I had done and seen today would beat my dad's worst nightmares. I had stepped a bit further into Domenico's world again, and what I found there was quite dark. But I could never tell that to my parents if I did not want to lose Domenico. Because they would do everything in their power to protect me. And that would mean that, on the one hand, Domenico's secrets would finally be disclosed, but on the other that he would disappear. He would vanish. I knew that. I felt it. So I had to keep silent, no matter the cost. All this was just too much for my nerves, and it felt like my head was going to burst under the pressure.

Mum saw immediately that something about me had changed and she pushed my hair to the side. "You did not tell me that you were going to have your ears pierced this afternoon, Maya! Whose idea was this?"

"Domenico's," I admitted. "But I have always wanted it!" a big, hard lump started to grow in my throat.

"Well, I think it looks pretty," Mum commented. "But I do not like the fact that you did not tell me first."

"Dad would never have let me do it!" I started to sob. "You know that. And I'm not a baby anymore. I want to be able to make my own decisions sometimes!" I sulked and pouted.

"I think we would have managed to persuade him, somehow," Mum said and she sounded tired. "Dad only wants what is best for you. I am going to tell him that I allowed you to do it. But next time I want you to trust us, Maya."

I sadly nodded and at the same time felt that a huge part of the tension had just been taken off me. Maybe I would get off with a slap on the wrist this time. And Mum had not even asked what studio I had got the piercing at.

She welcomed Dad at the door and told him about my earrings in passing while I stayed in the kitchen, laying the table. My lungs felt really tight all of a sudden but Mum handled it wonderfully. She was just amazing!

"I think they look very pretty on her!"

"Do you?" I heard Dad say. His voice did not sound very surprised, but still slightly sad. Our fight had not left him cold.

"Let's see those earrings, Maya," he said when he stepped into the kitchen.

I lifted my hair to the side so that Dad could have a look at the silver hearts. He nodded resignedly but did not say anything. His silence was worse than anything else. I would have preferred him to burst out and rant.

That night, I struggled to fall asleep. Again and again I thought about all the things I had found out about Domenico in the past few days. I was just lying there, staring at the sky through the window above my bed.

The next day, Domenico was not at school. I did not know whether this was because of his brother or his cold. During the ten o'clock break I dialled his phone number for the first time but somehow I already knew that he was not going to answer. The day passed extremely slowly without him; all the clock hands seemed to move at half speed.

My earlobes were flaming red and swollen, and I did not miss how Delia nudged Isabelle to point at me and giggle. I did not care. My whole world was turning around Domenico, and I could not even tell my parents about it. Patrick was the only one I could share my worries with.

In the evening I sent Domenico a short text:

Hey, how are you? Please, give me a sign!

He did not reply, of course.

On Thursday there was still no sign of him, and I was angry and slightly desperate because I had no idea what was going on. For the first time, I had serious doubts about our relationship. Was he just pulling me into a dangerous whirl of events, which I would maybe not be able to get out of anymore one day? What if Dad's fears were right?

Vaguely, I noticed that Mrs Galiani was standing next to me. "Maya, would you please give us a short summary of what we learnt about the African steppe last time?"

I winced. I had not been paying any attention to the class.

"Uhm…" There was a big blank in my head, and I had a totally wrong page opened in my geography book; in Southeast Asia somewhere.

"Uhm…" I said again. Everyone around me was giggling. Mrs Galiani was not used to me not knowing the answer and looked at me worriedly.

African steppe.

Domenico's horrible scars.

His dangerous leap into the water.

His bad cough.

His crazy brother.

"Are you not feeling well, Maya?" Mrs Galiani asked me sympathetically. Delia and Isabelle were grinning gleefully.

"I don't remember," I whispered, "I'm sorry!"

"Please, come to see me after the class." Mrs Galiani nodded encouragingly but my heart still sank. Oh no! I could not fail at school on top of it all! That would break my dad's heart completely!

I was nervously chewing my fingernails, which I normally never did, when I was standing in front of Mrs Galiani's desk at the end of the class.

"So, Maya, how can I help you? You have got something on your mind, haven't you?"

"N-not really."

She looked at me questioningly. "Is Domenico ill?"

"Yes! Please, could I get his address?" I heard myself say to my own surprise.

She frowned and gave me a serious look. As if she was trying to say: *Are you sure you want that?*

But then, she tore out a page of her notebook without saying anything, wrote down the address and handed it to me. When I read it, I suddenly had a vague idea, a sneaking suspicion.

Still feeling helpless, Patrick and I were standing together under the lime tree during the ten o'clock break on Friday, chewing on our sandwiches. We had given up calling Domenico. He either refused to switch on his mobile phone or he had given me the wrong number. A dark cloud moved in front of the sun, and I shivered a little bit. I had left my jacket in the classroom. Impatiently I waited for the bell to put an end to the break.

When we returned to the classroom I immediately saw the disaster. My jacket had been thrown on the floor and everywhere in the room small white book pages were fluttering around. I swallowed. I had completely forgotten that I had put my bible back into my pocket after Domenico had encouraged me.

"There she is, our little saint!" Delia jeered loudly. "Come on, Maya, stand on the table and preach!"

I did not reply. Silently, I bent down and gathered the pages. Patrick helped me. Everyone had gone quiet all of a sudden. I felt that everyone was staring at me. I slowly got up and looked around. I did not know what my eyes expressed, but one by one the others turned away and sat down on their chairs. I felt strength grow inside me, strength that I had never felt before. I searched every corner of the room until I had found all the pages. I forgot about everyone around me, when I walked back to my desk, pressing the pile of pages against me. Everything around me was blurred.

Over the weekend, my worries about Domenico grew worse and worse, and so, on Friday night, a plan began to form in my head, which I pushed aside for now though.

The atmosphere at home was still very cool and distant. I felt like I was losing my footing more and more. My entire world was crumbling, and I was scared.

I still worked on my plan again the next night. My doubts made me hesitate from time to time, but in the morning I had finally made a firm decision.

I would take a chance. I would go to his place. That way, I would finally find out what was going on with him!

16. The other side of the park

I did not even tell Patrick what I was going to do. I just thought it would be too much if the two of us showed up.

I felt physically sick when I left after school. I was getting into this deeper and deeper, having lied to my parents yet again. But I did not have a choice if I wanted to go ahead with my plan. They would never have let me go if they had known what I wanted to do. Instead, I had told them that Patrick had invited me for lunch and that we would revise maths afterwards.

I had figured out exactly what I would say to Domenico. Again and again I had repeated the words in my head, until I knew them by heart. My stomach turned when I thought about it, but I marched on resolutely. I walked past the restaurant at the lake where the path through the park forked into three. I had never gone any further than this except when I had walked up to the lantern. I did not really know where to turn now. The sun was shining onto my neck. I liked the smell of dry grass and hot concrete. It made me feel the summer in every fibre of my being. If only it had been one of those carefree summers. We could have had so much fun!

If the middle path turns out to be the right one, it

must mean this whole thing is a good idea, I decided. If it's the wrong way, I'll just have to turn around. And so I continued.

I could not really tell when the appearance of the park began to change. The big, wide fields had disappeared; there were only a few bits of worn-out lawn here and there. I slowed down and looked around, hesitantly. For the first time in my life, I stood in front of the gate on the other side of the park – at the gate to the other world.

The area around the gate was dirty; cigarette butts, beer cans, ashes and waste were lying around. The street behind it was narrow and full of parked cars and motorbikes. There was a sweet acid-smell in the air; a mix of dog poo, beer and urine, accentuated by the heat of the sun. I felt sick.

Several groups of young people were sitting next to each other on the shabby wall separating the park from the street. Probably they all met here because they did not want to go home after school. Most of them smoked or drank beer, and a ghetto blaster with its volume turned all the way up filled the hot summer air with loud bass rhythms. Some of the people looked as if they were actually homeless and spent their whole lives around this wall.

Now, I was scared. Dad had always warned me of this run-down area. But I just had not listened. If I was honest, I had known deep down even a while ago that I would come here, one day. I had just tried to fight the thought that Domenico was living in this miserable place, because it must be horrible. Now I regretted that I had not asked Patrick to come along.

I could still turn around. I had two possibilities. Either I made a U-turn, or I walked straight through that gate. The U-turn would definitely have saved me a lot of trouble. But …

No, Maya. You have already waited too long! Your cowardliness has been limiting you all your life, only because you cannot take a few seconds of tension! Go now!

And I made myself walk through the gate, leaving the park and my former life behind me. I took the next side lane, where I walked past a dingy sex shop full of graffiti drawings on the wall. I suppressed my fears and tried not to think of my dad. Instead, I walked on resolutely, past a run-down bar so full of cigarette smoke that I could not see anything inside. I looked up the shabby walls of the houses around me: the plaster was coming off everywhere and the windows were sealed with rags and sticky tape. It was a dark street with no front gardens, and somehow there was not even any sunlight.

I stopped. I had already walked too far. I was at number sixteen, but Domenico lived at number fourteen. But that was where the sex shop was. And then, I saw that between the two houses there was a narrow car park with a roof, forming a passage way. I mustered all my courage and stepped over the broken glass and the stones, squeezing past an old, dirty jeep and three rusty bike wrecks. I arrived in a dark courtyard that looked a bit like a waste dump. Techno music blasted out of an open window. But I did not see a door.

An elderly man with a pony tail and a cigarette between his lips was standing in a corner, hammering on a piece of metal. He was the only person far and wide, so I had to ask him. He turned around and stared at me as though I came from another planet. And somehow, he was not all that wrong.

"There ain't a lotta clean girls like you around here," he grumbled. "Bet you don't live here, right?" He looked at me from head to toe. With my school bag, the perfectly ironed blouse and my soft face I must have looked like innocence in person.

"No, you are right. I live on the other side of the park," I admitted.

"Yeah, with the doctors and the lawyers and all that lot! Sorry, no offense. And what are you doing *here?*"

"I … I came to see a friend. I heard he lives in this house. Do you maybe know him? His name is Domenico di Loreno."

"Yeah, course I know him." He shook his head disapprovingly and threw his hammer into a corner. "Everyone here knows those twin brats. No wonder, with that mother … Why would a girl like you hang out with that type of guy? The amounts of money I lent the two boys so they could at least eat something proper. I own this place, actually." He pointed at the sex shop. "What does your father do?"

"He is a doctor." I nearly whispered.

"Well, guess you were luckier than your little friend here, then. You were spared the real life." Now he pointed to a hidden cellar door on the other side of the sex shop. "You gotta go in there and walk through the cellar. The door ain't locked. But watch out, there's loads of tat in there."

"Thank you," I said politely and tried not to think about what he had just told me. His allusions made me feel dizzy and gave me ideas of a world I could not bear to set a foot in.

I stepped into a dark, moist cellar that smelt of mould. The techno music sounded pretty close now. My stomach turned again. I fumbled around for a light switch, but I couldn't find one. Suddenly, I stumbled over something on the floor and fell flat onto a pile of waste bags. An old sheet of metal crashed against the wall and made an awful lot of noise. I felt a piercing pain in my knee and had to clench my teeth to suppress a scream.

The light went on. Scared, I looked around. I could see a pale face with dark eyes peeking through a door crack.

"Nicky!" I said hoarsely.

He opened the door and stepped into the cellar. But then I realised that it was not Domenico, even though he looked nearly exactly like him. His hair was even crazier, standing up in spikes in the front, and his left ear was full of piercings, at least five or six. The cigarette in his mouth was nearly burnt down, and from his washed-out black t-shirt an ugly skull was grinning at me. Another skull hung on the leather bands he was wearing around his neck. On his left cheek, I could see a long, badly infected cut.

Mingo. This was Mingo!

I carefully got up, trying to put on a friendly smile, but my fear made it impossible. This boy looked dangerous and he gave me a hostile look.

"Who are you?" he snapped.

"I'm Maya. Domenico's girlfriend."

Mingo took a drag on his cigarette and gave me a cold, piercing look.

"He told you to come here?"

"No. I was worried because Domenico has not come to school for so long. I thought he might be ill!"

"Yeah. And you're the one who makes him ill! Since he met you, he started having stupid dreams again. About his perfect world down in Sicily. But there ain't no perfect world for us. Never was, never will be!"

I was scared when he suddenly lifted his arm. I saw the knife that he hid under his studded wristband. I stood back behind the sheet of metal to be ready to flee if necessary. Mingo's glowing eyes did not miss a move.

"He's gone totally nuts! Babbling around about a

lamp in Sicily and stuff. Jumping into that freaking cold water, cos he thinks he's jumping off a cliff in Sicily! And now he's ill. And it's your fault!"

"But why would it be my fault? I don't have anything to do with Sicily!"

"Cos he started to dream around again, cos of you! He's already been to a nuthouse. But I keep telling him that Sicily's too long ago. It's not possible he remembers anything. Now leave!" he hissed.

But I could not move. And right in that moment I saw the missing piece to the puzzle that Mingo represented to me. I saw the needle marks on his arms. They looked like mosquito bites he had scratched open and his arms were full of them. Now, I knew what Mingo's problem was! I stared at him, horrified.

At the same time, the door opened again and this time Domenico was standing there. He looked tired and unkempt, as if he had just woken up, and he was wearing his t-shirt the wrong way around.

When he saw me his face froze.

"Ma che … Maya, what are *you* doin' here? Vatinne di ccà! Go away! Leave us alone! Sparisci!"

I felt sick again. He had never given me such an angry and menacing look before. I could see an unpredictable rage burning in his eyes. I held on to the wall, slowly moving backwards. But I could not just leave now. I had to finish what I had come here for. I could not let my fear get the better of me. I firmly looked at him. His hand on the door handle was trembling nervously.

"I'm sorry, Nicky. I could not help myself. I was so worried about you. Please, don't be mad at me! I don't mind that you live here!"

He blinked as if he was blinded by the light in the hallway. His fingers were nervously fumbling at his pockets and when he did not find any cigarettes he swore silently. He looked at Mingo who shook his head and went back inside through the half open door.

Domenico stared at me undecidedly again.

"Can I come in, Nicky? I would like to talk to you," I tried.

He did not answer and leant against the wall.

"Nicky, please …!"

Why was he so stubborn! Carefully, I stepped over a stack of tat towards him.

"Just say something."

He closed his eyes and turned away.

"It's not like your house, Maya," he snarled, obviously fighting against his rage. Angrily, he opened the door, behind which I would have expected a laundry or a lumber room, but which led to the flat. Domenico had already disappeared inside but the door was still ajar. So I followed him. My knee hurt horribly.

There was no hall in the flat. I was standing in a shabby kitchen, which, even at second glance, did not really look like one if it had not been for the old stove that was standing in one corner. There was a huge pile of dirty dishes and leftovers in the dirty sink, which filled the room with a disgusting stale smell. From one wall to the other hung washing lines with wet clothes so that I had to I carefully push some t-shirts out of the way so I could follow Domenico. There was only one big wardrobe and anything that did not fit in there was piled in a complete mess all over the floor. I stepped on a tattered and mended rug and noticed how little daylight came through the small grilled window, since the flat was in the cellar. When I was about to step into the next room, where the techno music came from, I looked to the side and saw a table full of rubbish. There were half-full liquor bottles and glasses with cigarette butts. Suddenly, Domenico stood next to me and pulled me away from the table.

“Wondering how I can live like that, huh?” he hissed. I opened and closed my mouth like a fish, because I could not think of anything intelligent to say. He disappeared in the next room again and closed the door behind him.

“Nicky!” I felt that I absolutely needed to win this fight and banged on the door. The volume of the techno music was turned up even more, so that the walls started to vibrate. So, I pushed down the handle and opened the door myself. Domenico stood in my way immediately. He had a cigarette between his lips and his eyes were two thin, angry lines.

"You're not coming in here, Maya!" he spat.

"Nicky, stop being such a jerk!" I retorted.

"Manco morto!" He grabbed my shoulders and pushed me back with all his strength. He was incredibly strong. I stumbled and fell onto the kitchen floor. Shocked, he stared down at me. His cigarette fell out of his mouth and burnt a small hole into the rug. Finally, he sank down on his knees, beaten, and reached out to me.

"Sorry. Sorry, Maya. I didn't want that."

I put my hand in his. In that moment I could catch a glimpse of the room behind him and just about managed not to show my horror. No wonder Domenico was so ashamed!

The bleak dingy room looked as though somebody was planning on moving out soon. The mess in there was hard to describe. Except for two mattresses with linen full of holes, a stereo and a TV, there was no furniture. Instead, there were piles of waste and clothes everywhere. I stood up slowly. Food, school books, full ashtrays, cigarette boxes, magazines, coke cans, beer bottles – all lying around in a wild mess, spread over the whole room. And the smell was a biting mix of old cigarette smoke and mould.

Domenico was still kneeling on the floor and did not stop me from coming in, anymore. My eyes wandered from one corner of the room to the next. I saw crumpled up tissues with blood stains and old syringes. There were empty boxes of Rohypnol, a strong sleeping pill that Dad sometimes prescribed to his patients, right next to some empty, mouldy yoghurt pots. The only thing that seemed to make a boys' room out of this waste dump were posters of Metallica, that Italian rock singer Vasco Rossi Nicky had played for us in school, and a band called 883 on the ugly stained walls.

I took another step. Mingo was sitting on the floor in front of the stereo with a cigarette in his hand, trying to set the bass right. He only noticed I was there when my foot touched an empty tin. He turned around and looked at me contemptuously.

"Oi … girly, go home, it's time for the sandman!"

"No!" I firmly retorted. I let my schoolbag slide to the floor so that I did not have to just stand there rigidly. I saw another door in the far corner of the room, and I knew that what was behind it was none of my business. Mingo switched off the techno sound and played Metallica's Enter Sandman, singing along to the music: "I tuck you in, warm within, keep you free from sin, 'til the sandman he comes …"

"Will ya turn that off! A vo' stutare 'sta cosa, Mingo?" Domenico hissed and squeezed past me into the room. He picked up an old woollen blanket and threw it in a corner so that some especially big, dark stains on the dirty old rug were hidden. It looked a bit like dried blood, but I could not be sure of that. He came back to me and grabbed my arm.

"Let's get out, Maya."

"What is his problem with me?" I asked desperately.

"It's not you." Domenico dragged me through the kitchen, and I knew that this had been the first and last time I would ever be allowed to set foot in this flat. He noticed my hobbling and stopped worriedly.

"Hurt yourself on that stupid old metal sheet, huh?" I nodded.

"Happened to me before, too," he grinned. "It belongs to the landlord so I can't just get rid of it. I'm sorry … is your knee bleeding?"

"I don't think so. There might be a bruise or two but I will be fine." I smiled at him.

Carefully, he led me through the cellar door and made sure he did not shut it entirely. "If Mingo turns up the music again, he can't hear the bell," he sighed.

"Don't you have a key?" I wondered.

"We … we've only got one for the two of us."

The fresh air was great. Only a thin sunbeam made its way into the pebbled courtyard. We sat down on a low wall next to the run-down garage where I had met the man earlier.

"I'm sorry," Domenico said bitterly. "You shouldn't take Mingo too serious when he says things … he is … guess you saw what his problem is now?"

"Yes."

"And – you got it?"

"Yes. I think so, yes."

"You've got no idea what drugs can do!"

I shook my head. For the first time, Domenico was talking to me of his own accord.

"He started taking that stuff a year and a half ago. I really tried to stop him, but he had to try it, 'sto scemo … And now he's stuck with it. Can't get off it."

He lifted his head and looked into the blue sky.

"He's doing really bad! Guess you saw that. The stuff has destroyed him, è completamente rovinato … He even had to go to hospital cos he had jaundice. He's sold nearly all we've got to get dough for heroin. We ain't got nothing left. You saw it. I gotta watch out for him all the time!"

"I understand," I said silently. "But could he not do a detox?"

He looked at me as if I had lost my marbles. "Have you ever seen a drug addict on detox?"

I shook my head. Of course I had not. Drugs were an absolute taboo for me, one of the subjects that were strictly banned at home. So this was something I knew nothing about.

"You can't imagine how it is then. He tried. It was hell, I tell you. Addiventò loccu! Screamed around, destroyed half our flat. I had to sit on him and hold his hands down, so that he couldn't run off or keep destroying stuff."

"Oh, no …"

"He was in youth prison for a few weeks. It was really

bad. I don't want that to happen again, you know. But recently ..."

Suddenly he was shaken by a brutal coughing fit. I put my hand on his shoulder. Why had I not thought about bringing some coughing syrup from dad's practice? We had tons of it!

When he managed to breathe again, he continued: "Recently, Mingo passed out a few times, cos he had taken bad dope. Then he just lies there, not moving. And I freak out every time, cos I dunno if I'm gonna be able to wake him up again. It would be the worst thing in the world for me ... lose him. You know, a twin brother ... it's more than just a brother. He's part of me. Here." He pointed to his heart. "And I'm part of him."

I nodded, deeply touched. "Yes, of course."

He leaned back and nervously ran his fingers through his wild hair. "Last Tuesday, when we were in city, he attacked some guys with a knife. He was going nuts cos he was out of dope. I had to drag him off. And that was too much, visto come ... In the evening, my fever hit forty!"

I could not hide that I had to gasp for air for a second. Gloomily, he let his head hang down.

"Now you know it. Bet you don't want anything to do with me anymore, righ'?"

I did not know what to say. I felt like I was sitting on a roller coaster. The whole world around me was spinning like crazy and I could not stop it. Maybe, the roller coaster would turn into a hurricane soon and make me completely loose the ground under my feet.

"It's all my fault!" His voice was trembling. "I had abandoned him. You know … cos I was with girlfriends all the time, he was always alone and then went with bad guys. I was crazy … you know, I wanted to make out and stuff all the time, and Mingo was suffering. But he never said a word. You imagine that?"

I shook my head. "Did he not have a girlfriend?"

"The girls are all afraid of him. You see, he looks bad. And he was always really shy. Too shy to get girls. And then there was the thing with Janet …"

Janet, the beauty and the beast rolled into one … Why had Domenico been so fascinated with her?

"Janet deals with H. That's heroin. She wanted to sell me some too, but I said no. And then she gave some to Mingo and his friends. When I heard about it, I beat her up and dumped her. That's why she hates me so much now. And … You wanna hear the whole story? That's why you came here, innit?"

I guessed that the bitterness in his voice was not meant personally, but it was hard to ignore it.

"Where is your mum? You don't live here by yourselves, do you?" I asked.

"Nah!," he snorted contemptuously. "She comes home in the middle of the night, strapiena, wasted, and pukes on the floor or something. I'm happy if I don't see her."

Suddenly, I could see ice-cold anger flaming up in his eyes. He brutally grabbed my hand and pulled me to my feet.

"Righ', come on! If you really gotta know!"

Surprised, I let him drag me through the garage to the front of the house. In front of the sex shop, he stopped and angrily stared into the window. On the background of a red curtain, pictures of half-naked women were displayed. I did not understand what we were doing there.

"There! See that woman on the right? That's her!"

What? What did he mean? My grey matter took a while to process this information. I was staring at the picture of a very beautiful woman with dark curly hair and big sad eyes who could not be much older than 33.

"That's my mother!" he shouted and punched the window so violently that the people who were walking past looked around. "I can look at her, naked in a shop window! 'Unn è bello? Talé ..."

"Does she still do that?" I looked around, slightly embarrassed.

"Not anymore. They chucked her out, she always missed her appointments."

I studied the picture. Her eyes seemed to look right inside me, just like Domenico's. Yes, he had inherited some of her looks: the high cheekbones, the beautifully shaped eyebrows, the small nose. No wonder he was so handsome! I secretly looked at him and tried to imagine what I would feel like if my Mum was in that shop window. It would be horrible, that was for sure.

"What do you think what she looks like without all the makeup? She's a hag. Horrible!" he said bitterly.

When we slowly walked back into the courtyard, we came across Mingo. In the daylight, I saw how pale and skinny he really was. He stopped and exchanged a few quiet words in Italian with his brother. His teeth were in an even worse state than Domenico's, and he was smoking again. Domenico took a cigarette too, lighting it with Mingo's. He shouted something after him when he had already left.

"He buys the dope at the gate to the park" he explained quietly when Mingo had disappeared. "Sometimes, I have to go for him, when he's … you know …"

No, I did not know anything … I felt like I had entered the suburbs of hell. At least, I had finally got answers to some of my questions. But there were still so many left. And there was something I tried to suppress with all my might. I nervously played with my earrings. I just had to stop thinking about it!

"You can split up with me if you want," he suddenly said when we sat down on the low wall again. "I don't want you to get in trouble with your dad."

"So what? I don't care."

"You dunno what you're getting into!" Something in his voice worried me, but I had made up my mind. I was going to stick to my decision, even if I had to fight a whole army.

He just looked at me for a while, not saying anything. I could see my silhouette in his pupils. But suddenly, the picture blurred as his eyes filled with tears. Quickly, he flicked away his cigarette and turned his face away from me.

You should not see my tears, Maya. How did you manage to open that door that I keep everyone shut out with? Who are you that you managed to make me let you into my world? You're like a light shining into my darkness, leaving nothing inside me in the shade. And now, I can see the mess everywhere even more clearly! Don't look at it, please, don't look at it any longer! Otherwise you're gonna go away or I have to disappear!

"They tore up my Bible." I did not know myself why I suddenly changed the subject. I just had to say something.

"Delia and the others?" he asked silently and looked up. I nodded.

"Just ignore them, Maya! I think it's great that you believe in God," he continued hoarsely and coughed again. "I never had a girlfriend like you. I would never leave you. I wish I could believe in God again, too."

"But if you look at nature … the trees, the flowers, all the animals and humans … I just cannot believe that it all came to be just by coincidence! There has to be a brilliant and awesome Creator behind all this," I said.

He closed his eyes. “I know. I used to say prayers. That was a very long time ago. If there really was a God … someone who’s your friend, who you can talk to and stuff … someone who gives you answers and protects and comforts you and tells you what to do …,” he murmured, his head on his hands, pensively looking at a lonely little daisy that had managed to live between waste and stones.

“Don’t listen to the others, Maya,” he said again. “Keep your faith in God, I think that’s great!”

He picked up a few pebbles and resignedly threw them into the courtyard. His hair fell into his face. He still looked ill and tired. I would have liked to ask him more questions. About those dreams of Sicily, for example. But that would have been too much.

“Are you coming back to school tomorrow?” I asked.

“Dunno. Can’t say.” He stood up and turned his back to me.

“You should go home now, Maya. This is no place for you. And I don’t want you to come back, mi capisci? Ever! Can you promise that?”

I nodded silently. But then I remembered something.

“My schoolbag! I left it in your room!”

He turned around again. “Alrigh’. Wait here, I’m gonna get it.” Of course. I knew that I was not allowed to go into the flat anymore. But I did not obey. I got up too and followed him to the cellar door. He joggled the doorknob, but it was locked.

“Oh, no!,” he groaned. “Mingo forgot it again!” He looked at me with a strangely nervous expression in his face. “Man! I told you to wait there!” he snapped. “Go back!”

But I was standing there, paralysed with fear. He closed his eyes tiredly, turned around and kneeled down. He had turned his back towards me, his t-shirt fluttering in the soft summer breeze and I had to think about his scars, when I realised that he was trying to hide something with his body. He was fumbling at the house wall with quick movements and suddenly held a big key in his hand. I was still standing behind him, waiting, unable to move. But when he pushed me to the side hectically to unlock the door, my limbs came to life again and I did something that required more courage than anything I had ever done, before. I knew that it was not very polite, but I just could not bear it any longer. I wanted to know about his secret. When he had got into the house, I kneeled down and scrutinised the wall. I could not see anything, so I started to feel the cracks and openings, pushed a stone to the side and another one …

And there was a hole! A deep hole in the house wall. It was a hiding place. But what for? I was breathing quickly and my thoughts took that dangerous direction again. The direction I did not want them to take … I put my hand in the hole and touched something metallic. I took it out.

It felt heavy and cold in my hand. In a hand it should not be in. A bunch of keys. The heavy summer air was filled with a strange silent emptiness. Slowly, the ugly truth started to dawn on me in all its hideousness. Within seconds, I had finally completed the puzzle. The spire on the gym. The money for the earrings. The burglary at Mr Biedermann's.

It was the bunch of keys that had gone missing at school!

A shadow fell on me. Domenico was standing there and handed me my schoolbag. His eyes looked so menacing when I lifted my head that I felt like I was falling down a cliff.

"Nicky!" I whispered. I could not speak anymore. I thought I would suffocate. Everything we had built up from nothing, so carefully, was destroyed in this terrible moment. I held the keys up with a shaking hand. I started to cry and, when I looked at him, I saw that he was crying, too.

"I … I just cannot believe it! I can't! So it was you, after all!"

"Maya." He leaned against the wall. "I can explain it to you. I can explain it, Maya! It's not how you think!" He looked at me pleadingly. "Please … please believe me!"

But it was as though we were sitting on two sheets of ice that were drifting apart. It was him! Him! Everything went black. He was a thief! A criminal. And even worse than that: he was a liar!

"You stole the money. And you unlocked the door to the spire. All the keys are on there! You used the stolen money to buy my earrings, because you do not have any money yourself. I cannot believe it, Nicky!"

The heat of the day was slowing our movements down. It was as if we were no real humans, but characters in a story that did not exist. But no nightmare I had ever had was as bad as what was happening right now.

"Maya … I've gotta tell you somethin' … I knew that it was crap … oh man … I'm so sorry …" He pressed his face against the wall and punched the door with his fist. "I'm an idiot! Quantu sugnu scemu!"

"Well, that does not make it any better now! I will never be able to trust you anymore!" I forced out between my clenched teeth. My whole body was shaking as if I was the one with a fever now. How vicious! They had all been right. Dad, Janet … all of them. He was a criminal, a thief, a liar! He had fallen so deep that he did not think twice about stealing from an innocent man and lying to me.

But I also knew, somewhere deep inside me, that I had had my doubts for a long time. I had thought about it for the first time when Mrs Galiani had told us about the burglary. But I had not wanted to believe it. I had blocked it out.

We looked into each other's eyes, but there was a wall between us. A wall of sadness, anger, fury and the remains of a broken dream.

Why? Why did you do that? Who are you really? Do you even exist? Or is the darkness inside you so powerful, so deep, that nobody can ever reach you anymore, not even you, yourself? Can you even control yourself?

His eyes were piercing my heart so painfully that I could have screamed. There was silent pleading in his eyes when he was reading my thoughts.

I trusted you, I gave you everything. I even stood up to my father because of you. You knew it, but it no longer touched your heart. You were already lost when I was still full of hope.

The pleading in his eyes extinguished.

"You are so vicious!" I screamed in fury, so loudly that my voice echoed in the courtyard. I pushed him away and ran off, past the car, onto the street. I ran and my throat was aching. This was the end! It was over! Our friendship, which had been so great, so unconditional, was destroyed. It had vanished, reduced to ashes from one moment to the next, blown away by the wind. Forever! Never to be found again. The promise we had given each other under the lantern was broken!

17. A nightmare

I had stopped on the square in front of the mansion next to the lantern, trying to calm down a bit. I picked leaves from the bushes and tore them up with my fingers. Never before had I wished so strongly to be not Maya, but someone else, anything else. I would have preferred to be a bird, a cat … even an ant would have done the job! Ants were humble and simple workers, and they did not know much about what was going in the world. They did not know tears.

Obviously, I did not even have a tissue and so the tears were just flooding down my cheeks, wetting my blouse. I could not return home with puffy eyes like this. My parents would immediately guess the truth. They were just like that. I could not hide anything from them. But the pain was so awful that I could not stop crying. I sat down on one of the benches and looked up at my good old lantern. Mum had told me that it had been the first electric lantern of the city at the time. The mansion used to belong to a rich family before it was turned into a museum. This lantern must have witnessed many stories … Why was I thinking about that now?

I felt like I was going to throw up any second. My whole body was trembling. It had just been too much for me today. The truth had turned the sensitive, hurt boy into a cold-blooded thief and liar. Everything he had given to me in the past few weeks had been blown away and left a painful emptiness inside my heart. I would have put up with anything: the drugs, his craziness, his strange brother, anything but not this big fat lie. This abysmal viciousness.

I suddenly realised what a difficult situation I was in now. Was I not obliged to tell Mrs Galiani and the police what I knew? Was I not even complicit if I did not say anything? I was involved in a burglary against my will! God, what should I do? There was no way out of this anymore. Wherever I turned to, the poisonous tentacles of lies, pain and sadness were reaching out for me.

After a long while and still undecided, I started to walk back home. When Mum asked the question that just had to come when she saw my red eyes: "Oh dear, Maya, what happened?" I had a flash of wit and gave her the only answer that could save me: "I had an awful fight with Domenico again this morning. I cannot take it anymore. We ended our friendship." It sounded plausible and explained my swollen nose and puffy eyes.

"Oh, you did?" Mum frowned. "How come? Was he back at school, then?"

"Well …" Once you start a lie, there is no turning back. Now I had to stick to it.

"He … he beat up some boys. I do not want to have anything to do with that. I would only get into trouble. It just doesn't work."

But Mum's eyes stayed on me, and I realised that she

knew very well that this had not been all. I had to stop her from digging deeper.

"Mum, could you let me handle this? I would like to sort this out with Domenico myself. It was just too much, today!"

I left her standing there, but I sensed that she was following me with her eyes when I climbed up the stairs. Upstairs in my den, I fell on my bed and cried it all out, all that was in there.

Why did I care so much about him? I had only known him for a few weeks. Because of him, I even screwed things up with my dad! And he had just played with me in cold blood! He had been acting so cleverly that I had not even wanted to believe he could be this vicious.

Dad was obviously very happy when he heard about our split but he still made an effort to comfort me, even though I did not deserve it at all, I thought. I felt mean and dirty.

"You see, Maya, I know what is good for you after all. I saw immediately that this boy is no match for you! You are much too young for that kind of thing anyway. I do not want you to be with boys yet. All in good time. When you are old enough, you will find the right one, I am absolutely convinced of that."

At least, *one* of us was happy in this whole mess, I thought bitterly.

"No, Martin, it is not that easy," Mum said quietly and a bit snappily. "You cannot help your feelings. Domenico was Maya's first love. I was in love when I was fourteen, too!"

I was not hungry and just poked at my carrot salad with my fork while my parents discussed whether it was allowed to fall in love at fourteen or not. I really wished I had as little to worry about as they did.

The weather changed that night as if it adapted to my depressed mood. The window over my bed was still wet when I woke up with a heavy head the next morning. I had barely sat up when the horrible reality came flooding back like the rain outside. I could not eat one single bite of my cornflakes and tried to avoid my parents until I set off for school with a heavy heart. It would be a morning I would never forget.

Mrs Galiani's eagle eyes observed Domenico's empty seat even more suspiciously than the days before. And inevitably, she did what I had wanted to avoid desperately: she told me to see her at the end of the class.

"Listen, Maya, I am quite worried about Domenico. He has been away from school for quite a long time now! Is there anything you would like to tell me?" Her eyes looked unusually soft and compassionate. She obviously really cared about him. I had to pull myself together with all my might to stop the tears from streaming out and to manage a polite smile.

"He is still ill. Because of the cold water."

Mrs Galiani nodded, but I felt that her eyes saw right into my heart.

"Well, I do not want to interrogate you, Maya, but if there is anything I can do to help, let me know."

I nodded and left. Patrick waited for me in the schoolyard with a big question mark on his face. But there were too many unwanted witnesses at the lime tree, so we hid in a corner next to the school gate.

Patrick did not need to say anything. He must have seen from the expression on my face this morning that something terrible had happened. I told him everything: about Domenico's burglary and his lies, about Mingo and his drug addiction, about the run-down flat where the brothers lived, about their mother who was in it deeply and about the end of our friendship – everything.

Thoughtful as he was, Patrick had a pack of tissues ready. We could both use it. Patrick was devastated too. Domenico, his secret hero, who had protected him, who had helped him out of his loneliness, turned out to be a criminal liar. Patrick looked like he was going to cry, while another thought began to torture me.

"I think, w-we have to tell Mrs Galiani," Patrick guessed what I was thinking. "We c-cannot keep this t-to ourselves."

It was inevitable. However much I used to like Domenico, even used to love him, his lie had destroyed it all. If I was going to break the promise we had made to each other under the lantern now, he had broken it a long time ago. So I nodded. And kept nodding. Carefully, Patrick took my hand and squeezed it. Yes. This really was it. I had to accept that I had been wrong about Domenico. He was twisted, unstable, dangerous even. Great. Dad had been right again.

"My Dad warned me," I admitted. "He knew straight away that Nicky is criminal."

I literally saw the blood leave Patrick's face, and suddenly I felt his fingernails digging into my palm. I noticed a shadow behind me and swirled around. Petrified, I saw Domenico standing behind me, his arms crossed in front of his chest, immobile and calm like a statue. His face did not show what was going on inside him, but his eyes looked straight at me without blinking, unlike usually.

I felt panic creeping up my back. He was so unpredictable. Could he, *would* he be able to hurt me? Had he come here just to spy on us?

Patrick squeezed my hand even harder and quickly pulled me away, towards the fountain. I looked to the ground and did not dare to turn around. Had I looked up just a split second earlier, I might have prevented what happened next. But it was too late. Delia and Isabelle were approaching us, and Delia's voice was so loud and shrill, that not only I could hear her, but the whole schoolyard, too.

"Oooooh, look at that, the slut is on to the next one already. The fatso suits her far better anyway. Finally, she's realised Nick is no good for her. But if only Daddy knew how many boys she's already read the Bible with …"

I froze. The whole tension from before turned into one big wave of fury. I wanted to do something, answer back, but I did not get the chance. It all went really fast. Delia had apparently not seen Domenico, and I only heard a thunk when he leaped at her and hit her in the face as hard as he could. I saw how his eyes flashed angrily; I had never seen him look this furious and dangerous. Delia's deafening scream echoed throughout the schoolyard. Domenico grabbed her and violently pushed her to the ground. His strength was so incredible, it was downright scary.

"Shut up, you miserable bitch!" he snarled.

She screamed and helplessly lashed about, blood dripping out of her nose. It was awful! I could not even look at them and my whole body was shaking.

"Nicky, please, stop!" I begged. "Stop it!"

"You horrible monster!" Isabelle shouted and desperately tried to free Delia.

But he did not stop. And he did not pay any attention to Isabelle. Overcome by headless fury he hit Delia's head on the ground again and again, until she lost consciousness. Patrick and I were holding onto each other. Isabelle was crying and screaming for help.

The others approached. A group of boys leapt at Domenico and hauled him off Delia. Two others knelt over her and checked for any kind of reaction. But she was just lying there, passed out, more and more blood streaming out of her nose and her head. It looked as though life was slowly streaming out of her. When a teacher turned her to lie in the recovery position she groaned terribly.

"Oh, my God!" I whined, terrified. "Oh God, no! Please!" I felt physically sick and had to hold on to the fence to make sure I did not fall. Everything blurred in front of my eyes.

"Quickly! Someone call an ambulance!" a teacher shouted.

My eyes met Domenico's. It had never hurt this much to look at him. He staggered backwards slowly, like an animal being cornered. He looked around caught up by panic. It seemed as though he had lost control of himself. Then he turned around and ran off.

"Stop him!" someone shouted. Some boys hurried after him. Isabelle marched over to me, started to slap me and tore on my hair like crazy. "This – is – all – your – fault – you – stupid – sod!"

I was so shocked that it nearly took my breath away. At first, I did not even feel the pain in my head and only vaguely noticed that Isabelle had torn out a whole tuft of hair in her fury. Suddenly, I realised that she was right! Domenico had attacked Delia because of us! I felt like everyone was staring at Patrick and me.

Mrs Galiani had arrived, too; she asked a few questions and felt Delia's pulse. I heard them say Domenico's name several times. Nearly the whole school had gathered around now. Nobody cared about the bell anymore. Finally, an ambulance arrived. The paramedics wrapped Delia in a blanket and lifted her onto the stretcher. A puddle of blood remained on the ground. The sight of it was so painful that I covered up my face with my hands and started to cry again. "Dear God, please don't let her die! Please!" But in spite of all this, I could not stop myself from thinking – even if it was just for a split second – that she somehow deserved it.

I felt Patrick's hand on my shoulder. Suddenly, I saw Janet. She more or less punched her way through the crowd, straight towards us. She towered over us and roughly grabbed my chin. She came really close to my face.

"What have I told you? Now you see how he really is, your junkie boyfriend!" And while she talked, I could feel her spit on my face as she sprayed the words at me. And I smelled her breath. It smelled somehow weird. Mint and cigarette and …

"Domenico does not take drugs!" I shouted angrily even though I was not so sure myself anymore. Janet laughed tauntingly.

"You've got no idea! He's hanging out at the Xenon with his brother all the time. You know the Xenon, don't you?"

I closed my eyes. The Xenon was so notorious that

even Dad knew about it. It was the club with the worst reputation in the whole city. It was on the other side of the park, probably quite close to where Domenico lived, actually. There were reports about drug trafficking and police raids in the newspaper and on the radio every few weeks.

I opened my eyes again. "That is just not true!"

"Oh yes, girly, it is! He's lying to you. You should be happy that someone finally tells you the truth. You still wanna go out with him? There's a lot more I could tell you." She grinned broadly and reached out to grab my necklace.

"He gave that to you, right? Where do you think he got it? Stole it at the mall!"

I was petrified and could not find any more words. Suddenly, Mrs Galiani stood next to me.

"Maya, could you please come to the teacher's room with me?" I nodded indifferently and followed her. Everyone else stayed outside, talking to each other excitedly.

Mrs Galiani sat me down on the sofa. She offered me a glass of orange juice and sat down next to me.

"Now, Maya," she finally said, "I know that it is not easy for you to talk about it. You have spent a lot of time with Domenico recently, haven't you?"

"Yes."

"Do you maybe know the reason why he attacked Delia so brutally?"

"I … he did it because she was ridiculing me. Domenico became so angry that he …" My voice failed and I started to cry again. "Oh, Mrs Galiani, I'm so sorry! I … I didn't …"

"You do not have to be sorry; it was not your fault." She gave me a pack of tissues. "What a state this class is in! You have had problems with Delia before, if I am not mistaken …"

She stood up and paced up and down the room in thoughts. I tried to dry the tears but they just kept flowing.

"I have noticed that his behaviour has improved significantly since he started spending time with you. You have had a positive influence on him. I was very happy about his grade in the English exam. I assume you studied together a lot? Oh, and Patrick is friends with the two of you as well, isn't he?"

I nodded.

"Well, I think that was extremely good for him. I have always appreciated you and Patrick very much." She sighed. "But this thing with Domenico is not easy at all! Do you know a few things about his life?"

"Yes and no. It was always really difficult to find out anything about him. He never wanted to talk about himself."

"You see, I thought so. I had hoped that he would confide in you. But he did not. So I will have to talk! By the way, would you like some more orange juice?"

I shook my head tiredly. "Is there anything else you can tell me about him?"

"Well, what do you know?"

"I … I was at his home, yesterday … I know that his mum is a drinker and that she works as a model for … err … you know!"

"Yes, I know. A dirty, degrading business. I feel very sorry for her."

"And I met his twin brother. He is a serious drug addict."

She nodded. "For nearly two years now."

"You know his brother?"

"Of course. Their former teacher is my husband. We do not teach at the same school, as you know. I have known his twin brother for a long time. My husband was very patient with them. We tried to help them several times to sort their lives out."

I looked at Mrs Galiani with big eyes. "Domenico never mentioned that."

"No, of course not. He is constantly acting. But I have figured him out. What I am going to tell you now is more than I should, Maya."

For a moment neither of us spoke. My thoughts were riding a roller coaster. Should I tell her about the burglary now? The opportunity was perfect. But I just could not bring myself to start. And when Mrs Galiani continued her explanations, I did not want to interrupt her anymore. "Domenico's fits of rage are no news. At his former school, he hurt several students in this kind of state. His brother is even more aggressive. He attacked others with a knife. I had hoped nothing like that would happen at this school! …"

"I don't think anybody takes care of them at home. Domenico does not even have a proper dad."

Mrs Galiani nodded, her eyes closed pensively. "So, you know about that."

"Yes. And … a girl from school told me a horrible story. She said that their mum had not wanted to keep them after they had been born and that she wanted to get rid of them. But I don't know … the girl is known to be a liar."

Mrs Galiani sighed. "You are talking about Janet Bonaventura, aren't you? She has got a bad reputation, yes. Her father works at the psychiatric clinic and … alright. This is a long, sad story and I will summarise it in a few sentences. But you have to promise that you will keep it a secret."

I promised.

"Maria – Domenico's mother – was only seventeen when she gave birth to her children. She was a runaway from a small village and worked as a dancer in a strip club in Palermo. Since she was very pretty, she said that she had got offers for a promising modelling career. One day, she fell in love with a young German tourist who spent his holidays in Sicily. But he did not care about her. Trying to charm him, she did everything to seduce him and became pregnant. The young man did not know anything about it and one day just left. The pregnancy was obviously going to ruin her career and so … well, she let herself be talked into committing this horrible crime. One of the boys even suffered slight brain damages. No one knows what really happened the night the boys were born, but they must have had a mighty guardian angel! All I know is that an elderly nun found the babies and took them to her convent and gave them their names. She looked after them during the day, so that Maria could work. But it was too late for her modelling career. Maria was so tortured by the feeling of guilt about her deed that she sought relief in drinking. Seven years later, Maria suddenly picked her children up again and came to Germany. This is all I can tell you, Maya."

I closed my eyes. I felt like crying out loud, but I was too embarrassed in front of Mrs Galiani. Also, time was too precious and I still had so many questions.

"Who told you all this?" I asked with a trembling voice.

"I cannot tell you everything, Maya. I am bound to professional discretion."

"Is there anything that can be done? I tried to help him but it seems impossible!"

"I tried too, Maya." She walked back and forth, shaking her head, looking out of the window sadly. This was something I had never seen before: Mrs Galiani not knowing what to do.

"I cannot do anything else. The only possibility I had was taken away from me ..." The bitterness showed on her face when she returned to sit down again. "The foster family did not work. They could not handle the boy. Unfortunately, I cannot help you either at the moment. It is such a sad story. You should go home now. I am going to exempt you from the remaining classes of the day. I will inform Patrick about it and call your parents later today, okay?"

Tired and caught up in thoughts, I walked home. Now the bubble had burst. I could still not really grasp the whole story or make any sense of it. I was not even sure anymore whether it had all just been a bad dream! And I had still not told anyone the bitter truth about the burglary. And above all this, there was the scary question: How was Delia?

I was sitting in front of my parents on the sofa, my head hanging down. I had never seen Dad this angry.

"Mrs Galiani told me what happened. Can you imagine what could have happened to you!? If that boy had touched you! I cannot bear the thought of it! I knew something like this would happen!" His deep, loud voice resounded in my head. I was just sitting there, in pieces, crying and not able to say any of the things I wanted to.

"Do you see now? This is exactly why I did not want you to be with this boy! Just look what happened: He nearly beat a girl from your class to death! This is bad!

This boy could be a murderer; a … he could be anything!"

Why could Dad not just stop torturing me? I could not bear any more of this. Yes, I made a thousand mistakes. How much longer did he have to rub in the fact that I was the biggest idiot in the world?

"Martin, stop! Please stop! We are not getting anywhere like this," Mum pleaded.

"I want this horrible story to end once and for all!" Dad shouted. "I want to be entirely sure that Maya never has anything to do with this boy ever again!"

I buried my face in my hands. Before I could think about what I was doing, I got up and ran up to my room.

A few minutes later, I heard my Mum come in and close the door behind her. Silently she came over and put her arms around me.

"Maya! Your dad's worries are justified. You know, Dad only wants you to be safe. But I do understand that Domenico really needs help. Mrs Galiani said some very nice things about you, Maya. And about your friend Patrick. She trusts both of you. Apparently you have had a very positive influence on Domenico. But – she has told us something else. They are not sure whether Delia is going to be okay again. It is possible that she will be left with a disability because of the damage that was done to her head. It is very, very bad!"

I sat there, battered, and could barely breathe.

No, this could not be happening! Even if I hated that

horrible girl, I did not want her to be disabled for the rest of her life! It just could not happen! I felt awful. Pressing my lips together I prayed: "No, God. Please don't! Please don't let this happen!"

"We are going to pray for her together," Mum whispered softly and rocked me in her arms. Tired, I closed my eyes and felt as though I was caught in a waterfall. "And as for Domenico. The consequences would be unthinkable if Delia ..." she did not finish the sentence.

The thought of that caused another stab of pain in my heart.

"Mum!" I groaned. "Why is everything so unfair in this world? Why are there children like me, who have everything, and then children like Domenico, who have got nothing except for bad luck? Why does God not help him?"

Mum smiled. "But God is helping him! By sending Mrs Galiani and you, for example!"

"Yes, but ... he still does not have any parents!"

"No. You know, we do not always get an answer to every question. God is almighty but he cannot just get his magic wand out and make it all work out. He needs people and hearts that help him. People like you. I believe that your friendship has helped Domenico a lot. Mrs Galiani told me how many good things have happened thanks to you. Believe me, God sees every sorrow and he cries every tear with us. And his eyes are looking for people who can help accomplish his work day and night. We humans often expect some great miracle when God's helping hand is so close. It can be a nice neighbour who gives you flowers, a man who donates money for hungry children or a girl like you who takes care of her friend. Or even a butterfly that sits down on your hand and shows you that God likes you. Or a beautiful sunset. Or a bird that sings God's love songs to you. Or a lantern that shines for you. If you look for God with all your heart, you will find Him. If you knock on His door, He will answer and then even a garden full of thorns can become a garden full of roses. We can never grasp everything that happens between heaven and earth. But we can decide whether we want to believe in God or not. And if we believe in Him, we can keep our eyes open for the things God wants to do for other people through us. Do you understand what I mean, Maya?"

I had my eyes closed. This was Mum's special poetry; the way she explained things so beautifully. If only things were not that complicated. Mum's cool hand touched my forehead.

"Come on, honey, you should sleep a bit now. I am going to excuse you from the art class. You have had a bit of a shock. But you will be fine. I am sure that everything is going to be okay in the end."

The images were dancing wildly in front of my eyes when I was lying in my bed. They spun around my head faster and faster; I was caught up in a storm of impressions. The spinning finally made me so tired that I fell asleep and only woke up sometime in the late afternoon.

It was the most awful evening I had ever had. Time had never gone by as slowly. The weather had gone completely crazy; the wind had turned into a wild thunderstorm that had been raging over the city for hours. They were reporting the damages it left everywhere on the local radio station. Meteorologists called it the most violent storm in a decade. Cellars were flooded, houses were hit by lightning and trees were uprooted. There had been a power cut in the northern part of the city for the past hour. A man was dangerously hurt when a power pole hit him. The citizens were asked to stay in their houses. The world around us matched the world inside me. And there was no end in sight. I sat in the kitchen next to the radio, listening to the news reports. But nothing was as bad as the report they repeated every hour about what had happened at school this morning:

"Completely out of control, the offender hit a girl's head on the concrete ground several times until she lost consciousness and had to be taken to hospital, severely injured. She remains in a critical condition. The offender is on the run ..."

Domenico had managed to be on the news again, I thought bitterly.

"According to police information, the offender is a sixteen year old student who has come to attention previously due to his violent temper," the speaker indifferently closed the report.

I could not think or do anything sensible anymore. I spent the whole evening in the kitchen, staring out of the window with my head hanging down. I saw only rain. Just rain.

18. A stormy night

I was tossing and turning in my bed, covered in sweat. I could not stop thinking about Delia: the horrible puddle of blood, her face becoming paler and paler until life seemed to have flowed out of her body. And then I had to think about Domenico's terrible fate that had just become even worse. Gloomy visions of the future turned in my head. Visions of his future. Trapped, locked up in a place where all his hopes would be buried forever – just like himself. Young offenders' prison. Sentence. He would be marked forever; it would stay with him for the rest of his life: he is violent, he has got a criminal record. *What I want to be when I'm grown up? I used to want to become a famous athlete!*

I dug my fingernails into the pillow with such force that the fabric tore apart. No! No! This could not happen! My face was swollen and wet with tears. And those tears showed the truth that I had carried deep inside me all along: it was not over. The decision I had made under the lantern was unshakable. *No matter what happens, I will always stand by you.*

This was what I felt inside. This was what had taught me to fight in the past few weeks. What had torn me out of my safe world and brought me face to face with reality; a life with less securities.

I got up and aimlessly walked around in the darkness of my room. Was there not anything that I could do? Where was Domenico? Was there any chance I could see him at least one last time to tell him that I would stand by him, no matter what? I sat down on the window sill. There was no point in trying to sleep. The storm had finally subsided. I could see the lantern shining through the leaves of the trees. Far away, the thunder was still rolling. Suddenly, I knew it! I opened the window widely and put my head out into the dark, windy night. This was it! I knew where Domenico was hiding!

It was ten past eleven already. I listened for any noise in the house; the TV was not on anymore. I did not hesitate. This crazy idea had grabbed hold of me and no fear in the world could stop me now. On tiptoes, I went over to my wardrobe and pulled out a jumper to wear on top of my pyjamas. Shoes, however, were out of reach. They were all stored in a closet downstairs. So I would have make do with my slippers for this mission. Why not, anyway?

I had to be as quiet as possible, so I figured out a plan how to leave the house without my parents noticing. It involved the apple tree outside my window. I would climb on a branch and carefully find my way down the trunk, just like I did when I was a little girl.

I sat on the window sill and my feet felt for the thick branch that touched the house wall right underneath. Hopefully the wind would not get any stronger! Even in the dark, I found the branches I had to hold onto to climb down to the wet lawn safely. Domenico would have been proud of my acrobatic skills, I thought wistfully. I ran through the garden and over the street into the park. I nearly got pushed over by a strong gust of wind, but, strangely enough, I was not afraid. I only knew that I had definitely turned into my parents' nightmare, but I did not care right now. Everything had fallen apart and I had to move on in the ruins, where suffering further bruises was unavoidable.

The path seemed twice as long as usually when I hurried through the park trying to avoid the puddles. At that time of night and especially with that kind of weather nobody was in the park anymore. The restaurant at the lake was only dimly lit and seemed deserted. What scared me most was the botanical garden. Walking through the park like this was quite dangerous actually. I hurried over the slippery wooden bridge and up the path. My slippers were soaked already. Finally, I reached the small square lit by the lantern, which was shining in its imperishable beauty.

Slowly, I walked closer and looked around. But I could not see anyone. Everything was quiet; only I was shaking like a leaf. Hesitantly, I whispered Domenico's name. And once again, this time a bit louder. But then I shook my head. This was really stupid.

But suddenly something moved in the hedge next to the benches. I winced. "Maya, is that you?" I heard a voice asking warily from behind the plants.

"Yes, it's me! Are you in there, Nicky?"

Carefully, he crept out and stood in front of me grudgingly. His eyes wandered around nervously; he did not manage to look straight at me.

"What are ya doin' here?" he asked with a hoarse voice. "I thought you was angry with me?"

"I wanted to see how you are coping."

"Me? Why?" He waved his hand dismissively and tried to step out of the light. "Leave me alone, I'm a freakin' loser."

"No, you're not!"

"Yeah, I am! You are okay as you are. Leave me alone! Go away! I ... I'm just scum."

"No, you are not! Come on, let's sit on the bench." Pleadingly, I reached out to him. After a brief moment of hesitation, he followed me and waited for me to say something.

"I have been thinking a lot. What you did was wrong. But I am trying to understand you. Look, you injured Delia very badly. Mrs Galiani said that she might be disabled for the rest of her life."

His lips quivered and his whole face was twitching. "I heard it on the radio. It's so awful! I really didn't mean to ..."

"I know. But it still happened. Now we have to deal

with it. And so many other things happened, too. I can't sleep anymore, I'm so worried!"

"Man, I really didn't wanna drag you into this! Just go!"

"No, I want to help you," I replied firmly. "I promised you I would always stand by you!"

"You can't help me. What do you think they're gonna do with me if they find me!"

"I know the police are looking for you."

He did not say any more and stared up the lamppost. In the light of the lantern, he could not hide his desperation. I tried to grab his hand but he pulled it away. The wind blew his hair into his face. There were still flashes of lightning shooting through the sky, followed by the low growl of thunder in the distance.

"I think we're safe here till tomorrow morning," he mumbled. "If it don't start raining again."

And then?

He lifted his head and looked at me with glowing eyes. Did he sense that I knew more about him than he had shared with me? Yes, I was sure he did. He had this talent to see right into people.

What are you planning to do, Domenico?

It was as clear as the light of the lantern that was shining down on us. There was no way around it and he did not even need to say it out loud.

I'll do what you've guessed for a long time. I'm gonna become a memory. I'm gonna disappear.

"Nicky," I whispered, "you cannot leave!"

"If I stay here with you they're gonna lock me up," he muttered.

I winced when I heard a noise behind my back in the hedge. Had somebody found us? I grabbed Domenico's sleeve, but he stayed calm. Mingo crept out of the leaves and slowly stood up. The silver skull around his neck shone in the light of the lantern, flashing like a warning sign. His threatening aura paralysed my limbs. The cut on his cheek looked almost black now.

"Mingo, leave her alone. She's no threat," Domenico said and laid a protective arm around me.

"If she tell anyone where we are, I gonna kill her," Mingo hissed through his teeth and I knew that he was serious. I panicked and held my breath. Mingo lifted his hand and splayed out his fingers. In the sleeve of his leather jacket I could see the pointed blade of a knife. He opened the studded leather band around his wrist, and the next moment he held the knife in his hand. With a quick movement, he sent the knife shooting through the air, landing just a few centimetres away from my feet, point stuck in the ground. I did not doubt for a second that he was capable of the worst. I had never seen a fifteen-year-old who was this messed-up. He seemed much older to me.

"Mingo, put away the stupid knife!" Domenico barked. "Don't you dare hurtin' her! She's my girlfriend.

And the best friend I ever had!" He held me even stronger now.

"I am not going to tell anyone," I promised breathlessly.

Mingo still stared at me with his glowing eyes.

"Course she gonna blow the whistle on us, Nick! Gonna run to mummy 'n' daddy or to that teacher and tell'em everything. She's still a baby. A little girlie who reads books on ponies and stuff!" he hissed and then he started to swear in Italian.

Domenico spit something back in Italian and then they were caught up in a fierce discussion which I was not supposed to understand, it seemed. I realised that Italian was not only their mother tongue but, in this case, it was also their secret language.

Finally, Mingo was quiet. Without looking at me, he pulled the knife out of the mud, wiped it on his trousers and put it back under his wrist band before he lit a cigarette.

"Don't worry," Domenico whispered to me. "He is okay, really. He just wanna protect me, you know."

I nodded weakly. What was I supposed to say now? Domenico took the cigarettes from his brother's hand and tried to light one for himself in the violent gusts of wind. But he did not manage and finally threw the cigarette away, swearing. He was at the end of his tether. And so was I!

I put my hand on his shoulder, and he rested his head

against my arm. Mingo walked up and down in front of us and finally sat down on the other side of Domenico, handing him his half-smoked cigarette.

"Where are you going now?" I asked sadly. I had to speak up a bit, since the wind had become stronger again. Somewhere close to us, we heard a loud rattling noise. Domenico hesitated for a moment and blew out the smoke, caught up in his thoughts.

"To Sicily."

His words were followed by silence. They sounded heavy and irrevocable; somehow they were stronger than the wind. Now, he had said it out loud.

No, Domenico! You cannot become just a memory! Anything but that!

I could not say any more. The thought nearly killed me. Mingo looked at us silently.

"And school? What about school?" was the only thing I could come up with after a while.

"I'm not gonna manage anyway! Mingo's given up a long time ago."

"Stupid crap!" Mingo hissed. "I never gonna learn to read anyway. Never!"

What did he mean? Could he not read? An impressive bolt of lightning cut through the sky and made me feel even more worried. The realisation that there was nothing I could do about it all started to sink in.

"I would really like to help you two, but I just don't know what I could do! I really have to go home now. My parents cannot notice that I left the house. I climbed out of the window."

The twins looked at me in surprise.

"You climbed out of you window just to look for us?" Domenico asked disbelievingly. "Man! You're brave!"

Mingo showed a crooked smile and looked at me from head to toes. His eyes seemed to nearly devour me and I felt extremely embarrassed.

"Hey, Nick, look at that! She wears a pyjama!"

I looked down at myself ashamed. Did he have to make fun of me like that? But then I saw that Mingo's smirk had turned into a smile. For a brief moment, I forgot all about the problems, the pain and the strong wind and smiled back. Mingo lowered his eyes. All of a sudden, I felt very clearly how strong the bond between the two brothers was, how much they cared for each other. I would have liked to know more about them; right now, I would have loved to follow them to Sicily even. But this desire quickly subsided again. That would obviously never work. It was over. The end. We had to go separate ways.

"Come on, Maya, I'm gonna walk you home," Domenico said. "Don't want you to get into even more trouble cos of us." He stubbed out his cigarette on the bench so that it left a small black and brown burn mark on the wood.

"That's nice of you," I replied and looked at the mark disconcertedly. Why did he do these things? It seemed to me like an everlasting burn mark that would forever remind me of this night …

I wanted to say goodbye to Mingo, but he already retreated to the hedges with a brief wave of his hand.

"He's really shy," Domenico explained. "He's always like that when he likes someone."

"Mingo likes me?" I shook my head in surprise. The first raindrops had begun to fall again. I grabbed Domenico's hand. Our shadows were dancing in the light of the lanterns along the path. I studied our silhouettes and saw that Domenico was only a little bit taller than me. The tense silence between us was worse than the eerie sound of thunder above us.

"It's all just because of my stupid fits of rage," he finally mumbled. "I just couldn't watch her pick on you all the time. I got so angry that I didn't even know what I was doing anymore! It's really bad."

"Does that happen to you a lot?"

Embarrassed, he rubbed his nose. "Uhm … it's not the first time, I guess."

When we stood at our garden gate I mustered all my courage.

"Is it true that you take drugs? I mean, not like Mingo but …"

He nervously tried to avoid my gaze. "Who told you that? Janet?"

His hair was moist from the rain and it hung down onto his face. I pushed it to the side with my hand so that I could see his eyes. He did not give me an answer but I knew it anyway. The day on which he had jumped from the tower into the ice-cold water and his mood had changed so suddenly from really down to super-jivey had showed it clearly enough.

"I better let you go in ..." he mumbled.

"No, wait!" The pain in my chest became stronger and stronger. "When ... when are you going to leave? Will I see you again before you go?"

He took my hands and slightly squeezed them. The rain was pouring down on us mercilessly now, but neither of us really noticed.

"We're gone tomorrow morning," he said silently.

I nodded grimly and tried to swallow my tears. But they were stronger. He smiled a bit and carefully wiped them away with his fingers.

"Man, I'm gonna miss you real bad, you can be sure of that! But if I stay I'm probably gonna end up in jail. And then we ain't gonna be together anymore anyway, right? And it would kill Mingo if he was alone. Did you see how sick he is because of the drugs? I never wanna let him down ever again. He's the best friend I've got in the world."

His face was wet, and I could not tell whether it was from the rain or from his tears. "And now there's you of course," he silently added.

"Nicky, believe me, Mrs Galiani is really understanding about the two of you!" I nearly shouted. "I think she could help you. You and Mingo!"

"She can't help us. Look, Maya, I'm not stupid, I know that I've screwed up big time."

"But it's not your fault that your parents have never looked after you."

"No … but that's not an excuse for everything."

There it was again. This clear, undamaged spot inside him. I did not understand it really and could not explain how I knew it, but I just felt that this spot existed. And as if he sensed that I had found something there, he began to listen to himself, trying to bring out something that he was trying to understand. I would have waited the whole night out in the rain for him to explain it to me. He obviously struggled to find the right words to make it more or less clear.

"There are those dreams of Sicily. They've come back. I dream that our mum is waiting for us. Our real mum, you know, not this … you know! And I dream of a lantern in front of our house. Mingo always says it's all rubbish, but I dream of it every night!"

"Tell me more, please," I begged when he stopped talking.

"And then – I don't know. I always feel real bad when I wake up. I'm really sad and all cos it's not real."

"When did you start dreaming about it again?" I had a faint idea.

"I can tell you exactly. On the night when we came to the lantern together, that's when it started again."

"And how was it really in Sicily? Do you remember any of it?"

"Nah. It's a long time ago. Oh man! Stupid rain … I gotta go … Mingo's waiting for me!"

"Wait, just a moment, please! Is that why you want to go back there now? Because of the dreams?" I insisted even though time was rushing away with every drop of the pouring rain.

He shrugged his shoulders and obviously seemed to struggle with all my questions. While he nervously tried to find a cigarette in his pockets, I searched for the right words in my head. He had to stay a few minutes longer! And now I knew what I wanted to tell him.

"Nicky, do you believe in God?"

"God? I dunno. Why would he bother about me, anyway? I'm not a good person. I stole … and maybe I ruined Delia's life …"

I feverishly tried to figure out what to say. Mum always had such good answers. But then I suddenly had an idea.

"Nicky, if I like you as much as I do, even though you have done some bad things, then God must like you a thousand times more even! It does say in the Bible that God is love!" I was worried that this sounded a bit too soppy and pious to him. Too pretentious maybe. But I was still glad that I had said it.

He looked at me in some resignation.

"This all sounds very nice, Maya. But my life is just a pile of rubbish and waste."

His eyes were darker than ever before, and I could see how the darkness spread around him and threatened to swallow him.

"But rubbish and waste can be cleaned up. And then you can sow seeds on the clear ground and you can take care of it, water it and finally, one day, roses will grow out of it!" I continued to fight.

"That sounds so easy. No … my last bit of life is buried. It's all buried under a rock," his voice was very small now. "Shovels and watering cans ain't gonna help. You'd need an excavator. But even that would probably fail …" He inhaled deeply. "If Delia don't get well again, my life's over. Even God can't do nothing about that."

"But God will forgive you if you ask him to. He is going to forgive your mistakes so that you will be able to make a fresh start."

"You think?" Something in his eyes had begun to glow. Was it possible that he had not lost all his hope yet?

"Nicky, you told me once that you used to believe in Him and pray to Him too. Don't you remember?"

"Yeah …"

"Was that when you lived in Sicily?"

"I dunno …"

"But I do! You used to live in a convent with a nun. She looked after the two of you," I said. "Mrs Galiani told me that."

He closed his eyes. "Yeah, everyone says that."

"It's true, Nicky!"

He only shrugged his shoulders. I would have loved to know what he was thinking and whether he believed me. But his expression did not reveal anything.

"I believe that your dreams and all those pictures you have in your head are real," I said silently. "The nun was like a mother to you because your real mum did not take care of you. And maybe there was a lantern in front of the convent, too. You are just trying to block it all out!"

He opened his eyes again. "You're really crazy, Maya!" he said and suddenly began to smile again. "Except for Mingo, I am probably the worst screwed-up guy ever and you … you're always really nice to me. I'd like to be like you. I'd give anything for a fresh start! I'd never steal again or swear or smoke. And I would never beat anyone up anymore. I'd so much like to have a dream for my life, like you … Maybe I manage to start all over again in Sicily."

I looked to the ground pensively. And then I did something I had never dared to do before: I hugged him. He threw away his cigarette and pressed me against him. For a while, I remained like this, my head resting on his shoulder. I thought of a thousand things I wanted to say to him in this one moment. But I had to accept that we had run out of time. I had shed many tears because of Domenico, probably more than in the past fourteen years of my life put together. There was only one thing to figure out now.

"Will we ever see each other again?"

"I don't know, Maya. I don't know if I'll manage. But I'll never forget you."

"We could call each other!"

"No," he said. "No, we can't."

It was a clear no, not allowing for any more questions. He pulled out his mobile phone from his pocket and handed it to me.

"Keep it. It's a present. So that you've got your own now, okay?" After a brief hesitation, he added: "I've nicked it though."

"Nicky …" I sighed. I did not know how I would deal with all this. And there was no time for all the questions I still had in my head.

He turned away from me and coughed again silently. I was really worried about him. He was soaked, which was the worst that could happen in his state.

"Promise me something, Nicky: promise me that you go home now immediately and put on dry clothes. And that you go and see a doctor first thing when you arrive in Sicily. And that you stop smoking!"

He nodded as if thinking: "Anything else?" We silently walked over to the apple tree. Domenico helped me to climb up to the branch leading to my window. From there it was easy for me to get in. Without making a sound I jumped through the window into my warm room. When he was standing in the pouring rain under the window, looking up to me I had a thought. I had to be quick, but I thought it was of great importance.

“Nicky, wait!” I whispered and ran to my bed. On the bedside table there was my small Bible, stuck together with tape. Quickly I grabbed a marker, the tip of which was already drying out, and wrote on the first page: For Domenico from Maya. I love you! Don’t forget me. And always remember: Jesus is on your side!

“Nicky!” I silently called him when I was back at the window. His dark eyes looked at me with a hint of longing. “Catch this! It’s a present!” The small book fluttered through the rain, losing two or three pages on the way, and fell right into Domenico’s open hands.

He whispered a silent “Thank you,” pressed the mangled book against his heart and quickly hurried out of the garden.

I waved after him sadly until he was gone, and then I looked over to the lantern in the park for a long while. Something inside me began to hurt incredibly. The fact that this had been the last time I would ever see him slowly started to settle in and spread through my whole being like a creeping weed. My tears fell on the window sill. The rain hit my face with all its power. It was only when the church bell rang half past twelve that I closed the window, tore the soaked pyjamas off my body and lay down on my bed to cry myself to sleep.

Only an hour later, I woke with a start after a horrible dream and ran over to the window. The mansion in the park was pitch black. No light in the dark. I suppressed a yell. The lantern! What had happened to the lantern? Or was I still dreaming?

The walls of my room seemed to turn and twist when I struggled to find the light switch. I could not bear it any longer and started to sob loudly. It was not long before Mum stood in my room and picked me up from the floor to carry me over to my bed carefully. Her cool hand softly stroked my cheek, wet with tears, and her voice slowly lulled me back into sleep.

But even sleeping did not help. I was haunted in my dreams by Domenico and the lantern and I fidgeted around in my bed restlessly. When I finally fell into a short deep sleep, the new day had begun to dawn, and when I woke up again I knew that this day would bring a lot of change.

19. Mrs Galiani knows it all

Chaos reigned outside. It was not raining as strongly as the night before anymore, but some roads were closed because of fallen tree branches and water damage. I looked around hesitantly and opened my umbrella. To my utter relief, Mum had decided not to interrogate me this morning even though I was sure she guessed more than I would have liked her to. My wet pyjamas must have revealed a lot for a start …

A boy with a baseball cap worn the wrong way round and a cigarette between his lips stepped out from behind a tree. I only noticed him properly when he blocked my way. My heart skipped a beat.

"Nicky?"

He pulled the cap into his face and looked at me with watery eyes. It was only then that I saw the scar on his cheek.

"Mingo?" I could not forget about his threat with the knife the night before and my body automatically prepared to run away if necessary. But it was not.

"Wait!" He awkwardly searched for something in his worn-out leather jacket and finally produced a big, very crinkled envelope, handing it to me.

"My brother told me to give that to ya." His voice sounded dull, somehow quite out of it. Curiously, I turned the envelope in my hands. On the front there was a beautiful heart with my name in it. A raindrop fell right onto it and blurred the colour of the marker. I pressed the letter against my jacket and looked at Mingo.

"Where is Domenico?"

"Can't tell. The cops're after us."

"Please! It is important to me."

"Nah. Nick battered the lamp last night. Was really messed-up." He took a deep drag of his cigarette so that his cheeks hollowed.

I was cold in my thin jacket. The temperatures had fallen drastically. What he told me made me stop breathing for a few seconds. Our lantern … the sign of our friendship … battered?

"Why did he do that?"

"Dunno. He just freaked out! Came back, cried and all and threw a stone at the thing. Man, believe me, Romeo was bleedin'."

"Because of … me?"

"What you think? He's mad about ya!" His eyelids twitched nervously.

"Oh, Mingo, please tell me where he is. I won't tell anyone. I promise! I just can't bear this any longer!"

He flicked his cigarette to the floor and stubbed it out with his foot. I could see that he was wobbling a little. I nervously tugged on the sleeve of his jacket.

"Alright," he finally gave in. "Let's go a bit away from here. Your parents shouldn't see me. You live here, righ'?"

Yes, of course. Dad had not gone to his practice yet and could come out of the house any second. And Mingo with his skull necklace, the old leather jacket and the scar on his cheek would probably have made him freak out entirely. Even worse, since he did not know that Domenico had a twin brother, he would probably have thought that Mingo was Domenico.

We hid behind the neighbour's shed. I made room for Mingo under my umbrella and waited impatiently for him to light another cigarette with his trembling fingers. It fell out of his hands and he had to bend down to pick it up from the ground.

"Nick is with a friend. We slept there last night when the rain was … eh, worse. He told me bring that to Maya, cos he couldn't do it himself. He's really down."

I closed my eyes for a moment. I had to stay calm; just had to. The day had only just started and I would have to face a lot today.

"How are you going to travel to Sicily? By train?"

"Nah, Mike gonna give us a lift to the Swiss border. He's the guy we stayed with last night. We gotta get away from here soon, or Nick gets loads of trouble. Cos he beat up that girl from the school. Man, I really don't want Nick to go to prison, Maya! He's really good, he can do everything! He can make summin' in his life. No hope for me, I'm done. Drugs mess it up for me. I'm in it deep. Guess you can see that … I bet Nick told you."

I nodded shyly. His face was contorted with pain

when he continued: “Get what I mean? I’m complete rubbish, can’t even read. The whole thing with the alphabet and all. They made fun of me at school cos of that. Never gonna go back there again. Never!” He nervously wiped his eyes.

“I know that … I was bullied at school too!” I tried to comfort him. “Not because I could not read, but because of the Bible.”

This made his eyes come to life for the first time this morning. “Yeah, the Bible. Really good that you gave that to Nick. He carry it around with him all the time. Maybe it gonna help him. And I protect him, too. He never fall into this misery like me. I gonna kill everyone who try to do summin’, I swear! Like that!” He got his knife out and held it under my nose, so that I moved back terrified.

“Don’t be afraid. I never ever do that to you.” He carefully touched my shoulder.

“Does your mum know that you are going away?” I asked.

“My mum? Forget it! She’s happy to get rid of us. The booze made her nuts. She come home in the middle of the night with men, strangers, puking around … everywhere. You know what it’s like … sleep out in the park cos your mum’s screamin’ around, fighting with her johns? When she’s sick in bed whole day? She’s a wreck, I can tell you. But you’ve got a nice mum. Nick told me.”

“Yes. It … it’s so difficult. I would really like to help

you, but I can't. What are you going to do in Sicily? Do you know anyone you can stay with?"

"Nick wanna go to a convent. He's gone mad. Wanna find our real mum. Always he dreams of her. But that's just psycho dreams. Made-up stuff. We ain't got no other mum. I don't care where we live in Sicily. I just want Nick to be happy. Gotta go now, Maya, or I gonna be late. We wanna take off at eight."

"And you? What about you?" I asked and held on to his leather jacket, as if I could stop him like that. "Do you think you are going to be happy in Sicily?"

He shrugged his shoulders. "If they all leave me alone there and I can get my stuff, I'm fine. Sicily's gonna be great, I'm sure. Don't have no choice now, righ'? They gonna lock Nick up."

"I guess …" Suddenly Mingo was my main concern. It hurt to see that he did not worry about himself at all.

"You should really try to get off the drugs, Mingo. It's such a shame. You could make so much of your life! You are so nice!"

He looked at me slightly shocked. "Long time I don't hear that," he mumbled. Before I knew what happened, he put his arms around me and briefly hugged me. I was overwhelmed, for I realised that this hug was something special and that Mingo rarely hugged anyone, if at all.

Without saying anything else, he turned away from me and ran off at break-neck speed, nearly hitting a parked car. I stayed there rooted to the ground, not able to move my feet. I felt the envelope in my hand, but it took me another while until I was able to tear it open with shaking hands. Several strange things were in there: a letter, three sheets of paper with drawings, an article from a magazine with the picture of a good looking athlete and a crinkled poster of an airplane. My knees felt weak and I looked for somewhere to sit down. I forgot about everything around me when I read the few lines of the letter that had already started to get blurred by the rain:

Deer Maya,
I'm sorry that I killd the lantern. Wos completly nuts last nite. The picturs are 4 u, I made them wen I wos yunger. U can keep them please giv Patrick the pictur of the plain. Plees Maya if Delia gets well can u tie this band to the lantern? Do it on the last day of hollidays cos a frend of us will travel to Sicily and he will tel me if the band is there and so I no if Delia is OK or not. Tel her that I'm sory if u speek to her.
I wil neva forget u. Ti amo! Domenico

I had another look in the envelope and found one of the leather bands with the silver thorns he had always worn around his neck. On the last day of school holidays – if Delia got well again. I shivered thinking about it.

The ringing of the church bell reminded me to hurry up. I wanted to cry but I could not. I still felt this hard lump in my throat and did not even notice that the rain had become stronger again. I pressed the letter against my chest briefly and had a look at the drawings. They were extraordinarily good but I could not figure out their meaning immediately. I did not have the time right now anyway.

I had a quick look at the photo of the athlete, too, and then I put it all away in my school bag. I ran to school as quickly as my legs would carry me. When I arrived, soaked, I just saw Mrs Galiani leave the teachers' room. A wave of panic took hold of me and nearly forced me to the ground. If only she did not hold me back and interrogate me now! That would lead to a catastrophe!

But Mrs Galiani had either not seen me or ignored me on purpose. Her poker face did not show me anything about what I needed to know so desperately. I wished I could keep my cool as well as she could. But I looked like a plucked chicken, and Patrick, who had been waiting for me in front of the classroom, was visibly shocked by my state.

"W-what happened?" he gasped. "H-have you g-got any news f-from Nicky? T-they are talking about him in there. They all h-hate him now! It's r-really bad!"

His eyes widened when I handed him the envelope. I

wondered how I even managed to stand on my feet right now.

It took a while for Patrick to understand. He read the letter and stared at the drawings. Carefully, he took out the poster of the airplane and pensively flattened it with his hands, as if it was a precious treasure. His eyes were wet. But we did not have any more time as we heard familiar steps on the stairs.

Quickly, we tried to find our way through the classroom without attracting too many evil looks. How on earth should we concentrate on irregular French verbs now? But to our surprise Mrs Galiani entered the room instead of Mme Dupont. Mrs Galiani looked so serious that everyone stopped talking immediately.

"You do not need to get out your French books!" the teacher said with her low voice. "I have swapped classes with Mme Dupont. She will teach the last periods of the day. We have got something important to talk about, and I can imagine that you would struggle concentrating on anything else right now." She gave Patrick and me a quick look. Was there a hint of a smile on her lips? A small ray of hope?

"You are probably all very concerned about yesterday's incident. So am I. I would like to tell you a few things. First of all, Delia will presumably not be left disabled. I think we do not need to worry about her too much anymore. As for Domenico, he will most likely not return to your class. To be entirely clear: what he did was terrible! But before you all judge him and talk badly about him, I would like you to know that he had an extremely difficult childhood. He grew up without parents who were there for him like yours. From a very young age, he was on his own. Many things went wrong in his life and those things have all left their marks. Maya and Patrick were his friends, and I would like to point out that what happened is not their fault. It was never Maya's intention for Domenico to hurt Delia! He may have done it for her, but Delia provoked it by bullying Maya for no reason. Maybe you should all think about that, too."

Her words obviously had an impact. It was so silent that I began to be afraid that everyone could hear my heart beating like crazy. Delia would get well again! I was so glad for her! And Domenico would not have to live with that horrible burden. There was nothing in the world that could have been a greater relief for me right now. I took the big envelope I had hidden under the table and touched the leather band.

Manuela shyly held up her hand. "And what will happen to Domenico now?" she asked.

"Well, we do not know that exactly for now. But I will let you know as soon as I receive more information. Above all, I do not want you to spread any invented rumours. If there are any more questions, please come to see me."

We spent the rest of the class discussing class spirit and outsiders. I thought it was a good idea to bring it up, but Patrick and I felt a bit uneasy because we were at the centre of attention. Mrs Galiani called us to her desk at the end of the class. "Maya and Patrick, would you please come to see me in the teachers' room in the ten o'clock break? I have to talk about a few things with the two of you."

This was it! I started sweating when I thought about the promise I had made to the twins. We had to keep it a secret that Domenico and Mingo had fled to Sicily, no matter what!

Shortly after ten, we nervously made our way to the teachers' room. Mrs Galiani offered us biscuits.

"Please sit down and help yourselves," she said. "I have already made sure you are exempted from the next class. This is extremely important. Have you got any news from Domenico?"

"No," I said, my heart beating wildly, hoping that I would not blush. We sat down on the small sofa, while Mrs Galiani sat on an office chair opposite us. My hands were wet.

Mrs Galiani leaned over and looked at me attentively; nearly a bit motherly. "Maya my dear, believe me, you are not helping Domenico by lying for him! I already know that he has fled towards Sicily."

I gawped at her. And then I could not withhold my tears any longer. I broke my promise and under sobs admitted what had happened at the mansion in the park the night before. Mrs Galiani stroked my hair, trying to comfort me.

"What the two of you did is amazing! I was really impressed. Nobody managed to gain Domenico's trust ever before. He has changed for the better since he started spending time with you. However, you are no mental health professionals. You could not have mended everything that had gone wrong in the past fifteen years. Do you understand that? It is not your fault! I offered him my help so many times, but he did not want to accept it. I think he has just had too many bad experiences to be able to believe in anything."

"Oh, Mrs Galiani, Domenico is a nice boy, really!" I blurted out. "Everyone only ever sees the horrible, mean criminal in him, which is not true. He is very intelligent!"

"I know, Maya. I understand better than you think, even if I was always very strict with him. I really like him. And I know that he has got potential." She stood up and started to walk up and down, thinking. It looked as though she was fighting with herself, debating whether to tell us something she should not.

"The police were here this morning. They wanted to interrogate you as witnesses. But I managed to hold them off so you will not have to face them. When they came here after the burglary at Mr Biedermann's, I tried to protect Domenico with everything that was in my power. This might come as a surprise to you, but I knew straight away that he had stolen Mr Biedermann's money. He did things like that at his old school, too."

"You knew that?" Again, I was perplexed.

"Of course," she said quietly. "It put me in a very difficult position. I knew that he was the culprit and I could have told the police straight away … but I did not have the heart to do it. I wanted to leave the police out of this, to prevent him being convicted again. But Mr Biedermann insisted. I spoke to Domenico privately in the teacher's room to discuss the incident, but he just denied it all."

So many knots dissolved in my head. Mrs Galiani got up and came back with a packet that was wet from the rain.

"He put this in my letterbox yesterday night, or made somebody deposit it there. It is nearly the full amount that was stolen. I was very happy because this is the first time that he is trying to make up for what he has done. I think he did this mainly thanks to your friendship." She looked at us appreciatively.

"Mr Biedermann does not know about it yet, and he will never find out who stole his money. The three of us are the only ones who will ever know; we will keep it to ourselves, do you understand?"

I could not believe it. She was the most decent, nicest and fairest teacher I had ever met! If only Domenico had trusted her!

I fished the drawings out of the envelope, the meaning of which I had not quite understood. I hoped that Mrs Galiani would be able to fill some gaps. She took the pictures carefully and looked at each one of them thoroughly.

"Yes, Domenico is very talented. Mrs Wilde showed me the portrait he had drawn of you, Maya. I would have liked to help him make something out of that. He was always extremely good at sports, too. He dreamt of being discovered by a talent scout one day. And then move up the ladder! Because of his success and his looks he had many admirers in his old class, especially among the girls. But he could not deal with it. He became arrogant and was bossing around the entire class. He beat up other boys who tried to compete with him. Exactly like he did when he arrived here, before you became his friends."

"Was his brother as talented as he is?" I could not forget Mingo's sad statement of this morning: *No hope for me, I'm done.*

"At that time, Mingo had a complete break-down. His performance at school suffered enormously because of his drug consumption. Plus he is dyslexic. Which means that he has difficulties when it comes to reading and writing. This has always been a big problem for him. He recognised single letters by their shape but he could not read entire words. He just could not gather the words and sentences in their totality. Therefore, we had to separate the brothers. We had fought for Domenico to stay at Leonhardt School; he is far too intelligent to drop out of school. But we could not help Mingo. I do not think it was easy for the two brothers to be separated."

Mrs Galiani concentrated on the drawings again and put the first one of them down on the table. It was quite ugly; showing a scary skull with a cigarette between its teeth and a syringe piercing through its temple.

"The message of this one seems fairly clear," I said and Mrs Galiani nodded. "Yes, Domenico started smoking at a very young age."

"He seems to be really bothered about it," I continued. "But he told me that he cannot manage to stop."

"Yes, there is a sad story about this. His coach had cautioned him several times because he was smoking so much, and then he finally threw him out of the team. It was a very heavy blow for him, for his dream to become a famous athlete depended on that team. Nevertheless, he did not seem to find the strength to stop smoking and he suffered a lot from his failure. I really hope that he will not follow his brother into his severe drug addiction! I find the drawing with the syringe in the skull very worrying in that context."

The second picture was much more mysterious. As opposed to the first one, it was very pretty and it had been drawn with coloured pens. It was the portrait of a little girl with big dark eyes, brightened by a ray of sunlight. Her long, black hair seemed to gently caress her face, like a veil. The drawing was so fantastic that I held my breath and Mrs Galiani even smiled.

"I know this picture," she said. "He drew it in art class at his old school and it won him the school art competition. The girl is the twin's little half-sister. She has got a different dad than Domenico and Mingo. Her name is Bianca and she lives with her father. Their mother had married him in Germany, but the marriage did not last very long. The man was violent and beat his wife and the children. Domenico and Mingo looked after the baby girl when they were still little themselves while their mother had to stay in a psychiatric ward for some time. I give the two of them a lot of credit for that!"

"And Bianca now lives with that mean man?"

"Apparently, yes. Unfortunately, I do not know everything, Maya."

We were now looking at the last picture, and I guessed that it would answer one of my most important questions. It was so terrible but looked so real that it made me shiver all over. It was drawn mainly with red marker and ball pen and showed a knife that divided the page with a gaping wound. Drops of blood were running down from it and flowed together to form a cross at the bottom of the page.

How could he draw such a horrible picture? Mrs Galiani did not say anything, looking at it for a long time. I saw how she nodded very subtly. She knew something about it, no doubt. Was she not allowed to say anything about it or did she not want to? I looked at her questioningly.

"Okay, I will tell you the story. But you have to promise that you will keep it strictly to yourselves. Because I am officially not permitted to talk about it!" She got up and closed the window. The air in the room was damp and heavy. I could feel the sweat running down my spine.

"When Domenico was excluded from the sports team, he had a breakdown. He did not cope well with the situation and hated himself so much for his failure that he inflicted very bad wounds on his body with a knife. He even cut his wrists. Now you know where he got those scars you saw and why he did not want to swim with everyone. It was also the reason why I did not make him take off his t-shirt. And as for the wounds on his wrists …"

"… he hides them underneath the leather bands!" I realised the horrible truth. Oh God! If I had known that! None of the reasons I had figured out for him to wear all those wrist bands was as upsetting as the truth.

"But why did he not just join a sports club in his free time? There are so many of them!"

"Yes, of course. But he did not have the money for that. His mother worked as a model, but never earned very much. And she always spent the money on alcohol. I suggested to Domenico that my husband and I finance his subscription to a sports club. But he did not want to accept any kind of help! Can I see that magazine article he gave you, Maya?" Mrs Galiani asked.

"I do not know who that is supposed to be. Some athlete, but I really have no idea …"

But Mrs Galiani had an answer to this too, and one that left us speechless.

"It is possible that this is his father."

"His …?"

"His real father!" she repeated.

"But this is a famous athlete. Like …"

"Domenico's mother insists that this is the man by whom she got pregnant at the time. You know the story, Maya. She is convinced it is the man on the pictures." Mrs Galiani looked at me and Patrick, but she did not want to tell the story again.

"Do you think that it is true?"

"I do not know. It is not impossible. Do you see the man's ginger hair? And it would explain Domenico's talent at sports. But it is all just a guess." She handed the picture back to me.

"Was this the reason why his mother came to Germany with the children?"

"I cannot tell you that, Maya. I do not know why they left Sicily."

We sat there for a while, not saying anything. The picture was nearly complete now. But one question still bothered me.

"How do you know all this? I mean … Domenico did not tell even us an awful lot. How come you …?"

Mrs Galiani's face looked very tired all of a sudden. But she had already told us so much that she apparently decided that she might as well reveal this last bit of information to us too.

"I have already told you, Maya, that my husband used to be the twins' former class teacher. If you always wanted children of your own but could not have any, then you are even more touched by the fate of a child who was not wanted or rejected. You might be touched a lot more than usual. My husband and I had thought about having Domenico and Mingo live with us. We spoke to their mother a lot when she was in the psychiatric ward. She cried and complained that she could not cope with her failed sons. The boys supposedly attacked her in their anger and hit her sometimes, too. She even said Mingo had threatened her with a knife. She was afraid of them."

Right now, I really wished I had not heard any of this. I did not want the nice memory of Domenico being blurred and destroyed by this horrible picture. But the look in Mrs Galiani's eyes clearly showed me that I had to face reality. After all, this was the reason why she had told us all she knew.

"We would have liked to offer them a stable home, but the twins refused to live with us. They are like two wounded animals that cannot be caught. You have seen it yourselves," she added silently and returned the drawings to me, too.

"I cannot tell you any more. I have to finish this story without getting to know the end. A jigsaw puzzle I have to put aside, unable to find the last pieces."

"D-do you think the t-twins will find their p-peace in S-sicily?" Patrick enquired worriedly.

"I really hope they will! They had their only bit of normal childhood in Sicily when they lived with this nun. And maybe this will help them. I cannot do any more for them now." It was a brief answer that did not leave room for any more questions. We would probably never find out what Mrs Galiani really thought about it. She got up and walked to the office. "There is one last thing I wanted to tell you: I have spoken to the headmaster and to the other teachers. You can change classes if the situation does not improve. The incident with Domenico and Delia may be a turning point, but we will have to wait and see. Maya, how about you visit Delia at the hospital and apologise in Domenico's name? He wrote something along those lines, didn't he? Maybe it would be a good chance to bury the hostility between you two. What do you think?"

I nodded hesitantly. I was thinking about something else too: about Domenico's leather band that I had to tie around the lamppost on the last day of the holidays.

"I will let you know as soon as Delia is discharged from intensive care. But now you have to go back to your classes. And I have to prepare some important things for my next class."

"Oh, Mrs Galiani, can I ask one more question? A very personal one?" I quickly asked before she could hurry off. "Is it allowed to accept a present of which you know that it has probably been stolen?"

"Hmm. I do not think so, no," Mrs Galiani replied. "What exactly is it?"

"I cannot tell you that. But could you still give me some advice? Please?"

"Well, you could try to find out where it comes from and offer the shop to pay for it. And if you do not know who it was stolen from, you could donate the monetary value of it to a charitable organisation. Is this any help?" Mrs Galiani asked with a knowing smile.

"Yes, thank you very much!" And with that, Patrick and I ran back to our classroom.

When I came home for lunch, Dad was waiting for me in the living room. My body started to shake when I saw his eyes which were looking at me sadly but very lovingly at the same time. And suddenly – as had happened so many times already these days! – I started to cry. I had a dad who worried about me. Domenico, however, did not even know who his dad was! Dad might have been a bit complicated sometimes, but he was still my dad and he loved me! Should I not be extremely grateful for that?

Dad picked me up when I fell to my knees, sobbing. He held me, hugged me and stroked my head. And I cried on his shoulder. I cried it all out; everything that had cost me so much energy in the past few weeks. Dad just held me and did not say a word. There were no reproaches or criticism. Nothing. When I had finished crying, I felt like a lot of pressure had flooded out of me.

20. A new light

About two weeks had passed. I was on the way to the hospital with a huge bunch of flowers on my arm. Honestly, I was nearly as nervous as I had been when I had gone to see Domenico at his place. But I guess I had started to get used to nerve-racking situations recently. I had nothing to lose anymore now. I said a silent prayer and walked through the glass doors. The woman at the reception told me the room number.

Bravely, I turned to the lifts. My heart was beating at the speed of a pneumatic drill. I really wished Patrick had come with me. But Mrs Galiani had explicitly recommended to me to go alone.

The door to the room was slightly open, and I could see that Delia did not have any visitors. With a shaking hand, I pushed the door open further and stepped in.

Delia did not look at me to start with. She was concentrating on a magazine. But was this really Delia? No make-up, pale, hair tied back to a pony tail and watery eyes? No varnish on her fingernails? Was this Delia Samantha, the prettiest and most powerful girl at school who was lying there on the big bed, small and almost a bit helpless? She was still very pretty, but she seemed as unremarkable and average as me. Not even her hair looked as golden as it used to. Domenico had been right! Below the make-up she was incredibly pale!

All this I saw before I walked closer and mumbled a shy “Hello.” Delia looked up and her eyes widened in surprise when she saw me, of all people, standing in front of her with a huge bunch of flowers.

“You?” she asked incredulously.

“Yes …” I could not bring myself to say anything else.

“Why?”

“I wanted to talk with you about a few things … Is there a vase for the flowers?”

“There’s one over there!” She pointed at the windowsill. I went to get it and walked over to the sink to fill it with water. This was weird. All of a sudden, my nervousness was gone.

“How long do you have to stay here for?” I asked when I returned to the side of the bed.

“About another week. But I can only go back to school after the summer holidays. The head injury was not exactly harmless …” She turned her head and pulled her hair to the side so that I could see the massive wound on the back of her head. It had been stitched.

“I … I am extremely sorry that Domenico did this to you because of me. I really did not want anything like this to happen.”

“Oh, well, I guess it was my mistake, too,” Delia said, much to my amazement. “I have been thinking a lot. You can’t help thinking when you nearly … well … end up with permanent brain damage!”

“What do you mean?”

"Well … you never did anything to me. If I'm honest …" She was chewing her fingernails nervously.

"And why did you always bully me?" I asked carefully.

"I … I don't know! I …" And suddenly the words came flooding out. "It's so stupid! I've got a little sister and we are fighting all the time. She's such a cheeky brat and she makes my life hell whenever she can. The worst thing is, though, that my dad likes her a lot more than me. She's a lot better at school, much cleverer. For my dad, that's what counts the most! Oh, I know that this is no excuse, but I always envied you. For your parents, for your house and everything! You're so clever and I … well, I'm not. I can get nothing straight. I'm just a bit too stupid to get all the stuff at school … maths, physics and French and all. My dad always says that he'd rather have an ugly, intelligent daughter than a pretty, dumb one like me! Oh Maya, I just hate it! All I want for him is to be proud of me for once, too! But I guess that's never gonna happen …"

I sat there, staring at Delia in disbelief: the girl who had made my life hell so many times and for whom I suddenly felt extremely sorry now. I could only guess how hard it had been for Delia to confess all this. I was surprised, once more, at what could be discovered in others once their mask had gone. I had learned a lot about this phenomenon in the past few weeks.

"Oh, Delia, you will not believe what I always thought," I heard myself say. "I always wanted to be as pretty as you. I had looked at myself in the mirror for hours sometimes, thinking how boring and ugly I was."

"Oh, man! And I made you believe that! But you're not ugly at all, Maya. You're pretty. What a stupid cow I am!"

All anger I had felt towards this girl for years just melted away like snow in the sunshine in this one, brief moment. It felt as though someone had opened a window in a hot, stuffy room.

"No, I get it, Deli! If you get hurt you have to let off steam somehow," I said understandingly. "It was the same for Domenico. Just a lot worse."

"Domenico? What do you mean?"

"He did not have anybody to look after him. He does not even know his real dad. His mum wanted to strangle him and his brother when they were born. Oh, I should not have said that ..." I held my hand in front of my mouth shocked.

"I'm not gonna tell anyone," Delia promised immediately. "But what's that you're saying? That sounds horrible!"

"His brother has got massive problems with drugs and he cannot read properly. Can you imagine that?"

"No!" Delia looked at me with big eyes. "Is that really true? He told me an entirely different story. I always thought he was so great, because he was so experienced and handsome and strong and mainly because he was older than me."

I nodded understandingly. "I think he only beat you up because he was so desperate."

"Mrs Galiani explained something like that too, but not in that many words. And you couldn't help him?"

"We tried."

Delia closed her eyes. "Mrs Galiani also told me that he has run away with his brother Mingo. Do you know more about that, Maya?"

I just wanted to start when the nurse came through the door reminding us politely that the visiting hours would be over in five minutes. So I just said: "Let's talk about this next time! But one thing you should know: Domenico always suffered severely from his violent temper, and he was extremely sorry he did this to you. He told me in a letter to tell you this."

"I'm not angry at him …" Delia's voice sounded tired now. "Oh God, compared to his problems, mine seem ridiculous! There's so much I still need to think about." Her pale blue eyes rested firmly on me. "How are you feeling with all this? I mean, with him being gone and all?"

I could not reply straight away. I thought about the past two weeks. I thought about the morning when Patrick and I had finally had to give evidence to the police. How horrible I had felt, because I had to give away Domenico's secret. I thought about the picture of little Bianca that one of the policemen had showed me. Bianca, who had been reported missing a few days before and who they assumed had been abducted by her brothers and taken to Sicily. And then I thought about the horrible moment when the picture disappeared in the policeman's folder again and I was not allowed to get any more information whatsoever about her. I thought about how I still cry nearly every night before I fall asleep, staring at Domenico's drawings for hours. I thought about his life, his past, his secret, about everything I had never been allowed to understand entirely …

"I miss him. I constantly think about him. If only I knew that he is fine, it would be half as bad. But he did not want to stay in touch. He left me his mobile phone so that there is no way for me to reach him."

"Are you always gonna wear his necklace?" Delia looked at the red heart-shaped pendent on my neck, which used to belong to her. I nodded silently. Yes, I wanted to keep it. I was determined to.

"It looks a lot better on you than on me." She turned to the bedside table and searched for something with her hand. Finally, she took out a small box.

"Look, you can have them if you want. They are really small golden rings, hoops. I don't know if you like them … but you got your ears pierced recently, didn't you?"

I carefully opened the small blue box and admired the finely worked jewellery. "Thank you!" I said, touched. It was the first time that I could be happy about my pierced ears without feeling guilty. And suddenly I realised that I was going through something like a small resurrection. A new, soft wind was blowing through my life and a silver lining seemed to shine through all the ruins. Mrs Galiani had been right! I promised myself that I would thank her again, especially for convincing me to visit Delia at the hospital.

Suddenly Delia said something different, something unexpected.

"I never really believed in God and I laughed at you because of your Bible ... But I heard the doctors say that it's a miracle that I'd not sustained lasting damage ... So, I don't know ... maybe all this isn't as stupid as I thought. You know, believing in God and that ..."

"I prayed that you would get well again." My heart was beating loudly when I said that, and I had to think about the story with the kitten when I was a little girl again. I had to pause, because I just realised something: I had found the last piece to the jigsaw puzzle. I could see the entire picture now, and I recognised that so many of my prayers had been answered. My life had changed in the way that I had always wished it would. The fight was over and won! Delia looked at me silently and admiringly for a while.

"You have to tell me more about that," she said quietly. "I think there is still a lot we need to talk about!"

Suddenly, she seemed to have an idea. "My sister and I are going to visit my grandparents in the mountains over the holidays. You know, I really like it there. The doctors said that I have to relax to get better. But I will write you letters. And after the holidays, when we're back at school, everything will be different for you, Maya. I promise."

Before the nurse finally chased me out of the room, I told Delia something I had thought of in the last second: "If you want we can study for the exams together next year."

Delia did not have the time to reply. But the glow in her eyes was enough said.

One week later was the last school day before the summer holidays. I had not been in the park at the lantern since that fateful night. I just had not been able to. But now I had to carry out a mission. The lantern was mine and Domenico's secret, so I did not even take Patrick with me, even though his company would have been a comfort.

It was a quiet, nice summer evening; the sun sent its beams through the trees and flooded the forest with mysterious light. The birds were singing songs full of longing above the thick green canopy of leaves. My thoughts wandered off, far away, and I imagined a deep red sunset by the sea. The sound of the waves splashing against the rocks, the fresh sea breeze that swirled up the sand, caressing my legs. Lava rocks. A country far away, in a different world.

When I arrived at the mansion, I immediately saw the

pieces of broken glass on the ground. Hesitantly, I looked up at the destroyed lantern and felt a burning pain in my heart. I bent down and picked up one of the pieces. The glass was massive and reflected the sunlight onto my t-shirt.

Remember that every time you see the lantern!

I walked over to the hedges where the twins had hidden in that stormy night. At the spot where the twigs were squashed a little, I carefully pushed them aside and cut those that would not move with the piece of glass from the lantern. Domenico and Mingo had almost artfully caved their own den here. A perfect hiding place that could not be seen from the outside. I crawled in and lay down on the ground that had been tidied so that two people could lie here. The thought of the two boys having to spend the night here on the spiky twigs because they could not stand it at home was terrible.

I'm there nearly every night!

I looked at the piece of glass that was still lying in my hand and finally put it in my pocket. I swallowed my tears when I got up again and crawled out to send Domenico this last message.

I tied the leather band around the lamppost twice, made a thick knot and checked that the metal pendant was well visible. Delia had not only got well again, but she had also become my friend. This was what our relationship felt like now, anyway. I unrolled a tissue and got out a piece of chalk with which I wrote on the lamppost:

I love you! PS: Delia is now my friend!

Maybe this would reach him.

I stopped at the door to our classroom, looking at it apprehensively. Next to it, there was a new, shiny plaque that read 9a. The morning sun drew patterns of light onto the yellow wall. Everything seemed quiet and peaceful, nearly beautiful somehow. Ninth grade. The first day at school after the summer holidays.

Six long weeks had passed. Six weeks in which neither school nor homework, nor teachers or other students had been important. Six weeks of swimming, travelling, camping, playing and being lazy. Six weeks that had brought some distance between what had happened and what was going to happen. During these weeks, together with Patrick, I had tried to come to terms with the experiences I'd had. We had talked about everything for so long that Domenico's name had become a myth; he had become the hero of a legend that belonged to the past. And we had to face the future now, as hard as it was.

I carefully touched the door handle. Today Delia would be back. From today on, everything would be different in our class; she had mentioned that several times again in the letters she had sent me, as promised, from her holidays. How would the others react to the change? Andrew and Isabelle and Manuela and Ronnie and Danny?

I played with my earrings before I finally pushed down the handle and bravely walked into the classroom. I had tied my hair to a pony tail for the first time today, and I was wearing my new t-shirt with the shiny sequins that my parents had bought me in the holidays.

Everything remained quiet, nobody moved, nobody paid any attention when I made my way over to my desk, slightly embarrassed. I had immediately noticed Delia: she was sitting on her desk and some people formed a circle around her. She was wearing a plain t-shirt, and her hair was tied up in a pretty braid. It seemed as though she had become older and wiser during those few weeks.

When I slowly came closer, Delia looked up and stopped talking. She carefully pushed Isabelle to the side, moved down from the desk and walked towards me. I stopped and only managed a hoarse "Hi, Deli," still insecure as to what would happen next. Everyone had stopped talking now and their eyes attentively waited for Delia's, the leader of the class', reaction.

"You're wearing my earrings!" Delia said loudly, breaking the silence. "They look pretty."

"Thank you," I whispered.

The others did not move.

Hesitantly, Delia took the last step towards me and then, suddenly and in front of all the surprised faces, gave me a hug. The ringing of the bell startled everyone, and when we heard Mrs Galiani's steps in the hallway, we all hurried to our seats. Together with Mrs Galiani, Patrick appeared in the room and sat down next to me, on the chair that used to be Domenico's.

Mrs Galiani spoke a few admonitory, but also encouraging words in front of us new ninth graders. She welcomed Delia and then returned to teaching her class as usual. But I knew now that behind our class teacher's cool reserve there was a kind heart. Mrs Galiani was someone you could trust. Patrick smiled at me. Life would go on.

During the next break, Delia, Manuela and Isabelle stood in front of us. To have my three former archenemies standing so close to me made it hard for me to breathe. I could smell Isabelle's strong perfume, saw Manuela's soft eye shadow and Delia's thin gold chain with her initials engraved. Manuela bent over and placed her elbows on the desk.

"Can we ask you guys something?"

"Yes, of course." My voice was barely audible.

"What happened to Domenico? I mean … have you got any news from him?"

"No, unfortunately not," I said and nervously played with my notepad, not knowing where to put my hands. Patrick's face was deep red with apprehension.

"This girl, Janet, told us that he stole the money from Biedermann. Is that true?" Manuela probed.

I hesitated. We had agreed with Mrs Galiani that we would not tell anyone about this. But what should I say now?

"I think you have to ask Mrs Galiani about that," I finally replied.

"That's so typical!" Isabelle jeered. "Daddy's little girl is trying to be mysterious!"

"Stop it, Isa!" Delia shouted. "No more of that, got it? If Maya doesn't wanna talk about it, she doesn't have to. And Janet's not at this school anymore anyway."

"How do you know?" Manuela was perplexed.

"Some guy from her class told me. Janet's … well, she was expelled."

Isabelle rolled her eyes contemptuously. "The whole fuss about Domenico is getting on my nerves anyway. He's a stupid ass, that's it."

"You haven't got a clue what he's been through!" Delia suddenly shouted angrily.

"Oh, come on! My parents give me trouble too."

"Yeah, but I don't exactly think that's the same!" Delia turned away from Isabelle to look at Patrick and me.

"I … I wanted to ask … whether … you wanna be my friend now, Maya. Only if you want, of course. And you too, Patrick."

"Oh, no, what do you want from those nerds? Have you gone completely mad now?" Isabelle's voice sounded shrill. Apparently she did not know what had been going on between Delia and me during the holidays. I saw how much evil there was in the eyes of this girl. She would remain my enemy in the future; there was nothing I could do about that.

"I don't care if you think I'm crazy," Delia said firmly. "It's better to be … decent, even if I have to be slightly crazy for that." She looked at Patrick and me expectantly.

Suddenly, I had to fight against tears again. How I wished Domenico had seen this. I missed him so much! He had left a huge gap inside me.

Delia's eyes rested on me firmly. She looked kind and surprisingly timid. She was still waiting for an answer. Patrick nudged me in the side.

"Yes, that would be great!" I finally blurted out.

And a second later, we were hugging again. Manuela stood next to us, not saying anything anymore, and briefly looked at Patrick. Isabelle turned around and hurried off. The clacking of her heels sounded cold and hollow. Andrew had, somewhat hesitantly, started to throw paper balls over to us. Patrick knelt down and picked them up.

"I keep telling you," Ronnie mumbled, "girls gotta be aliens!"

"If I hear you saying alien one more time I'm gonna beat the crap out of you!" Andrew barked, but his voice sounded strangely hoarse and throaty.

It was a mild, beautiful autumn evening when I looked out of my window and saw the light in the park. The wind softly pushed the twigs of the trees to the side and freed the view toward the lantern. It was alight again! Finally, somebody had mended it. And the light was even brighter and more intense than before.

That same evening, Mum brought me the letter. The envelope had my name on it in withered letters, nothing else. But I recognised the handwriting, and my heart made a huge leap.

I took out a beautiful picture and a letter.

Deer Maya,
Wen my frend gifs u this letta it means that the lantern is shining again cos I told him to only gif it to u wen its on again. I got yur mesage and I'm xtremly reliefd. The pictur is 4 u! I dont write alot cos I start to forget my english doun hear. But I will neva forget you.
Ti amo, Domenico

Tears were streaming down my face when I looked at the picture. He had used oil pastels, and it showed a bright lantern with a red sunset and rolling waves in the background. And behind the lantern there was a white cross in the middle of a rose garden. It was a fantastic piece of art, and I looked at every line on it, trying to understand the message he wanted me to read in it. When I carefully put the picture down on my desk, I thought that he understood now what I had told him about God and the power of love.

The dreams I used to have about the lantern never returned after Domenico had gone. Something inside me had changed. Life was beautiful now. I was not afraid of school anymore and I no longer thought that I was ugly. I felt this new strength, and the tears that used to flow so easily hardly ever welled up these days. I was almost popular in my class now, and suddenly people had started listening to me. I had learned how to get respect from others: that it was okay to be who I was. I had stopped wishing I was prettier, stronger, fitter, more fashionable or different in any other way. I was just me, Maya.

Delia, Patrick, Manuela and I were always together, and we had a great time. Delia's grades had become better and better after we had started studying together. She was not chasing after the newest trends and hippest clothes anymore and had left the position of the class leader to Isabelle. Andrew and his boys were calling Patrick a "womanizer" now because he was always hanging out with us three girls. But apart from that they left him alone.

My relationship with Dad had changed, too. I felt I understood his worries and fears concerning me a lot better. It did not bother me so much anymore when he did not (or not yet) allow me to do certain things. Of course, good old daddy could still be extremely complicated and, well, annoying sometimes! Especially with his interrogations and quick judgements. But I always knew that he only wanted what was best for me. I firmly intended to trust both of my parents a lot more and, above all, never to lie to them again. The constant lying had been awful, and under no circumstances was I going to let it take up any space in my life anymore. I wanted to stay true to myself.

Deep inside, I knew of course that I had gotten off from this whole story with a slap on the wrist. My parents and Mrs Galiani made me promise that I would choose the places I went to and the people I spent my time with more carefully in the future. Not everyone had a soft spot like Domenico and Mingo, after all. Someone else might have taken advantage of the fact that I was so good-natured, affectionate and inexperienced. And Mum, who, as I had expected, had found out about my secret trip to the park in the middle of the night, had told me – in private – that I should never do anything that dangerous ever again. I understood her perfectly and took her request very seriously.

And then there was the thing with Domenico, which still swung back and forth between making me happy and hurting really badly. I would never forget him. I had put his drawing in a frame and hung it up above my bed. When I was alone in my room, listening to music, I still could not help crying when I looked at it. Apart from the pictures and his short letters, there was nothing left of him. But there was still another very nice surprise: The leather band with the metal pendant I had tied to the lamppost was still there a few weeks later! So I took it home with me and hid it in the bottom drawer of my desk, protecting it like a treasure.

And even after a long time, when memories had already started to fade, I still frequently wondered whether Domenico was happy where he was now, and whether his brother Mingo had managed to get away from the drugs. I wondered whether he might come back one day and tell me all about his time in Sicily. I could not give up this last bit of hope. There was still so much I wanted to tell him! He probably did not know what a difference he had made in my life and how he had turned my world upside down. He was the boy from my dreams whose name I could never remember, who had his leg bandaged and was holding a cat on his arm. The cat stood for the miracle that, in spite of all the problems and anguish, had helped me become stronger inside and believe in myself. The bandaged leg stood for the wounds in Domenico's heart that had finally started to heal. I sent many prayers to God, asking him to protect and guard Domenico's life so that one day he would be able to answer all the questions I longed to ask.

The light of the lantern always reminded me of how deep our friendship had been and how much this adventure had changed my life.

To be continued ...

I would like to thank:

God, who gave me this dream and also made it come true in the end.

My parents, who read a lot of stories with me when I was a child and who never got tired of painting and drawing with me.

Robert and Edith, who supported my dream with their prayers.

Aline and Julia, who loved the story and who kept encouraging me.

Kai, without whom I would never have been able to realise this book technically.

Gideon, who read the first draft and who gave me a lot of good advice.

Kerstin, who gave me even more good advice.

The students Sandra, Nadine, Johanna, Eva, Cornelia, Noëmi, Sheryl and Debora for their test reading and their constructive feedback.

All my dear friends and family who always encouraged me to have this book published.

And last but not least, the editors of Fontis-Verlag for working with me.

About the Author

Susanne Wittpennig, born 1972 in Basel, has been writing stories since she was a child. She also illustrates them herself. Her first booklet was written by her when she was only five years old, her first novel when she was ten. That was the time when her brother, two years her junior, was killed in a car crash. She took her first notes on Maya and Domenico when she was eleven.

After her apprenticeship as a chemist, she jobbed in an airport and in a laboratory. Then she worked as a webdesigner and graphic illustrator beside writing her first published novels. Finally, she packed her bags to study three years at a Norwegian film academy. At the moment, Susanne Wittpennig lives and works in the Norwegian capitol Oslo and enjoys the country, the people and life itself.